My Mini Library Romance

LINA JUBILEE

Chapter One

"There are *children* in this neighborhood."

Mrs. Whithouse was walking her little dog again. The dog's name was Cupcake. She was a cute pile of fluff drowning in thick, white curls, all snarling and teeth whenever anyone but her owner approached. Hardly as sweet as the name implied. I had to forgive her, though, with that woman as a dog mom.

"Huh," I said sweetly—too sweetly, my smile practically cracking my cheeks. "And here I could have sworn all those big, yellow vehicles stopping by twice a day were giant bumblebees. Guess they're school buses, after all. For the children in the neighborhood."

Mrs. Whithouse *harrumphed* and moved on her way, Cupcake's rapid, perky steps in perfect echo of her white-haired owner, who strode down the sidewalk with her nose upturned. Mrs. Whithouse's black workout shorts and blue workout top that pinched and squeezed and showed off every one of her broad-shouldered body's dimples showed she meant business—only, it wasn't just her workout that demanded her attention. It was all of the neighborhood's business, too. Nothing got past her without a complaint to the perpetrator's face, followed by a complaint to the Condo Association President.

Luckily for the rest of us, Evangeline was patient enough to hear her out and then proceed to do virtually nothing to address her ridiculous complaints.

Which was why my Mini Donation Libraries still stood here at one end of the collection of cluster mailboxes.

I loaded up the last of the all-ages books I'd gotten from the Friends of the Library sale this morning: some culinary-themed cozy mysteries with only minor wear on their spines, the hottest YA fantasy trilogy from a few years ago—the library had ordered so many copies of that one—a few middle grade books, one about superheroes and another about a bratty little brother, and the holy grail of my All-Ages Mini Donation Library: two barely worn hardcover picture books, one with a puppy on the cover and another with a colorful worm.

You know, for those kids I supposedly didn't know lived in the area.

I had *more* than gotten my money's worth out of getting up early to be the first to show up for the sale and fill several grocery bags for $3 a pop. I shut the door of the All-Ages Box, latching the barrel bolt closed, admiring, not for the first time, the colorful unicorn traipsing across the side of the white box and following a rainbow path that led around the clear glass showcasing the books from the front.

My hand grazed the golden horn. Dad had made these boxes back when he and Mom and had lived here two years ago—built with Evangeline's permission and the enthusiastic support of at least three-fourths of the condo community. The other one-fourth being mostly non-responders and one uptight Mrs. Whithouse.

Before he and Mom had taken a semi-early retirement and moved clear across the country to New Mexico, all in the service of leaving cold Midwestern winters behind.

Me, I thrived on a cold, cozy day as an excuse to cuddle near my space heater under my leopard-print Slanket. The best kind of day to enjoy a good book under my reading light and a warm cup of tea or coffee. The only problem was, add a thick, wooly sweater, a pair of book-quote writing gloves, some fuzzy reading socks, and one gray-striped lap cat named Darcy, and I was bound to meld with the recliner for a whole day if allowed.

In any case, the two-bedroom condo Mom and Dad had moved into after I'd gone to college was mine now, thanks to generous parents who'd allowed me to move in with them for a couple of years after graduating and a series of job interviews that had gone nowhere. Now I was freelancing—writing, editing, remote administrative assistant work, even the occasional grocery delivery—hustling, whatever I could manage to get the bills paid.

And caretaking for the two Mini Donation Libraries Mom and Dad had crafted and left behind. That mostly meant making sure they stayed tidy and combing book sales and heading to book conventions on occasion to make sure the libraries stayed full. Of course, everyone was welcome to donate, but there were usually more books taken than returned. Just how I liked it.

And yes, I did cull the occasional overlooked book. But only after rearranging its positioning several times and giving it many months of opportunity to find a loving home.

But there was also just the junk.

Today's selection was an old, worn middle grade book from the 90s, two dog-mouth chunks taken out of its top and bottom corners, some sort of brown stain on the first few yellowed pages and blue crayon scribbled across several pages on the inside.

Yuck.

I tossed it into the empty paper grocery bag, being careful to hold on to it by the minimal amount of surface space of my index finger and thumb.

Some people mistook the "leave a book, take a book" guideline to mean my libraries functioned as book garbage cans.

Some books, no matter how much you might wish otherwise, were beyond saving. Milly, my best friend and a librarian a few cities over, had schooled me well on the fact that sometimes books just had to go to the dumpster.

Mini Donation Libraries were one way to save them from that fate—but they had to be in a shape that might prove worth saving.

"Uh-oh. Did Cupcake leave a surprise in one of those boxes of yours?"

I jumped in place at the sound of the tenor voice with a teasing edge. Bodhi, a friendly, handsome man about twenty years my senior who rocked the "silver fox" look with slicked-back salt-and-pepper hair and just a hint of crow's feet to mar his dark brown skin, stood in front of his mailbox, his keys already in the metal door. I hadn't heard him walk up.

"Oh, uh, no." I laughed. I *had* been looking at a brown paper bag—albeit a much larger one than the typical dog walker needed for their dog's mess—as if it contained something stinky rather than just someone's trashed book. "Though Cupcake's owner made sure to remind me that the Ooh-La-La Box is an affront to all the children in the neighborhood."

Laughing, Bodhi stacked one arm with the junk mail, bills, and small packages accumulating in his mailbox. He had on a golden-colored shirt dotted with a pattern of palm trees. It was starting to get a bit warm and sunny here in late April, but it was hardly ideal weather for that kind of shirt, his Bermuda shorts, and his open-toed sandals.

"You and Rory just back from vacation or something?" I asked, referring to his husband.

He winked at me. "Two weeks in Palm Springs." He took a deep breath, as if the crisp, spring Midwestern air could pass for the heat and humidity he'd left behind. "I told Rory I want to move there."

I gasped, picking up the second brown grocery bag full of books and swapping it out with the nearly empty one on the white, slatted bench between the two Mini Donation Libraries. "But who will help me add books to the Ooh-La-La Box?"

Bodhi chuckled and waddled over, his arms stuffed with multiple days' worth of mail as I unlatched the soft pink box that carried only romance titles.

There were sweet romances in there, sure. They went plenty fast.

But the spicy, hot, not-safe-for-work-type of books? They vanished from the shelves at supersonic speeds. I couldn't find enough of them to keep the box stocked.

"Oh, you know I'm not going anywhere," Bodhi said, setting his stack of mail down beside the paper bag. "Rory loves his job and we do have a lot of friends here." He wrinkled his nose. "Even if it's impossible to see them whenever it snows."

"I know you have a lot of dinner parties. I can hear your laughter from the street," I said slyly.

"Yes, and so does Mrs. Whithouse and her awful little bark-monster, Cupcake." Bodhi opened the top of my bag and started riffling inside. "Luckily, all it takes is inviting Evangeline every so often, and she doesn't seem to mind we might imbibe a few too many when playing party games." He pulled one book out and clicked his tongue. The black cover featured nothing but a BDSM crop in gold. "Hmm, hmm, hmm. You know, Quinn, maybe you need to take us up on one of our invites sometime. Fantasy is great, but once in a while, a girl needs to get some outside of her head."

"Ha ha," I said, snatching the book from him. My cheeks flushed. I *had* enjoyed this title quite a lot all by my lonesome. *Quite a lot.* So sue me.

I moved aside the very few remaining titles from my last fill-up three days ago to make the three small shelves inside neat and tidy. Romance readers were ravenous in more than one way, as the haphazard state of the few remaining books could attest. It was a grab-and-dash-type affair, getting a hold of your next read from the Ooh-La-La Box, with its deep red hearts and sexy, puckering lips and pop-art-style woman offering a sly wink painted on either side.

Dad had been an art teacher before retirement, and he still taught some Art and Wine classes over in his desert-dwelling (slight exaggeration) life now. Mom was the romance reader who'd recommended the second romance-only box idea, in addition to passing her love of everything spicy and steamy down to me. It wasn't like Mom and I had a book club or anything—it could get awkward going into the details of what you found hottest about this or that romantic hero with your mom—but we often passed along recommendations with a wink and a whisper and a finger to our lips.

I missed book swapping with Mom. There were e-book gifts, but it wasn't quite the same.

"I'm just *saying*, we have quite a few single friends. Half of them are straight or bi—oh, and there's a really cute lesbian friend who just got out of a long-term relationship with *such* a drama queen. You would be so refreshing for her."

My neck was on fire. I slipped the book with the riding crop in beside one of the few books remaining from the last fill-up: *North and South* by Elizabeth Gaskell. I hoped it was because it was a classic any interested reader could get for free in e-book form and not because of a lack of interest. Brooding Mr. Thornton was every bit as dastardly dashing as the more famous Mr. Darcy.

"I'm fine single," I said promptly. "But thank you." When would I have time to date? I was almost always working, and if not working, then I just wanted to veg out in front of the TV and watch a Hallmark flick—or of course, read a good book. Occasional baths, complete with waterproof Kindle so I didn't humidity-warp any pages of my precious book collection, were about the extent of excitement for me.

The paper bag crinkled next to me. "Quinn Simmons!" Bodhi put a hand over his mouth as he stared down into the open bag. "You did *not*."

Bodhi was about as scandalized as if I'd come out to curate the libraries wearing lingerie, black tights, and high heels. I double-checked my attire just to make sure.

Nope. Black lounge pants—a little form-fitting, but not so tight that I'd have to peel myself out of them —and a pale pink sweater and brown slip-on flats. I was about as unscandalous as could be.

Bodhi flipped the book around to show me the couple on the cover locked in a hungry embrace. The man was—of course, and whoa, Mama, yes and thank you—shirtless, his carefully crafted muscles on full display. The woman wore jeans like he did—so tight, they'd need a shoehorn to get them off, maybe—and also a lacy, black bra.

"I didn't... what?" I checked the title. Had I read that one? No. It'd just looked like a good pick today at the book sale. I'd been shoving romance books in decent condition in that all-you-can-fit paper bag like there was a fire and I had two minutes to save as many books as I could from the unforgiving wrath of the flames.

"This book." Bodhi's eyes widened and he cuddled the book—actually *cuddled* it against his chest as he let out a dreamy sigh. "Oh, this book, Quinn. Tell me you've read it! It is to *die* for."

I hadn't—unless the cover had changed. I took it from him, though the man only let it go reluctantly. *Corrupt Me* by V.L. Breedlove. I'd never heard of it. Never even heard of the author.

I flipped it over for information on her—or them, I supposed, but there was a good chance it had been written by a woman—but all it said was, "V.L. Breedlove brightens up a dull life by writing naughty romances in the dark. Cuffs in hand, always looking for the next empirical experience to inspire another book."

I chuckled, but a tingling bolt of energy shot up my toes.

"You dare laugh?" Bodhi took the book back and cradled it in his arms again.

Shaking my head, I took another stack of books from the bag to load the Ooh-La-La Box up with. "I just wondered how she *writes* in the dark..."

Frowning, Bodhi took a look at the back of the book. A wide grin broke out over his face. "By *living* it, sweetheart."

"Please. Romances are fantasy. I love them, but they're fantasy." A little sigh escaped my lips as I stacked the second shelf.

"Spoken like a woman who *needs to get laid* already. Quinn, you're how old?"

"Twenty-six," I admitted.

"And when was the last time you dated?" It wasn't the first time he'd asked. He had so many friends, I could understand why he might not remember—but that bastard, he remembered, all right. He just wanted to rub it in.

"It's been a few years, okay? You happy?" I snatched the next pile of books from the bag roughly, mumbling under my breath.

"*Since college*," Bodhi said. "You are *crazy*. I know these books probably help deal with a lot of pent-up *energy*, but unless you're on the ace spectrum—and bless you if you are, you'll find no judgement from me

—you need to close the book every once in a while and look up and see what the real world has to offer."

"I'm not. Asexual," I mumbled. "Well, I don't think I am. I'm fine just imagining, though."

Before I could grab another stack for the Mini Library, Bodhi slipped the paperback copy of *Corrupt Me* into my hand. "Okay, then you're coming to dinner this Wednesday."

"I can't," I said quickly, before the invitation had even really sunk in. "I have a deadline Thursday, and I'm sure I'll still be working—"

"You have four days to figure that out." Bodhi gestured wildly at me, as if to say to *figure me* out. I tossed my long, honey-blonde ponytail over my shoulder and behind my back as if to hide it from his judging glare. I glanced at my short, unvarnished nails and the slightly dry skin on my blush-tone hands. I glanced back at the supermodel with wavy, lush, brown locks in the lacy bra on the cover.

Yup. Fantasy.

"Hmm..." Bodhi looked at the Ooh-La-La Box's shelves—two-thirds of which I'd filled again —and ran a finger over the spines. "Don't mind if I do," he said, pulling out a sexy MLM romance with two beefcakes holding one another on the cover. It was one of Mom's favorites, so I'd had to snatch it at the sale in her honor. Bodhi tucked it beneath his arm and smiled slyly at me. "You've read this one."

"How can you tell?"

He chuckled. "Your eyes always light up when someone's about to read a book you think is good."

"Hmm…" I said, nodding. I tucked the book he'd recommended under my own arm and went back to work.

Bodhi let out a little snicker as he gathered all of his mail again. It was practically going to topple out of his grip.

"You got all of that?" I asked, haphazardly setting down the last of the books I'd bought this morning on the third shelf of the Mini Library. I helped him balance his mail better, adjusting the boxes and stacks. "You know, you could have asked me to get your mail. I never go anywhere."

"Oh, don't I know that," said Bodhi. "I can't even get you to walk down a block to join me and Rory for dinner. But you are this Wednesday." His brow arched at me sternly.

"Fine. I am." What was the worst that could happen? I'd get a free meal out of it. And Bodhi and Rory were fun to be around. I just didn't like hanging out with more than a handful of people. Even Milly and I only got together once a month or so despite living within forty minutes of one another.

"Thatta girl," Bodhi said. "Maybe next time I'll put you on mail duty. We didn't want to bother you. We did ask some friends to pick it up. It's just been a few days since any of them came."

They had more friends than there were days in the month. They'd probably rotated on a daily basis so no friend ever had to inconvenience themselves more than once.

"See you Wednesday!" Bodhi called over his shoulder as he waddled down the street. "Seven o'clock!"

"Okay!" I shouted back, waving.

Mrs. Whithouse was across the street now, walking Cupcake on the other side. She glared at me as Cupcake did her business on a fire hydrant, clearly as disgusted by me waving and shouting down the block as if she'd just seen *me* relieving myself against a fire hydrant in the same manner as her dog.

Cupcake growled in my direction for good measure.

I plastered on a smile and waved at both of them—the sexy book Bodhi had recommended still in the hand I used to wave at her.

She visibly shuddered, her mouth agape, before tugging on Cupcake's leash and skittering down the path. A new email was already being composed in her head, no doubt. *"Dear Mrs. Evangeline Vanderberg. It has come to my attention that that pornographic amateur librarian is at it again, flagrantly waving her material for all in the neighborhood to see..."*

I giggled to myself at my little joke. Chances were, Evangeline *was* about to receive something similar. Tucking *Corrupt Me* back under my arm, I went to work straightening the last of the new additions.

There was a lingering book at the end, one of the rare ones left behind. It was almost shoved there in the dark, out of sight, as if whoever had put it there was embarrassed for it to be found.

Because I didn't recognize it, so I knew it hadn't come from my last trip to the thrift store.

I took it out—to make sure it was in presentable shape, of course, and maybe just *a little* bit to see if a sexy new read wanted to jump into Mama's shelves at home—and was taken aback.

This was the *last* thing I'd been expecting.

I pulled the book I'd tucked under my arm out to compare the two to make sure. The book hidden in the dark corner of the Ooh-La-La Box almost matched the one Bodhi had recommended to me. Same style font, same stark, dark cover. A gorgeous couple locked in an embrace, this one with foreheads touching, their mouths open and clearly hungry for one another.

Thrill Me by V.L. Breedlove.

They were from the same series.

I checked out the spines, the backs—same series, though *Thrill Me* had come out first, but they could be read in any order, it said, thus why Bodhi hadn't warned me he'd been recommending a sequel, I presumed.

Of course. Bodhi. I knew he added books to the Ooh-La-La Box all the time. Made sense he'd add an extra of one of his favorite series, as this clearly seemed to have been.

But this one from the Mini Donation Library was *pristine*, as if it had never before been touched, unlike the slightly worn copy of the sequel I'd gotten from the Friends of the Library book sale. Had Bodhi really gone out and bought a brand new copy, hoping it would soon find a permanent home in a booklover's shelves? I flipped open *Thrill Me* and nearly dropped it.

There was a signature in there.

V.L. Breedlove.

Harsh, small letters, as if to say the loopy, romantic writing I'd come to expect from romance readers was more suited for the sweet romances that inspired wholesome Hallmark movies.

As if to say Ms.—Mr.? Mx.?—Breedlove couldn't be bothered. She had dark places to bore into.

"Oh! It's book fill-up day! Check it out, kids!"

I slammed *Thrill Me* shut and shoved both it and *Corrupt Me* into a grocery bag, quickly gathering both that and the bag with the trash book in it and shoving them under my arm.

I'd just barely shut and latched the Ooh-La-La Box before I spun around to find Evangeline, along with her two kids, who ran right for the unicorn All-Ages Box.

"Good morning, Quinn," Evangeline said. It was still only just morning. She flicked her gaze over my shoulder at the full-to-bursting Ooh-La-La Box and nudged my shoulder. "Anything you recommend today?"

"Always."

We both snickered.

She was slightly taller than me, her angled bob showing off her straight, black hair. Her tawny complexion was near perfection, and she looked younger than I did—even though I knew she had fifteen years on me. Still, the long-sleeved navy blue sundress she wore gave her an air of professionalism, despite the white tennis shoes she'd paired with it.

Her kids, a boy and a girl aged seven and nine, were pulling out stacks of the new additions to the All-Ages Box.

"Just one each," their mother said.

"Aw," said Benjamin. Though he, like his sister, resembled his mother more due to their Singaporean heritage, he chose to wear his dark hair in a buzzcut like his father. "But look at these!" He showed off a chapter book about dinosaurs that had been there since earlier in the week, as well as the new picture book featuring puppies.

"You said you were going to take the dinosaur book this time if it was still there." His sister, her black hair in two buns on top of her head, was riffling through some middle grade books and even that YA fantasy trilogy.

"Can she read YA already?" I pointed out.

"Sure. But the issue is more that she wants too many at once." Evangeline moved forward and plucked the YA and a few others from her daughter and the puppy book from her son's hands, leaving them each with just one.

"There. Those are your picks," she said.

"Aw, Mom." Penelope widened her eyes and started pleading.

"Leave some for the other children."

The kids both frowned but set about flipping pages through their books as their mom put the other ones back and latched the All-Ages Box door, her keys jangling from her hand. Then she set upon the Ooh-La-La box, practically bouncing from foot to foot.

"You can't go wrong with Colleen Hoover." I slipped up beside her, my own picks still in the bag under my arm. "Oh. That Trish Fiona one's a good one." I pointed to my recommendation.

Evangeline bit her lip and slipped out the Fiona book, first studying the cover—a sculpted man in a suit that was open at the chest, his tie dangling off haphazardly down his shoulder—and then the back of the book.

My voice lowered as the kids began talking amongst themselves, Benjamin eager to see what Penelope was looking at and Penelope trying to keep her brother from staring over her shoulder at her book. "Mrs. Whithouse is going to complain again. About the Ooh-La-La Box."

"You mean the box I'm currently sorting through." She lifted the Trish Fiona book in the air and ran her tongue over her incisor. "This one definitely sounds like it'll do. Still... I have to be sure." She tucked it under her arm and began flipping through the other titles.

"She made a comment about children in the neighborhood again. I mean, it *is* freely accessible. I thought about a lock with a code of some kind only shared amongst interested residents, but I don't want to ban anyone from out of the neighborhood from taking books, either."

Benjamin was trying to snatch Penelope's book from under her arms now, sneaking up behind her and darting out.

"*Mom!*" Penelope called. "Make him stop!"

"Benjamin, stop bothering your sister," Evangeline said without even looking up. "Reading books is me-time, okay? You have your own book for some me-time." She flipped through one row of the romance reads. "Ignore that woman," she told me. "Hey, kids, do you want an extra book from Mommy's romance box?"

"*Ewww*," said Benjamin. He stuck his tongue out and plopped down on the bench, shuddering as he dove into his dinosaur book.

"Gross," said Penelope, not looking up from her own read.

"See?" Evangeline pulled out a book and took a long, solid look at the hot fireman on the cover. She lowered her voice as she slid the paperback back on the shelf and kept looking. "As far as the kids who might *actually* be interested go, well, it's up to their parents, and frankly, I've been raiding the romance section of my local library since I was at least eleven." She pulled out a vintage title, with the couple painted instead of photographed, the man's chest exposed through his flowy, white shirt and the woman's ruffly dress dipping down, exposing her shoulders, as she fainted backward in his arms. "Whatever gets kids interested in reading."

I giggled. "I bet you're a hit at the PTA."

"Well, I mean, my response will be that it's at a parent's discretion." She straightened up and slid the Ooh-La-La Box closed. "But preteen-me will be rooting for those likeminded kids who manage to sneak one or two home if need be." She gestured at the box. "There's plenty of sweet and classic romance in there, anyway. Let kids read, I say!"

Penelope nodded as she flipped a page.

Her brother was similarly engrossed in his own book.

"Okay, kids," Evangeline said. She'd taken my recommendation as her selection, I noticed. "Daddy's waiting."

"I wanna get the mail!" said Benjamin, jumping down off the bench and slamming his book shut. Evangeline handed him the keyring in her hand, and he scattered off down the concrete to collect the day's delivery.

"Say..." Evangeline tucked a piece of her short hair behind an ear, her cheeks coloring just slightly as she watched Penelope join her brother in scooping the contents out of their mailbox just up ahead. "You don't happen to have a new assistant curator for the Ooh-La-La Box, do you?"

I cocked my head. Had the selection seemed that radically different from usual? And hadn't she just seen me finishing up the task?

"No. I mean, everyone is welcome to add to it." We started down the sidewalk, her kids leading the way toward both of our condos. Evangeline's family had one of the largest first-floor models, complete with an office they'd transformed into a third bedroom. I lived one building over in a two-bedroom upper. The second bedroom had been for Dad's art before I'd moved back in every summer and then after college. Mom and Dad had gone for a full house again in New Mexico, a small ranch with space for a permanent art studio.

"It's just... I spotted a hottie there on Wednesday." She lowered her voice, though the kids were plenty ahead of us. They ran across the grass straight to their condo's front door. In the yard of the house I'd grown up in, they would have been kicking up dandelion seeds. Here, though, the lawn was immaculate. Not a sign of life anywhere outside of the carefully manicured grass and the trees every few feet.

I blinked. It had taken me a beat to figure out what she'd said. "A hottie?"

She giggled and held the book I'd recommended to her in front of her, tapping the front cover. "Easily as sculpted as this guy."

I gasped. "You exaggerate."

"I wish!" She laughed, then explained herself. "I mean, Lucas is handsome, and I adore him, but if I'd known the stuff of romantic cover shoot models was in town back before I'd married him…"

I nudged her with an elbow. "Naughty."

"A woman can *look*, can't she?" She gestured at her small frame. "Even one who's had two babies?"

I rolled my eyes. She looked amazing. And even if she hadn't, hell yeah, a woman could look. As long as she wasn't blatant about it.

"Don't you recognize everyone from the neighborhood?" I pointed out. We stopped at the end of the sidewalk leading up to her place. Inside her condo, its door left wide open, the kids were giggling and chasing around their little corgi, who was no doubt happy to finally see them after all of five minutes apart.

"Almost everyone." She shrugged. "I mean, we do have some people who value their privacy."

"Recluses," I said, knowing full well I was one—outside of curating the Mini Donation Libraries.

"I was trying to put it politely." She grinned. "But yeah… I think I would have recognized him if he were a resident. Thought you might have gotten some outside help from a brother—"

"I'm an only child."

"Or a cousin—"

"None of my cousins are *that* attractive."

"Or a… friend?" She bumped her hip to mine, her eyes sparkling wickedly.

"Ha ha. No. No super-hot male friends for me."

The paper bags crinkled under my arms as I shifted at just the thought of such a thing. What would I do with an unbearably attractive friend? How could I be myself if all I wanted to do was jump his bones?

No, better to not even imagine it. Besides, everyone's tastes were subjective. "He was probably just someone looking to offload an old book or two. We get some drive-bys. The closest other such neighborhood library is several miles away, and anyone is welcome to stop by."

"He wasn't offloading one or two books. And like I said, he was at the *Ooh-La-La Box*." Evangeline's eyebrows arched.

"If he's not from here, he might not know it's a romance-only box," I pointed out. "I've had to swap donations from one box to the other on occasion."

"He had a *box* full of books," Evangeline continued. "And he was lining them up so nice and neatly. I was curious about his book selection, but Penelope had a game and Lucas and I had to get going." She whispered conspiratorially, cupping her free hand around her lips, even though no one was within earshot. "I stopped by the next morning. Pickings were getting slim, but I think I spotted what he'd added on the bottom shelf."

"Oh?" This whole adventure had to have taken place after my thrift store score fill-up earlier that day.

"There was a line of identical books. I snagged one myself." She fanned herself. "Sorry I didn't bring it back for someone else to read. It's too damn good. I slid that sucker into Mommy's special shoe organizer under the master bed."

"The one with your sex toys?" I laughed, covering my mouth.

Evangeline wrinkled her nose. "I told you that in confidence. But yes."

"You just said your kids aren't interested in romance books—"

"They're not. But Penelope is getting to that age, and if she starts browsing my romance reads, I do *not* want that to be her first pick." She chuckled. "I'm being hypocritical, aren't I? But fine. I'll admit it. I just wanted to keep that to myself. Besides, he'd left so many of them—I bet most of the neighborhood already got the same copy."

"What was it called?" I asked, my curiosity burning. Both because of her reaction to it and the fact that a reportedly gorgeous man had gone to the trouble of leaving a box full of potentially the same title.

"*Thrill Me* by V.L. Breedlove. And, Quinn, my copy was signed!"

My knees went weak and I almost reached out to lean on the bush dividing the lawn from the sidewalk.

"They were probably all signed," I said, riffling through the grocery bag with my own picks and pulling out the copy I'd taken. "This one was, too."

Evangeline practically screamed. "You have the next book?" She snatched *Corrupt Me* out from my hand, but her face fell when she opened it to the front. "This one isn't signed."

"I got that from the Friends of the Library book sale," I told her. "The first book was in the Ooh-La-La Box. No wonder a pristine condition book this spicy was left all alone there. If the man you saw left a box full of them... Probably everyone in the neighborhood got a copy."

"Everyone but Mrs. Whithouse." Evangeline giggled and handed the book back to me. "You're in for a treat. It was two A.M. and the kids had school the next morning by the time I finished the book, but I ordered the rest of the series on Kindle and read all of *Corrupt Me* before I got two hours of sleep." She yawned, even though she was talking about days ago. Her eyes looked bleary, though, as if she'd been having late nights for a while now. "I finished the rest of the series whenever I had a free moment over the next few days. Hard to find with two little kids, but I managed." She scrunched her shoulders.

"Well, I'm looking forward to getting started, then," I told her. "I have some work to do, but tonight... Tonight, I'm cracking open *Thrill Me*."

She waved and started heading down the sidewalk leading to her condo, her dog's barks echoing out into the air. "I hope you don't plan on working the next several days. It's a six-book series so far, and the author has another series! Buy frozen meals or make sure you have your phone nearby to order delivery! You'll be stuck to your seat!"

I waved back and laughed. I'd been addicted to a series before. I could usually hold off long enough to reward myself for getting through another day of work.

At the very least, I could come up for a meal and a bathroom break on occasion.

I read the back of the books again as I headed to my condo, the bags and trash book tucked under my arm.

Everything Evangeline had told me about the mystery donator seemed strange.

But she hadn't brought the biggest mystery up—and I hadn't thought to, either.

What was this gorgeous man doing with multiple copies of the same book?

And at least two with signatures?

Did that mean he knew the author in real life? Was he helping promote his wife's—or maybe sister's or mother's if we singles could get lucky—books around town?

Did that mean V.L. Breedlove was a *local* author?

But what did that matter to me? Unless she started signing books at local events, I'd never meet her, even if she was typing out stories on the front porch of a house just down the street.

Still, it would bug me—the mystery. I wondered if I should keep a better eye on the boxes this week.

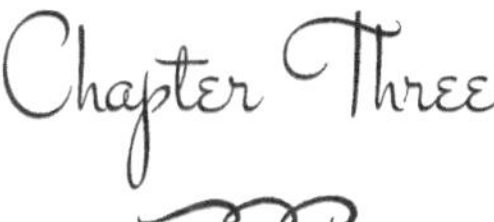

Chapter Three

Finding out if V.L. Breedlove lived near me mattered immensely.

I had to meet her—at least once. Not in a crazy stalker kind of way, of course. But if I were to stumble upon her at a public venue or if she—please, please, please—were to hold a signing.

Something. Anything.

Please!

She was my new favorite author. Hands down. I would always love so many romances by so many different people, but V.L. Breedlove—she just spoke to me.

Her heroes spoke straight to my loins, too.

I *had* managed to finish my work project on Saturday before I'd decided to sit down and crack open the first book. Fortunately, I had already eaten.

Come dawn, I hadn't slept a wink and I'd blown past *Corrupt Me* and moved onto Book 3 in

Breedlove's Maxwell Security Series purchased straight to my Kindle. Coffee and a piece of untoasted bread—still reading as I drank and munched, wandering around the kitchen and only looking down to feed Darcy, whose entire schedule had been messed up by me never coming to bed—and then it was on to Book 4.

I'd been a little ahead with work. I deserved a full day off once in a while, I'd told myself.

My stomach had rumbled something fierce, and my eyeballs had been about to bleed, but I got through Book 4.

Then I'd collapsed, still in the day before's clothes, on the bed, my Kindle still in one hand, me trying in vain to keep reading.

It was four in the morning on Monday when I woke up, Darcy asleep at my feet, my covers not even on top of me.

Against my ardent desires, I'd showered and changed and forced myself to fix some cereal.

I *had* to work today.

But then I'd thought it couldn't hurt to get started on Book 5 while I ate, getting a speck of cereal on my screen as I swiped through the pages.

Darcy reminded me the sun had come up, and it was time to feed him again. If not for him, I might never have gotten up from the kitchen table or haphazardly put the bowl of cereal in the sink.

By the evening, my eyes were burning as I sat in my favorite reading chair, but I'd gotten through the entire series, the Kindle screen showing the last page of Book 6 currently cradled against my heart, my other hand petting Darcy to the rhythm of his purrs.

My limbs were jelly. I needed coffee, but more importantly, I needed some kind of release.

I took a few moments to myself in the bedroom—thinking woefully how I'd teased Evangeline about her own box of toys. Mine wasn't a box; it was all in a drawer since no nosy kids would dig through my dresser.

I took another shower when I was done, then fed Darcy again and took a deep breath, just trying to let my feelings all flow through me.

What the fuck just happened to me? I clutched the kitchen counter, my stomach a rumbling mess, my lightheadedness at odds with the feeling of release flowing throughout my body.

Right. Back to the human race.

My heart thundered at thoughts of the six heroes in Breedlove's debut series. I needed to Google more about her—my god! Evangeline had told me she'd released a second series.

I needed to read it like *yesterday*—

No. No. I paced around the kitchen, then took a deep breath.

Nope.

I exhaled. My stomach rumbled.

Food.

No time or energy to make anything healthy.

I snatched my phone, dismissed a few texts from

Milly and my mom, then ordered a pizza and started a cup of strong roast in my Keurig.

May as well go the whole shebang down college-life road.

Scratch that. I'd never slept this poorly in college. Had never relied this heavily on coffee.

An email notification reminded me I had a deadline for a client—writing some content for their website—in less than twenty-four hours.

Shit.

V.L. Breedlove would have to wait.

I sat down at my desk and started my computer up, doing my best to breathe deeply and clear my mind as I got ready to work.

I sipped at my coffee. Brought up my browser.

Typed "V.L. Breedlove" in the address bar.

Nope, I told myself, backspacing.

I clicked on the browser button for my emails. I needed to review the assignment.

I didn't know how much time passed, but my doorbell rang and I got up to get my pizza.

I ate the pizza straight out of the box on a TV tray I'd dragged up to my desk, Darcy coming over to sniff at the air and tap my ankle for his share.

"No pizza for you," I told him. "Go back to your cat tree."

He just stared up at me. I swallowed down some coffee—it was cold now—between slices and wrote one-handed to get out the first few lines of what my client needed from me.

I stared at the screen. I had a headache from the lack of sleep and the abundance of coffee.

My stomach growled as the pizza hit it. That would rest pretty heavily in my weakened gut. When was the last time I'd eaten? I could barely remember.

What time was it? What day was it? What *was* time? What was life?

I put down the pizza and massaged my temples, thinking. Breedlove's heroes of Maxwell Security were no longer waiting for me. As one of her heroes, Gideon, had said to his lover, Bianca: "Partings can be such sweet, sad torture." Every couple had had their happy endings. Some had had kids while the others had hooked up. They were all living happy, fulfilled and very sexy lives in the fictional town in my head and the heads of other readers.

Who even knew what Breedlove's other series was about.

It didn't matter.

It could be my treat. Once I finished this.

Darcy, clearly having given up, trotted away and jumped up three flights of his cat tree. He stared down from the top perch with one eye open, as if to keep an eye on his crazy cat mom.

I slapped my cheeks.

Focus.

I hesitated.

Then I brought up a browser and typed in "V.L. Breedlove."

And hit return.

Sweet, holy miracles, the information that popped up would tide me over until I started the other series.

There were the usual suspects: V.L. Breedlove on Amazon, Goodreads, an author website that was titillating but basic and branded in black and red.

But there was an Instagram profile—most of the few images promotional for her series, giving nothing much away, except for the very top entry.

It was a picture of *my* Ooh-La-La Mini Donation Library.

"Love this Mini Donation Library design," she wrote as a caption. I'd have to tell Dad and Mom an author had shared Dad's artwork online. "So sexy! It's filled with only romance books. I may have just added a bunch of signed copies of *Thrill Me* this evening..."

The next photo was a zoomed-in picture of the bottom shelf of the Ooh-La-La Box. Sure enough, Breedlove had added at least ten copies of *Thrill Me* to an already picked-over shelf.

The post was flooded with comments asking where the box was, if they could have signed copies, and just saying whoever got one was lucky. Someone who identified himself as Breedlove's PA directed readers to where they could order a signed paperback but made no comment about the box's location.

V.L. Breedlove had over 500,000 followers—and yet I'd never heard of her before the other day. The books were *that* good and Bodhi, who had been out of town when Breedlove had stopped by to load up the Mini Library with copies, had clearly already read her work—and he hadn't recommended them to me before?

We would have words, he and I.

Going down the rabbit hole, I discovered that V.L. Breedlove was completely indie published, the publisher listed just a name that Breedlove used to only publish her own books. Agents had expressed interest in foreign rights deals and audiobooks, apparently, but the latter she'd had produced herself and the former she'd apparently also hired translators for. There were German, French, Italian, Spanish, and Czech versions of the Maxwell Security series on the way within the next year.

Breedlove had only started publishing the books last summer, and she stuck to a release schedule of about one book a month, which was why she had ten releases. That was awfully fast for an author, particularly an indie one, to have built up such a ravenous fanbase and afford all of that marketing and book expenses.

The books must have sold like hotcakes. They were ranked respectfully low on Amazon—though none broke the Top 100 overall, there were a few category bestsellers.

Which made it all the more strange that I had gone this long without reading them. I'd been too focused on what I could find for the Mini Donation Libraries, I supposed. There was always an older release or two I picked up for myself while I was at it.

And most people who owned V.L. Breedlove books

were probably not eager to part with their copies. No wonder they'd never shown up in the Ooh-La-La Box before.

That reminded me. Someone—Bodhi, at least—had failed me by not recommending the books earlier. I wouldn't do the same for my mom.

Clicking on *Thrill Me*'s e-book version, I selected the option to send it as a gift and wrote a note along with it to my mom. *Make sure you clear your next few days before you get started on this*, I typed. *And check out the author's Instagram. Dad should get a chuckle out of it.*

Of course, as soon as I sent that, the site recommended the rest of the series—and Breedlove's second series, which appeared to be about a motorcycle club.

Oo. Dark. Sexy. Illicit.

My cursor hovered over the first book in the series.

It couldn't hurt to buy it and send it to my Kindle.

When I went to the book's main page, the handsome, rugged model with his MC club "cut" ripped and showing off all his muscles, I saw I could buy the entire series at once.

"Yes, please."

One-click and sent to my Kindle.

I took a deep breath. Work. Work.

Focus. Focus.

Oh, but I *had* wanted to sign up for her newsletter.

I went back to her website and did so, excited to get the first email that included a short featuring *Thrill Me*'s couple happily married.

I sent that to my Kindle.

Surely, I *had* to read that one. I'd already finished that series and hadn't realized there'd been a bonus short.

Leaving the computer behind, I snatched up my Kindle and curled up in my reading chair, getting cozy under my shaggy blanket.

Darcy's head perked up and he jumped down from his tree, settling in on my lap.

Well, now I *had* to stay sitting until Darcy felt like getting up.

It was only polite.

Two guesses when it was I finally peeled the skin of my thighs off of that chair.

Chapter Four

Wednesday evening rolled around and I was a mess. An utter mess. Somehow, I had managed to eke out the bare minimum of work the past couple of days, but I was no longer ahead of schedule. I hadn't gone grocery shopping like I'd meant to earlier this week. I hadn't left the house. I'd barely slept.

My stomach rumbled as I fumbled out of a wake-up shower I'd taken at six o'clock in the evening. The sun was already working its way down past the horizon.

I stared into the mirror, at the puffy purple bags under my brown eyes. My wet, dark-blonde hair hung in limp strings. I looked like a ghost who'd climbed out of a well.

I wondered if my writing on that website I'd just written for was good enough for the client. I'd read it over, but my brain had been goo. I wouldn't be surprised if the client asked for rewrites.

Which didn't bode well for future work from them.

Sighing, I got to work brushing my teeth and applying toners and lotions to my face. I *thought* I'd done some of that over the past few days, but I couldn't remember.

My mind was a blur of V.L. Breedlove's writing. Forgoing sleep, I'd managed to finish everything she'd released.

Her next book came out next week, another install-ment in her motorcycle club series. I'd preordered that one and all five other books she had up for preorder.

There was a new series starting in June. A green-skinned alien romance. That was a new take from her. But I was in. I was in for life with V.L. Breedlove.

"Hell yeah," I said to no one in particular, pumping my fist in the air. I laughed at my pathetic reflection.

Outside of the bathroom door, Darcy meowed, one of his meals likely overdue. My stomach growled with it, but Darcy came first. I fed him, only just avoiding fumbling over him between my lack of balance and his incessant need to rub my ankles, then got dressed, pulling on a pair of clean sweats.

No surprise: I was behind with laundry.

My stomach growled, but I didn't know what to make. Those cupboards were getting bare. There was a half-eaten wedge of cheese in the fridge, maybe.

Oh, no. And leftovers from last week I hadn't thrown out. I could have eaten them all this time!

My phone buzzed with a message, so I checked it out. I hadn't written to Milly in days, so I quickly wrote back. *Sorry. Been in a book coma.* I linked her to *Thrill Me*, though it was hard to decide between that and *Kidnapped Desire*, the first book in Breedlove's MC series. It was even racier, though. A tingle went through me.

Yeah, better to ease her in. Start with *Thrill Me*.

Milly would understand. We could go days without talking to one another, especially when good books were involved.

Mom had sent a dozen smiley faces with hearts for eyes, thanking me for the recommendation. Dad was "tickled pink" about the Instagram post and thought about commenting on it, but he was afraid that might out the author's location. Did that mean V.L. Breedlove lived nearby? Mom wondered. She was already on Book 3. Of course. At least she was retired and ought to have time to get through the series. That, and Dad could take care of her, make sure she ate, slept, and bathed with regularity.

I needed me a partner who could do the same for me during my book binges.

Darcy licked his chops and stared up at me as I stood in the middle of the condo, my phone in hand.

Well, at least *he*'d notice if I passed out for days. Not sure what he could *do* about it. Maybe he'd cuddle against my side and provide some warmth at least.

The doorbell rang.

I blinked. I wasn't expecting any packages I had to sign for.

It rang again.

What day was it? *Shit.* Wednesday. Wasn't I supposed to go out to find some used books with which to fill the Mini Donation Libraries? Maybe some of the neighborhood was getting antsy for me to curate.

I headed down the stairs and peered through the peephole.

Bodhi. He was wearing a collared shirt, a light lilac sweater, and khakis and managed to look "casual chic" with the slightest of efforts.

I opened the door.

"What's up?" I asked.

His eyes widened as he took me in. "*What* in the world are you wearing?"

I stared down at my legs. Baggy, gray sweatpants and a baggy, gray sweatshirt to match. I looked like one giant baggy, gray sack. But I was comfortable. I wriggled my bare toes. I'd forgotten to put on socks.

"Loungewear?" I offered, flicking some of my hair over my shoulder. I winced as I realized I'd revealed a patch of dampness the size and shape of the lock of hair over my shoulder and down over my breast. I'd forgotten to blow-dry it, too.

"Please tell me you just got out of the shower and were about to get dressed," Bodhi said, clutching a hand to his chest. "I mean, *really* dressed."

"Uh, well, I just showered..." I steepled my fingers

and slapped my palms together. "Do you need something?"

Darcy, finally intrigued by the sounds of voices, appeared at my feet and I picked him up so he wouldn't go outside, cradling him against my chest.

"Quinn Simmons." Bodhi's brows narrowed into a thick line. "It is Wednesday. You agreed to come to Rory's and my dinner party." He gestured at me. "You are aware what day it is, correct? You look like you haven't slept in a week."

Not too far off.

My jaw dropped slightly as Darcy lifted his head and sniffed the air. "Right. Um, that was *this* Wednesday."

"People don't typically say, 'Wednesday' when they mean four months from the date." Bodhi shook his head. "I had a feeling you'd bail on me again, so I came to escort you there. Didn't think you'd come prepared to make this an uphill battle. What's your mommy doing, huh, honey?" Bodhi leaned forward to give a gentle scratch to Darcy's cheek and chin.

Darcy lapped it up, starting to purr.

"I honestly forgot," I said. My stomach growled and I felt a bit faint, my heart thumping wildly. It wasn't a big deal if I skipped, right? Then again, what else was I going to do for supper?

"Did you forget about the Mini Donation Libraries, too?" Bodhi asked.

So my curation work *had* been missed.

It was nice to know we had such active booklovers in the area.

I was only sorry my own love of books had led me to disappoint them.

"Been busy," I mumbled. "Work."

"Uh-huh." Bodhi studied me, pursing his lips. "You let me take baby boy here," Bodhi said, grabbing Darcy from my arms. "And we'll wait for you to get ready."

My mouth opened to protest.

My stomach growled.

"You're not going to say *no* again, are you?" Bodhi asked sternly.

"I'll get ready," I said. What was one more coffee and another Tylenol to counteract the caffeine headache and the bleariness my eyes experienced from too much reading?

"Oh, lookie, baby boy. It's Allen. Allen!" Bodhi, who cuddled Darcy against his chest, lifted Darcy's front paw and waved it at a light blue jeep as the driver stepped out of it.

Flushing, I realized whoever it was could see me.

"Let's get inside," I said softly, not about to shut the door on Bodhi when he was holding my cat.

"It's one of our friends," Bodhi explained, as if that made it okay for the person to see me like this, barefoot and wet and drowning in gray cotton fleece.

Yeah, that didn't help any.

The door to the jeep shut. My face burning, I didn't want to see another dinner guest notice me, so I didn't even look. If I didn't look, maybe they wouldn't see me.

I stepped forward to tug on Bodhi's elbow, but the slight vertigo I'd been experiencing due to lack of food and sleep made me stumble.

Darcy screeched as Bodhi tried both to catch me and keep a good grip on my cat.

He managed to stop me from falling flat on my face, but Darcy squirmed and landed on my head with a mighty yowl, jumping off it to get back inside the condo—but not before getting caught in some strands of my hair and yanking them upward—scrambling up the stairs.

"Hi, Allen." Bodhi let go of my shoulder with one hand and waved toward the end of the sidewalk. My cheek was flush against his sweater, some of my damp hair draped across his shoulder.

"Quinn, this is Allen Cox." Bodhi spit a bit and I realized my hair was on his lips.

I yelped and straightened up. "Sorry! Thank you. Sorry." My head bobbed at Bodhi with every word.

"Allen, this is Quinn Simmons," Bodhi said, as if I hadn't just left a patch of dampness all over his cashmere.

I turned slowly—so slowly—like if I moved slow enough, the dinner guest would just go away. Then I could pretend he'd never even been there, never seen the whole spectacle that was the-mess-of-me.

Instead, I found the man had moved closer. Tall and muscled, his broad shoulders filling out his navy-blue suit impeccably well, as if a tailor had crafted the fabric to show off every bulge of his biceps.

His chest practically strained against the cream shirt, his long, navy tie around his neck something my hand naturally gravitated to, as if I could reach right over and snatch the man out of fiction and to reality.

Because of course this man had to be gorgeous. Wavy, dark hair, a sharp jawline with just the slightest five o'clock shadow peppering his smooth, tanned complexion.

All dressed up and ready for anything.

Whereas I was standing here like a scrub, ready only for the ground to open up and swallow me.

"Much better." Bodhi was dangling one of Darcy's favorite cat toys over his head, and Darcy was wholly absorbed in batting the jingling dragon's feathered tail around.

Sighing, I adjusted my maroon blouse to make sure it tucked in nicely into my pair of black dress pants. It was the nicest thing I had to wear that still fit me just right—my butt had grown two sizes since college, and my stomach and bust were getting a little more filled out as well. But it was a bit chilly for this spring evening.

"Let me grab the suit jacket that goes with these slacks," I said.

"It's not a business dinner, Quinn." Bodhi let out a

little chuckle as Darcy leaped almost as high as his hip and snatched the dragon on a string out from his grip entirely.

"That man was all dressed up," I pointed out. "Allen." His name made my heart flutter.

Why? Besides the fact that he was gorgeous.

Duh. That was reason enough.

Was I really doing this? Going to a dinner with the stranger who'd seen me... like... like... me? He'd seen the real me.

Was that so bad?

Maybe.

"Allen's got a stick up his very chiseled ass," Bodhi said, his focus entirely on Darcy bunny-thumping his back claws against the dragon in his tough, little death roll.

"Did he just come from work?" My voice carried down the hall as I scoured my closet for the jacket. I found it—only it was way in the back. I held it out in front of me. It may have been a bit wrinkled.

Bodhi let out a *pft* sound. "That boy works from home. I've heard of Zooming in dressed up from the waist-up, but still walking around in a full suit after hours takes professionalism to a whole other level."

He worked from home? Looking *like that*? And here I thought my career was my excuse for my usual slovenly appearance.

"What's he do?" I asked. I was curious. And I couldn't imagine managing to ask the man myself this evening. I would do everything I could to keep him from noticing me. I slid my arms into the suit and tried to button it. Key word: *tried*. My bust strained at the top few buttons.

"Marketing." Bodhi let out a laugh as the sound of Darcy's thumping leaps into the air carried down the hall. "But I suppose it's best you ask him for more info yourself. He's very hush-hush about it. He's not very talkative, frankly. I would never have imagined making him a frequent dinner guest were it not for Valerie."

"Valerie?" My hands froze after undoing the top few buttons of the blazer to let the girls fully breathe.

"His sister. Twin sister. The pair of them…" Bodhi made a smooching sound, and I came to the doorway of my room in time to see him mime a chef's kiss. He turned to look over his shoulder. "She's gay—but taken." The way he looked at me, then, it was like he'd assumed I'd been about to ask.

I tucked my hair behind my ear—blow-dried hair now—and didn't flinch when Darcy stopped his game and came over to rub my ankles.

"Well, now there's cat fur all over your ensemble." He tapped a finger to his lip as he took me in. "But you know what? It works. Keep the jacket. Just like that." His gaze focused in on my cleavage.

I rolled my eyes. "Despite your frequent hints to the contrary, I'm *not* looking to get laid."

"Hmm…" Bodhi didn't respond. Then his Apple watch beeped and he practically jumped in place. "Ah! The fish! Rory won't know to take it out. Chop, chop." He clapped his hands twice and Darcy jumped backward into my room, staring at his playmate wide-eyed as if just discovering the man had turned on him. Bodhi didn't notice, as he was already down the hall and to the stairs, the front door swinging open. "*Now,* Quinn!"

I bent down to give Darcy some scritches and bade him to be good. I probably shouldn't have moved so quickly, though. I was still operating on too little sleep and food.

"Whoa," I said, grabbing hold of the bedroom door as I stood.

I took a deep breath. I could do this.

I snatched my clutch—the pattern was that of an illustration of a shelf of books, not exactly dressy enough for my outfit, but who would even notice? Then I grabbed my phone off the table and my keys from the peg near the front door as I slid on some plain, black flats, locking up behind me.

It was chillier now that it was getting dark, but Bodhi and Rory's condo was just a short walk away. The next building over, past the mailboxes.

My gaze darted briefly to Allen's jeep. It was shiny, clearly well cared-for, and it looked brand-spanking new. Still, it didn't quite fit my idea of a self-made businessman. I wouldn't have expected the driver to pop out wearing what he had.

Then the obvious thought hit me: Why had he parked this far away?

Oh. The next block came into sight. That was probably why. The curb in front of Rory and Bodhi's place was completely occupied with four cars. I could only guess how many guests that translated to.

They only had one of the two-bedroom places like I did.

As I passed the Mini Donation Libraries, I was satisfied to see my absence hadn't tarnished the All-Ages Box too badly. It was still half-full, if in need of a bit of straightening.

I stopped. I knew I was running late, but surely, Bodhi wouldn't miss me between his fish and the mass of guests in his small place.

Rushing over to the All-Ages Box, I opened it up and straightened the books inside. A lot of the books I'd put in it over the weekend were gone, and there were a few new middle grade books that looked to be in nice condition.

My eyes darted to the Ooh-La-La Box on the other side of the bench.

Practically empty.

But there was no time to run to the thrift store just now.

"I know Bodhi and Rory's parties can go on a bit long." The voice from behind me was gruff, and it made me catch my breath. "But I don't think you need to grab a book on the way. I can *promise* you won't be bored."

Chapter Five

"Bodhi sent me to get you." Allen stood there, mere feet from the Ooh-La-La Box, his suitcoat opened and his hands tucked into his pockets in front of the lapels, as if ready to go from all-business to something more casual at the first hint of play. He seemed to read my mind as a saucy grin perked up his altogether too-tempting lips. "Said you might get distracted on the way and he had fish to keep from burning."

I cleared my throat and latched the All-Ages Box up again. "I just stopped to fix these. It bothers me when the books tumble over in disarray."

He took a step closer. He was a head taller than me, and I could smell his aftershave. Something earthy. Rich. My toes curled.

"Neat and orderly," he said, and for a moment, the way he looked at me as he spoke, his gaze traveling up and down, I wondered if he was referring to me. Especially in comparison to how he'd seen me before.

Laughing nervously, I stepped back, putting some space between us, and tugged at the bottom of my suit jacket. "Well, I'd rather it get messy than not."

"Oh?" Allen's brow arched. "And why is that?"

The way those eyes lingered on me. And Bodhi had said the man was shy? Well, he'd said he hadn't talked much.

I cradled my clutch to my chest as if to protect my heart from those dastardly, brown eyes of his.

"It means it's well-loved, of course." Silence hung in the crisp night air between us. He smirked. My cheeks flushed. "The library, I mean." I gestured to it with my clutch. "People are taking lots of books and I can't keep up with it." My eyes darted to the Ooh-La-La Box. "That one's almost empty. I missed a drop-off today, and—"

Allen held up both hands in surrender, his suitcoat falling back into place, though still loose and unbuttoned. "I agree. Messy and well-loved beats neat and orderly any day."

I jutted my chin up a little higher. "But aren't *you* neat and orderly?"

He held out one side of his coat and examined himself as if just discovering that about himself. "Well, I did think the suitcoat would hide the wrinkles on the shirt."

There were some wrinkles in the fabric, now that I looked closer.

"Did you get ready in a hurry?" I asked.

He dropped hold of his coat and ran his hand

through his hair. "Maybe. But not as much of a hurry as you did. Quite the change." He nodded appraisingly.

"Hmm." I covered my heart—my boob—with my clutch again.

Allen cleared his throat and then pointed at the Ooh-La-La Box. "So, Rory told me you're the gal to ask about these."

"Oh?" Had he and Bodhi's husband been talking about me since that disaster of an introduction? It hadn't even been for more than a moment. Bodhi had at least spared me that, excusing us so I could get ready and instructing Allen to go on ahead before shutting my condo door in his face.

Allen cradled his chin between his thumb and fore-finger, examining the Ooh-La-La Box. "You're the volunteer librarian." His eyes darted to me. "Though I'd be able to tell that from your bag there."

I glanced at my library-pattern clutch and brought it to my side sheepishly. "Curator of the neighborhood Mini Donation Libraries. My mom installed them a few years back—Dad built and painted them."

"Oh? Your dad's the artist? They really catch the eye."

"That's maybe not a good thing," I mumbled.

He chuckled and turned to me. "What do you mean by that?"

"Well..." I tucked a pesky lock of hair behind my ear. "Some people in the neighborhood aren't fans of the Ooh-La-La Box."

"The... what?" His mouth hung open slightly.

Damn, those lips were enticing.

I blinked—hard. Had I just thought that? Also, had I *said* those silly words to this man? "The Romance-Only Box," I explained. "That's the... uh, name for it. You know, it wasn't my idea. It was my mom's." That didn't really make it any less embarrassing, now that I thought about it.

"What's wrong with that?" Allen asked. His chin dipped slightly and his voice rumbled. "Some people can be such prudes."

I laughed so hard, I hiccupped. "Well, it's not going anywhere—the majority of the neighborhood likes it."

A cool breeze sent a shiver down my spine, and Allen gestured as if for me to join him in walking to Bodhi and Rory's condo. "I imagine so," he said as I stepped in line beside him. "It was pretty full when I stopped by last week to pick up Rory and Bodhi's mail."

"I have to stock it twice a week," I explained. "I scour book sales, yard sales, thrift shops. Sometimes I make a day of hitting used bookstores up in Milwaukee. On occasion, I get a whole bunch of ARCs—that is, advanced reader copies—from a book convention." Allen seemed amused that I stopped to explain that part, but it may have just been the fact that I'd shoved my clutch under my arm and mimed reading a book, as if that were necessary to aid in the definition. "And the locals are good about adding their own used books to it, too—when they can stand to part with them, of course. Few titles actually manage to show back up on the shelves again."

"Must be because you know how to pick 'em." His eyes twinkled in the overhead street lamp as we made our way up the walk to Rory and Bodhi's place.

"I guess..." I thanked him as he held the front door to the condo open for me.

Immediately, I was hit by the warmth—Bodhi and Rory must have still had their furnace on. The hum of conversation wormed its way down the interior staircase, cushioned by the soft melody of jazz music.

Their condo was so similarly structured to mine, and yet it may as well have been on a different planet. Even the staircase leading up was decorated warmly, lush, framed posters from Broadway plays and pop art decorating the white walls. Mom had wanted Dad to paint something on our staircase walls, but he'd never gotten around to it before they'd moved.

Shifting aside so Allen could follow me into the small mudroom and shut the door behind us, I nearly backed into a coatrack weighed down with an assortment of coats.

Allen's arms reached out almost on instinct in order to catch me, but I saved myself, turning a stumble into a hop and hanging on to the staircase handrail.

"Smooth," Allen said with a smirk. "That's the second time in less than an hour I've seen you fall nearly flat on your face."

"At least you didn't have me flat on my *ass*," I said.

Then my heart practically stopped. "I mean, you didn't *see* my flat ass. I mean, *see me flat on my ass!*"

I screeched. Sinkhole, swallow me up now.

"Quinn, honey, is that you?" Bodhi's voice carried down the stairs. I *had* shouted about my flat ass. Not that I actually *thought* it was flat. Stupid gaffe. "What are you shouting about?"

"Yes, nothing, never mind, we're coming up!" I spoke quickly.

Allen's eyes blinked rapidly, but then his lips clamped together and he cleared his throat. "*Flat* ass?" His gaze darted tellingly downward. "I don't think that's how I would describe it—"

"Um, forget I said anything?" I offered, cutting him off. "Please."

"You have *definitely* been reading a lot of romance novels," he suggested.

"Yes, I have," I admitted. I gestured wildly at my face. I'd put on some concealer to cover the bags under my eyes, but it could only do so much to cover the truth. "I'm currently coming off a multiple-day book binge. My brain is..." I twirled my hands around my head, as if leaving the rest unsaid.

But really only because words had escaped me.

"Mush," I said after a while.

My stomach rumbled.

"And your stomach is empty." Allen gestured upstairs. "Shall we?"

"Yes, of course." Taking a deep breath and cursing my stupidity, I headed up the stairs.

Was I harassing this guy? Had my stupid brain fart qualified as harassing?

Or was this flirting?

God, my head hurt.

"There they are!" Bodhi put a large serving plate down on top of his counter and waved his oven-mitt-covered hands in the air.

I waved *hi* at a room full of four strangers and Rory, Bodhi's equally handsome husband, a tall, thin man with a white beard that almost blended in with his pale-white complexion. He was bald, and he had these bright blue eyes that were hard to look away from.

"Hey, Quinn! It's been a while." Rory beamed and pulled out a seat. Whereas my carpeted condo had a small, round table that could seat four at most, Bodhi and Rory had left a large, open space on their hard-wood flooring for a long, sleek dining table that could fit up to eight. I couldn't imagine having eight people crammed into my condo on any one occasion.

I couldn't imagine having seven other local friends I'd want to hang out with all at once.

"Thanks so much for having me," I said, placing my clutch under my chair and straining my mouth into a smile. I offered a polite nod to my hosts and their guests, who were all strangers to me. Of course, they were all gorgeous, too. I was surprised I'd made the cut, really, but it wasn't like the couple had chosen to surround themselves with beauty, I was sure.

At least I was pretty sure.

"I'm sorry I held things up," I said. "And that I

almost forgot... Been busy." I thanked Rory as he helped me push in my chair.

"Nonsense, you're just in time," Rory said, his voice higher in tone than one might have expected from his motorcycle-club-lite appearance.

I had V.L. Breedlove's MC series on the brain, that was clear.

Allen sat down right across from me as Rory went to help Bodhi plate the food.

"So this is the Mini Donation Librarian?" a va-va-voom woman who sat beside Allen asked as she set her glass of wine down in front of her. She was shapely and filled out a red dress like it had been poured onto her. A rosy, somewhat pallid complexion clashed with brown hair so dark, it was almost black. It spilled in waves over one shoulder.

"Who? Me?" *Of course you, you nincompoop.* "Oh, yes, yeah, of course. You've been talking about me?" *Why did you say that out loud?*

She chuckled, a tittering, airy sound. "Well, we can be gossips. You'll have to pardon us." The woman beside her—lanky and dark-skinned, with her head half-shaved and the rest of it dangling over one eye and dyed bright yellow—took her hand.

The two men I didn't know filled out the table on my side, leaving the ends for our hosts.

My stomach rumbled again as Rory set a plate of salmon in front of me.

I felt myself blushing as half the room broke out in stifled giggles.

"Bodhi's cooking does that to me, too," the man beside me said. He was a big guy, rotund and with a trimmed brown beard against a tanned complexion. "C.J.," he said, extending his right hand across himself to me.

"Hi." I shook his hand.

"Nickname," said the man beside him. He was also rather beefy like his presumed partner, though he was clean-shaven and had a tawny complexion. "But only I call him 'Charles.' A lot of nicknames in this room." His eyes flicked tellingly from C.J. to everyone seated across from us.

"You can call me 'Valerie' when you want to get my attention," said the woman dressed in red as she took a sip of her wine. She shuddered but spared a smile to thank Bodhi for her plate. "Just the sound of it makes me shiver. Mother only ever called my name when about to yell at me. I don't even like 'Val' much. Why can't I just go by my initials, like C.J.?"

I took a sip of water, eager to dive in to the food, the aroma of which was just about making me salivate onto the table.

"Your initials are too much of a mouthful, if I remember right," Bodhi said, grabbing for an opened bottle of wine and filling up Val's nearly empty glass. He made a face as if it hurt him to speak. "V.T.? V.M.?"

"Valerie Louise," she corrected dramatically. "Two grandmothers in one."

I spit my water back into my glass.

"Ah. How could I forget?" Bodhi wriggled his eyebrows across the table, like part of an inside joke.

I was still choking.

"You okay?" asked C.J.

"Yes, um, yes." My eyes flicked to Allen. He pressed a fist against his lips and looked away tellingly.

"So anyway, I'm Maya and this is my fiancée, Val," said the dark-skinned woman.

"Maya's an accountant." Valerie—Val—freaking *V.L.* put a hand on her fiancée's lap. I noticed she didn't say what *she* did.

"I'm Jake," said the man beside C.J.

"And you've met Allen," Bodhi said, holding the wine bottle out over my empty goblet. I covered it and shook my head. I'd better not, not on a dangerously empty stomach. "Val's his sister."

They did quite share some similarities in the structure of their faces. Siblings, huh? Twins, if I remembered right from what Bodhi had told me.

"Quinn," I said to the rest of the room. "Nice to meet you." My stomach roared out in what could only be described as agony.

"Oh, please dig in." Bodhi waved a hand as he poured C.J. a glass of wine. Rory stepped out of the kitchen, his arms full of salad bowls. "No need to wait for us."

He didn't have to tell me twice. I put my napkin on my lap and got to work, cutting into my fish with likely a bit too much relish and only just—only barely just—stopping myself from moaning when the first warm, flaky bite hit my tongue. I covered my mouth and my eyes widened as my gaze met Allen's across from me.

I swallowed and took another harried gulp of water to cover my embarrassment. Nothing I did around that man seemed to get past him.

"What do you do?" C.J. asked, taking a fork to his salad as Bodhi and Rory finally joined us at the table.

"I'm a writer," I said.

Maya gasped and looked down her side of the table.

Val elbowed her and mumbled something.

Shit. Could this really be?

Did I outright ask her?

Be cool, I told myself. But inside, my stomach was fluttering. It all made sense. She clearly knew the neighborhood.

"What kind of writing?" Jake asked.

"Oh, nothing fun. Business content, speeches, stuff like that. I also edit. Basically, I freelance, cobble together something resembling a living."

"You work from home," Allen said. It wasn't a question. The way he examined me in my ill-fitting suit, it was like he knew I almost never wore the thing.

"Yeah. So, uh, what do you all do?" I asked. "I mean, besides Rory and Bodhi, since I assume we all know that much."

Bodhi *tsked*. "There's more to life than just what we *do* for a living. Really, what a drab question, C.J." He winked at me, as if reminding me C.J. had asked the question first and assuring me I didn't have to keep the conversation going in that direction.

Drat. Normally, I'd agree with him, but I was hoping the question would get around the table and Val—V.L.—would talk about her writing.

If that was indeed her full-time job. Many authors juggled other jobs, too, I knew that much.

"Oh, say, Allen, did you ask Quinn yet?" Bodhi said right before popping a bit of pink, flaky salmon into his mouth.

My stomach flip-flopped. Ask me what?

Allen stared me down over the rim of his wineglass. "No. I didn't have a chance to ask her. I thought it'd be better if we got inside first. Bit nippy out." He winked at me and took a drink.

I shivered, glad for the suit jacket over my blouse. A bit *nippy* out indeed.

"He likes your boxes," Val said, straight to the point as she cut into her fish. "Said we should get some set up in our neighborhood."

Did brother and sister still live together, then? I opened my mouth to ask just that, but Allen stopped me with a hand out. "My sister and I live in the same building downtown. A converted old factory." He shrugged. "Our mother's in real estate. She offered us both first dibs on some condos that opened up at the same time."

"And they often work together," Maya added, clinking her fork against her plate. "So that makes it easier for them to get things done."

They did?

Here we were, back to the question of what they

did for a living.

Back to the thought that perhaps I was seated across from my new favorite author this very minute.

"I'd love to help," I said quickly. "Though it was my dad who built and painted the boxes—and he moved out of state."

"That's too bad," Val said, barely sparing me a glance. "They're rather cute."

"Jake's good at art," C.J. volunteered.

Jake chuckled nervously. "Well, I don't know if I could match the artistry on those boxes out there, but I can try. Allen, didn't you send me a pic of one of those boxes? The one with the hearts and the sexy ladies?"

Jake fished a phone out of his pocket, but before he could do more than tap the screen once, Bodhi reached over and rapped his spoon against the back of Jake's hand. "No phones at the table!"

"Right, okay." Jake chuckled and put the phone away.

Allen had snapped a photo of the Ooh-La-La Box?

Just like V.L. Breedlove had posted to her Instagram.

And what had I noticed when I'd been browsing the comments the other day? Breedlove had a personal assistant. And it had been a guy. Why had that detail stuck in my mind? Right. The screen name had just been "V.L. Breedlove PA," but the readers responding to the comment had engaged in a conversation with each other about getting a signed copy, and one of the women had mentioned "contacting *him*," that was how she'd gotten her copies.

Wait. That was my in.

"I, uh, saw the box online the other day." Clearing my throat, I went to stab another piece of food on my plate, only to realize I had eaten every speck of my dinner. Flushing at the heavy clank the fork's tines made against the plate, I set it down quickly. "I showed my mom and dad. They loved it. An author shared it to her account."

The room went quiet, the soft music in the background filling the silence. I watched Val like a hawk for her reaction, but she didn't so much as flinch.

"Oh, that's fun," said C.J. "Hope that means more books get donated."

"Well, she didn't share *where* the box was, but it's recognizable to those of us familiar with it," I said.

"That's quite a coincidence, then." Allen leaned back in his seat and held his wineglass aloft. "You stumbling on a post that didn't tag your Mini Donation Library's location."

A coincidence, indeed.

I wiped my mouth on my cloth napkin and set it down on my lap. "Not a coincidence at all." I stared down the table at Bodhi, even though I could feel Allen's eyes on me. Combined with my suddenly full stomach, the thought was making me grow rather feverish. "You know that book you saw me unloading into the Ooh-La-La Box the other day? The one you said was to die for?"

Bodhi pursed his lips for a second and then realization dawned on him, his jaw growing slack. "Oh. Yes. *Corrupt Me*. My *god*."

"Sounds spicy," Jake offered.

He and C.J. chuckled under their breath.

"*Corrupt Me*?" Val asked, looking up from her plate for the first time since the topic of the mysterious author had come up.

Of course. She thought the box had been loaded up with just copies of *Thrill Me*. Loaded up by her PA—

Oh, my god. Allen was the hot guy Evangeline had seen filling up the box, on behalf of his sister! It all made sense.

Now if I could just get either of these coy twins to spill the beans already.

Chapter Six

"Yes," I said, picking up my wineglass and trying to hold it casually like Allen was, only recalling when I glanced at it that I'd passed on alcohol for the evening. I picked up my water glass and leaned back in my chair instead. The tall, oblong water glass gave me less of the cool, collected sleuth vibe I'd been trying to go for. "By coincidence, I'd picked up *Corrupt Me* at the Friends of the Library book sale that morning, and I'd planned to leave it in the neighborhood library, but after Bodhi gushed over it—and Evangeline did the same—I had to read it for myself."

Val's eyebrow arched and Maya giggled. Before either could fess up to anything, Rory stood and started collecting plates. "We have a cobbler in the oven for dessert," he explained. "Best to plate it up while it's still hot."

Entirely unintentionally, I found myself fanning my flushed face with my free hand as he mentioned the heat. Thoughts of the heroes and heroines in Breedlove's Maxwell Security series had crept from my subconscious to my conscious entirely against my will.

"Oh, is it your peach cobbler?" Jake asked, jumping to his feet to help collect the plates. "Please tell me it's peach!"

"Cherry," Rory admitted.

"Come now, you haven't even *tried* the cherry yet," Bodhi said, joining them as they stepped past the counter and into the condo's kitchen area.

Maya and Val started talking quietly amongst themselves, and my ears strained to hear their whispers.

"So I take it the author of your book is the one who posted the picture."

I jumped in place. For a brief, bizarre moment, I'd almost forgotten about Allen, so focused I'd been on Val potentially dishing her secrets.

"Yes." Time to turn my investigation powers on him. "*And* my friend—the head of the Condo Association, who keeps a *close eye* on everything going on in the neighborhood—saw someone loading up the box with several *autographed* copies of the first book in the same series last week."

Allen didn't flinch, just set his wineglass down on the table and ran a hand absentmindedly across the collar of his dress shirt.

"Oh, that was probably Allen," said Bodhi, both his hands full with a small plate of cherry cobbler. As if he hadn't just blown open the subject I'd been tiptoeing around, watching for hints and cracks in facades, Bodhi set the pieces in front of Allen and me, giving us each a new fork, and strolled back toward the kitchen. "Didn't you mention you do promotional work for that author?" Bodhi flapped a hand in the air behind him.

I froze, my mind scrambling for words, but my tongue growing rather slack.

Allen chuckled, a deep, rumbling sound, as he picked up the new fork in front of him. "Among a number of things."

I watched Val for some reaction, but she and Maya only looked up when Jake approached with two plates of cobbler for them.

"Heavenly," said Allen to Rory, who handed C.J. a plate and sat down with his own portion. "Both of you outdid yourselves today."

"Oh, stop," said Bodhi. "But don't really." He laughed. "You're welcome."

Somehow utterly defeated, I picked up my own fork while my mind scrambled for words.

The cobbler *was* good. And it gave me the strength for another plan of attack.

"Bodhi, how could you not have told me you knew someone who did marketing for an author?" I turned to Allen. "Of course we would have gladly taken any copies of your author's books for the libraries—authors? Do you do marketing for more than one?"

Allen and Val exchanged a glance. "No," Allen admitted, wiping his mouth with his napkin. He was mum on giving me more.

He worked from home—promoting Val's work couldn't be the only thing he did. Then again, V.L. Breedlove books seemed to be selling like they were triple discounted on Black Friday, so maybe she could afford a living for them both.

But he'd mentioned he did "other things." Perhaps the PA work was more a favor to his sister than anything.

Look at him. How many cover-model men made a living off of being one romance author's PA?

"But, Bodhi, even just as a fellow reader—how could you not tell me about those books sooner?" I said.

Bodhi was sitting down with his own plate of cobbler now and he rolled his eyes. "I *did* tell you."

"Only when you saw the book in my hands!"

"Of course I would have told you, Quinn, when I got around to it. I was only introduced to V.L. Breedlove through Val and Allen before our trip. I just met Maya and Val a month ago at the club downtown."

True, Bodhi *did* seem to make a new friend every minute. I knew I was hardly the top of his call list whenever he had news. But I *did* think I was his go-to bookworm friend, considering the Mini Donation Libraries.

Fine. I would let that go.

I straightened my back in my chair. "I would love to meet Ms. Breedlove. Is she planning on doing any local author events?" My gaze darted between Val and Allen.

They did look at one another, as if waiting for the other to answer me first.

"Breedlove prefers privacy." Allen nodded at his sister and offered me a slight smile as he rubbed a thumb across the condensation on his water glass. "And what makes you think I work for a local author, anyway? The Internet makes everything possible."

I opened my mouth to retort—my gaze flicking to Val, who shared a knowing look with Maya, both barely able to contain their laughter—but he had me there. Even the autographed copies.

She could have sent them to him after he'd told her about the Ooh-La-La Box or even just for him to have on hand for any number of promotional activities.

But I still had a feeling that wasn't the case.

"You've never met her?" I threw back at him.

The rest of the men at the table watched the conversation with interest.

"I never said *that*," Allen offered. He picked up his fork and casually finished his cobbler, his mouth wrapping with relish around the last bite. My mind went immediately to what kinds of things his tongue was doing to that fork.

I bet *all kinds* of interesting things.

Shuddering, I tried to take my mind out of the gutter.

"Allen is *all about* his clients' privacy." Val patted him on the leg, and he visibly winced. Her cheeks colored and she whispered something to Maya, the two of them devolving into giggles.

"All right, you two, enough secret chatter at the table," C.J. said. He pushed his chair back and stretched, his fingers lacing over his stomach.

Enough secret chatter indeed.

"Well, how about this?" I asked. "I help you figure out the logistics of a Mini Donation Library in your neighborhood, and you let me tag along the next time you *meet V.L. Breedlove* in person. As long as she's aware I'd be there, of course—as an *incredibly enthusiastic* fan." My gaze darted to Val, who was entirely caught up in her own hushed conversation with her fiancée.

"I can pass on your fan mail." Allen nodded at me stiffly.

"A PA can *always* pass on fan mail!" I protested.

"I thought you just said you did promotional work for the author," Rory offered. "A personal assistant...?"

Allen's cheeks darkened somewhat, and he shrugged. "Many popular authors have PAs. We largely do promotional work. It's not like I'm fetching coffee and driving anyone to appointments."

"Though, speaking of, you promised to take me to my dentist appointment next week, remember?" Val pouted at her brother.

Allen let out a deep sigh and ran a hand over his face. "Is your car in the shop or something? You can borrow mine."

"It isn't in the shop and you know how I get about

dentists." She made a sour face and shuddered. "I have nightmares. And Maya has work, and *your* work is flexible, so—"

"Fine." Allen grunted.

"Looks like you're *someone's* PA," Jake joked, getting to his feet. "If not this Breedlove author's."

Oh, I wasn't so sure about that.

C.J. and Jake excused themselves shortly after dessert, and though I was about to collapse on my feet, I was determined to stay as long as my new favorite author did.

If only I could get her to admit she *was* my favorite author.

My eyes kept shutting, but I did my best to cradle the cappuccino Rory had made me as I leaned against the counter dividing the kitchen and the living area.

"We keeping you up past your bedtime?" Allen walked over, his own mug steaming.

I suddenly had this vision of him in the morning in my own condo—so similar, yet different, my own décor utterly lacking—walking over to hand me a cup of coffee as we greeted the day together.

My insides tingled, from my core out to my fingers and toes.

"I'll have you know I usually go to bed at two in the morning," I said. "It's just that... I may have skimped on sleep the past few days." I took another sip of lukewarm coffee, waiting for the buzz to kick in.

My body was already a jittery, crashing mess, though, and more caffeine at ten o' clock in the evening could only do so much to keep me awake.

He chuckled. "That's a writer's schedule if I've ever heard one."

"More like a ravenous reader's. But yeah, one of the benefits of being freelance." I leaned an elbow on the counter, laughter echoing out from the open patio door. The volume of Rory, Bodhi, Maya, and Val's conversation was likely something that would annoy Mrs. Whithouse. At least they'd shut off the music before opening the door late at night.

"Have you ever thought about writing?" Allen asked.

I cocked an eyebrow and set my mug down beside the last of the cherry cobbler, tempting me from its crumb-covered glass pan. "I do write. Almost every day."

"I mean fiction. Do you write fiction?"

My knees wobbled under the way he examined me. "I've never thought about it. You?"

"I've dabbled." He grimaced and seemed to use his mug to hide his face. "Had an agent once. She never sold anything for me."

"Sounds like more than *dabbling*." I blinked— hard. Were these twins both authors?

He shrugged. "I know why it didn't sell. It was this whole thing loosely inspired by my family. A man figuring out his identity, that sort of thing. Nothing interesting, really."

"Sounds like the type of thing most publishers eat up," I pointed out.

He set his mug down beside mine and stabbed the cobbler with the metal pie server, cutting the remaining portion into two equal pieces. "I was younger and a bit uptight. I had these lofty hopes for it. I hate the manuscript now. I'm glad it never saw the light of day."

"Hmm. But an agent liked it enough to represent you."

He picked up one of the slices and shifted it down to the empty half of the pan, closer to me. "An agent who stopped returning my calls almost as soon as it was clear no one was interested. I moved on." He set down the pie server.

Checking over Allen's shoulder to see if Rory or Bodhi would pop in and all of a sudden object to us messing with the last of their dessert, I hesitated.

But Allen walked into the kitchen, opened a drawer like he owned the place, and got us each new forks.

"Thanks," I said, using my fork to dig in, right in the pan, burnt bits clinging to the sides and all. I groaned as the deliciousness hit my tongue for a second time.

Allen smirked, his eyes twinkling as he took a more subdued bite of his slice.

My cheeks flushed and I put the fork down. "I'd like to read it. Your book."

He chuckled darkly. "Yeah, no one's going to read the manuscript in my drawer. Metaphorically speaking, of course. I'm not the type of guy who prints out his manuscript and forces it down everyone's throats."

"I see." I rapped my fingers against the counter. "And you're not the kind of guy who gives up secrets about authors with pen names, either."

"NDAs exist for a reason." He winked as he went for another bite of his slice. "But if you blow me away, I promise to put a good word in for you."

"*If* I blow you?" I asked. "Away?" I added quickly.

I'd only meant to ask what he'd meant by that. I hadn't meant to imply anything. I'd known he hadn't meant *that. Get out of the gutter, mind.*

If only my mind hadn't been marinating in V.L. Breedlove for days, I might have had a better shot of dragging it out of there.

Allen chuckled and set down his fork. "Well, I wanted to discuss payment with you. I know you volunteer for the Mini Donation Libraries here, but it's your neighborhood—and it sounds like it's your legacy. I wouldn't expect you to do the same thing at my place for free."

"Oh." My heart thumped. I was genuinely surprised he wanted to pay me. Frankly, just being able to openly gush with V.L. Breedlove about her books would have been payment enough—though my checking account probably would have disagreed with that. "Thank you. What did you have in mind?"

"A hundred dollars an hour?"

The fork between my fingers slipped and clattered to the floor. A hundred dollars an hour? What was he doing, growing a money tree in his apartment?

"Too little?" he offered, unperturbed. "A hundred and fifty?"

"Are you *nuts*?" I said. "I mean, someone needs to foot the bill for used books to fill the boxes, but even assuming your neighborhood is as voracious as mine—and that's a big *if*—that usually costs like fifteen bucks a week, max."

"All those books for so little?" Allen's eyebrow arched.

"You have to know how and where to shop. Sometimes Evangeline reminds people to Venmo me some cash to chip in, too, so it's not all on me." Though it mostly was, really.

"I see. In any case, we're discussing payment for your work, not for the upkeep of the boxes. Once you teach me everything I need to know, I can do that. I'll have Val and Maya help me."

I swept across the air with my hand in a karate chop move. Clearly amused, he jumped back out of the way and I had to clutch my wrist to keep myself from gesticulating wildly.

"You do realize my dad built and painted the boxes, right? I can't do that myself."

"Yes, you told me." He stared at my hand over my wrist, as if wondering if I'd chop at him again.

I'd been chopping at the ridiculousness of it all, not

him. My cheeks burned. "Then what are you paying me for?"

Allen rapped his knuckles against the counter. "You really know how to sell yourself, don't you?" He gave me a onceover. "You got dressed for success, didn't you? Then embrace it."

Fiddling with the hem of my suitcoat, tugging it down as if to straighten it—it was a bit short at the waist—I took a deep breath and mumbled, "It's not like I've had time to research the going rates..."

"Oh, yeah?" Allen's eyes positively sparkled as he leaned just slightly closer. "What is the going rate for 'Mini Donation Library Consultant'?"

"I imagine there is no such thing, but—"

"Were you going to negotiate for a better offer? Two hundred an hour?"

"*No*! I mean..." I stumbled backward. At this point, a small part of me was tempted to see how deep this man's pockets would go. Allen flicked back his suitcoat as he dug into a pocket and pulled out his wallet. "When's good for you?" He removed a business card from the fold and handed it to me.

It was black with gold lettering and it just had his name, email address, and a phone number. No specific profession or location. I turned it over. Blank.

"Looking for hidden messages?" he teased.

Feeling my neck grow hot, I quickly stuffed the card into my suitcoat pocket and crossed the room to where I'd left my clutch. "I have some work I have to catch up with," I said, making a point of keeping my nose in the air as I riffled through and found the small stash of business cards I'd kept for just such an occasion. A very rare such occasion. I wasn't sure I'd given these out to anyone at a social gathering before. "But why don't you tag along with me to the thrift store this Saturday to start? I'll show you what I do to stock my own boxes."

Allen appeared right behind me and try as I might, I couldn't stop myself from jumping slightly. I handed him a card. It was mostly white with blue accents. It had my name, phone number, and title: "Business Writer/Copyeditor." Granted, it was a title I'd given myself and I hadn't bothered to include the remote temp administrative work and grocery store app shopping that occasionally filled in the gaps.

Though depending on how many hours I worked on this project for this ridiculous man, I supposed there'd be no reason to pick up any slack this month. "No charge, I added."

"Pardon?" Allen looked up from examining my card.

"For the thrift store shopping. Since it's just you observing what I do for my box." Judging by the state of the boxes, I really needed to go sooner, but too much freelance work awaited, thanks to that reading binge. No more reading for fun, no more relaxing, until I caught up. Just work, eating, sleeping. And giving Darcy attention.

I could do this. I was a big girl. Besides, I'd read everything V.L. Breedlove had written.

At least until next Tuesday.

"You are a terrible negotiator." Allen's grin was broad as he tucked the card into his wallet.

"As are you, on the employer side, I might add." I arched a brow.

The conversation spilling into the condo from the open patio door turned both our heads as Rory, Bodhi, Val, and Maya stepped back in. My gaze shifted to my feet, as if caught doing something I should have been embarrassed of.

"Saturday, it is," Allen said. "Where and when?"

"I'll text you the details." Snapping my clutch shut tighter, I brushed past him, doing my best not to meet his gaze.

"Thank you so much for having me," I told Rory and Bodhi.

"Do you have to go already?" Bodhi offered me a hug. It was late, though. Perhaps he hadn't kept track of time.

"Yes, but I do appreciate you dragging me out for such good food—and good company." I smiled. "But I really do have to get back to work for several more days."

"You overwork yourself." Bodhi patted me on the arm.

Did I explain to him I hadn't been working much at all, despite my haggard appearance? I could save the details for another day.

"Nice to meet you," I added to Maya and Val, who had moved over to speak to Allen, my eyes lingering one long moment on Val, wondering, just wondering, if she'd let a hint slip out into the open.

Was this a rare night off? Did *she* manage to keep a good work-life balance? Maybe it was just me who let good stories wreck my life for days at a time.

"And you. I do hope we'll be seeing you." Val snickered a little haughtily, moving to cover her mouth. "'Partings can be such sweet, sad torture.'" She seemed slightly drunk, her words slurring.

She and Maya burst into giggles and Allen rolled his eyes, tucking his wallet and his hands back into his pockets.

So there it was. The author quoting her own book right at me.

I would get her to outright admit she was V.L. Breedlove yet.

And then... I would tell her how much I loved her.

Books. Her books.

Chapter Seven

Good to my word, I spent the next two days in a productive haze, catching up on sleep, eating better, cutting back on coffee, and getting back on track. I worked harder than I had in ages, and Darcy alone kept me company.

Mom wanted to Zoom—she'd said she'd gone into a book coma herself while plowing through all of V.L. Breedlove's available works—but I didn't have time for *that* whole conversation, not to mention my suspicions about Valerie Cox.

That conversation deserved an entire afternoon. I apologized via text and promised to chat with her this weekend once I caught up with work.

I didn't tell her about the prospective job offer from Allen. Job as in finite, contract work, of course. How many hours could it take, especially if he didn't expect me to build and design the box myself? Perhaps I'd get it all done on Saturday.

Milly texted, too. *I'm visiting my parents on Tuesday—want to have lunch?*

Her parents still lived locally. Not that Milly had moved *that* far, but far enough we didn't get together that often. True, I could live anywhere in theory, thanks to the nature of my work, but in practice, not so much. I was lucky Mom and Dad had paid off the condo—and didn't expect me to pay them back for it. My income was enough for income taxes, property taxes, utilities, the condo fee, my health insurance premium, groceries, my phone bill, and all the basics. Including books, naturally, though not always the most expensive, most recent releases. Thank god for libraries for that. Rent would put me in the red—and capitalism didn't look kindly on freelancers with fluctuating income when it came to getting approved for a rental or a mortgage to begin with.

Being alive was expensive.

But in any case, I liked it here and I liked the freedom of working from home. I liked curating Mom and Dad's Mini Donation Library legacy.

Milly lived with her boyfriend of two years, so she had no need of a roommate.

Sure, I texted. *You have off work?*

All week, she wrote back. *Swapped vacation with a co-worker last minute. Just doing a staycation this year.*

More time for books, I wrote back. Then I apologized that I would be too busy to text much over the next few days and I set my phone back on my desk, folding my hands in front of my laptop.

My back and butt had been getting sore at my desk, so I'd moved to my couch, stretching my legs out and editing a nonprofit client's upcoming speech about youth in after-school sports programs several states over.

The internet made for interesting sources of income.

Darcy chirruped as he jumped up by my feet.

"Hi, baby." I spared one hand to pet his cheek with my index finger. "I just have to finish this project and then I'm caught up to where I need to be."

Next week was pretty light on work, actually. It would have been much more convenient to have a book binge during that week.

But alas, I could not have stopped myself after cracking open that first book if my life had depended on it.

Darcy meowed more emphatically and then made for the laptop's keyboard. Panicking that he might leave one of his favorite edits of "lkjlkhjhlh" in the middle of my client talking about school truancy rates, I partially shut the lid.

Darcy wasn't having it. Locking eyes with me, he reached out a paw to the back of the laptop monitor and shut the thing entirely.

I ruffled his head. "I said, I'm almost finished! Come on, boy. You have to let me work."

He meowed again and my phone buzzed. Darcy happily settled onto my lap on top of the closed laptop. It was an email. I meant to push aside the responses from Mom and Milly, but I accidentally hit Milly's message, which just wished me luck getting all my work done and said she'd see me next week.

As I exited the texting app, my eyes lingered on Allen's brief response to the directions to the thrift shop of choice this week and the time of eleven A.M.

I'll be there.

That was it. Had I expected anything more? I shouldn't have.

But maybe, I thought with a tiny bit of heaviness in my gut, I really had.

Maybe I was rusty. It had almost seemed like he'd been flirting with me the other day.

There were two emails.

One was from Evangeline with a list of the month's condo updates. I scrolled through it and found a mention of donating to my Venmo for more funds to stock the libraries, and a *reminder* that *some* of the books in the Ooh-La-La Box weren't appropriate for children. "'Parental discretion is advised,'" I read out loud, chuckling. Evangeline also suggested more people dropping off books to the boxes when they were done with them and noted it would be more efficient a way to keep the boxes stocked than to rely solely on me for the job—since she'd been fielding complaints about the boxes being kind of light this week.

Well, *excuse me* for having a life. My gaze rested on the flannel PJ set I'd *changed into* this morning for the day's outfit.

Okay, a *bit* of a life. But did that mean I had to fill

the boxes up twice a week without fail? Even when my life got a bit hectic, even if I only had myself to blame?

I made a mental note to warn Allen that it was entirely possible his Mini Donation Library would cause a ravenous appetite in his neighborhood for a constant flow of books. Once he'd let that cat out of the bag, there'd be no turning back.

At least no one had complained directly to me.

The other email was a newsletter from V.L. Breedlove.

I actually squealed, making Darcy open one eye and flick an ear from his comfortable position on my laptop.

Hello, rockstars, the newsletter began. She'd called me "Rockstar" in the introduction newsletters, too. It was apparently her pet name for her readers.

Are we getting excited for Riding My Baby *coming out next week? Have you preordered yet? Anyone who preorders and sends my PA an email with proof will get a special surprise. Let's just say it might involve Gideon and Bianca learning how to deal with the terrible twos.* I grabbed a throw pillow off the edge of the couch and screamed into it, just softly, my face growing pink. Gideon and Bianca were the couple from *Corrupt Me*, and they'd had a kid by the end of the series. I couldn't wait to read about them dealing with their rambunctious little girl as a toddler. I had to email the screenshot of my preorder, like, yesterday.

I came up from the pillow for air to find Darcy's

judging look. I stuck my tongue out at him and kept reading.

What's going on in your life? Breedlove continued. I hadn't responded to an email yet, but she wrote as if she expected people to. I wondered if she wrote back or if her PA—if *Allen?*—wrote back for her, just telling her the highlights.

I've been busy writing and editing, as usual, but I try to get out for some fresh air on occasion. It's getting warmer here, but not so warm I'm ready to leave my flannel pajama pants behind. I looked down at my own red pair. It was like she was looking into my room—though the Val I'd seen at Bodhi's had been entirely more glamorous. Maybe she was a scrub when home writing, too.

I've had a lot of comments on my Instagram asking about the location of the Mini Donation Library I featured the other day.

I blinked, then read that line again. She was talking about *my* box. Well, sort of *my* box. She'd posted the picture from Instagram in her newsletter, too. There it was, in the broad light of day, Dad's sexy, romantic art all over it.

I found out who did the art on the box, but I haven't met him, she kept writing. Hey, did she really want to meet my dad, despite Allen and his "NDA"? Dad wasn't even a fan! *And no, I can't tell you where it is. It's too close to where I live.*

I screamed. Outright *screamed*. Darcy jumped off

my lap, flicking his tail. I'd make it up to him later with a bit of tuna flakes in his bowl.

Val was outright admitting it. Admitting it!

I've been inspired to create one of these romance-only boxes in my own neighborhood—but it won't look the same. Updates forthcoming! And no, I still won't tell you where you can find it.

She had been inspired, huh? And had delegated it all to her PA?

I mean, she *did* have books to write and edit.

But I wondered... If Breedlove was going to make this a whole saga in her newsletter, she was bound to be a part of the process, right?

I checked the clock. I had just enough time to get back to work before crashing into bed and getting to ask Allen all of my questions tomorrow.

But not before I sent off that screenshot for my special preorder bonus.

If looking for small crowds, weekdays were definitely better for hitting the local thrift shops, but this week, I'd been too busy, and besides, I knew this particular one often restocked on Friday evenings in preparation for a bump in foot traffic over the weekend.

Plus, it was nice. Run by a local nonprofit, decorated kind of like an antique shop. For some reason, despite the fact that this was purely a professional relationship, it had sprung to mind as a cute place for a date.

I didn't normally care what I looked like. Mom might even say with the ripped jeans I had on today, along with a blue plaid button-up shirt, I was *trying too hard* to not care what I looked like.

But Mom wasn't here to tease me.

Hesitating, I flipped down the visor and peeked at the mirror before I got out of the car. Full makeup. I'd even, as I couldn't help but observe in the mirror as I fluffed my hair, done my nails.

There'd been no time for a professional job. Besides, that was the kind of thing I did once a year with Mom or Milly.

But Allen was a possible *in* to getting a face-to-face in which Val might possibly acknowledge what she really did for a living. And besides, he was a client with deep pockets paying for a job.

Not that I was going to charge him for this taga-long for something I'd already been planning to do, but...

My cheeks reddened in the reflection and I shut the mirror closed.

If Mom saw me now, she'd be right. I was trying too hard—and also trying too hard not to appear like I was trying too hard.

I *really* was still working off that V.L. Breedlove binge. And a new release next week would just spiral me back down into my addiction.

I held my hands out in front of me, the gloss reflecting a bit of the sun. It was like I'd been *possessed* by Breedlove's heroines. Bianca had kind of gone through a homegrown makeover for Gideon, too. The way he'd held her hand and mentioned her long, beautiful fingers had inspired her to try a manicure for the first time. The way he'd taken that hand and *kissed* it when he'd seen her next...

A rap on the window made me jump. Allen's broad form was hunched over, his grin wide. "I thought that was you." His voice came out muffled through the closed car window between us, though it still managed to make my heart skip a beat.

Though that could have been because he'd scared me.

I'd let out a little yelp, too.

"Hi." I waved, then scrambled to unbuckle myself and snatch up my purse.

As soon as I started opening the door, Allen took over, holding it out for me.

"Thank you," I said, sliding my crossbody purse over my head and shoulder. Holding the door for me was purely unnecessary, but boy, did it make my insides do a little leap. I almost forgot to hit the fob to lock the car once he'd shut it. "I didn't see you pull up."

"I've been here twenty minutes already. I saw *you* pull in." He stuck his hands in his pockets—he was wearing jeans this time. In fact, we looked rather like we'd coordinated outfits now that I got a good look at him and I could bring myself to rip my eyes from his dazzling smile. He had on a button-up blue shirt, and I was almost shocked by how well the casual look suited him after he'd looked positively *made* for the business attire he'd worn the other day.

Who was I kidding? He could wear a plush banana suit and still look sexy.

"You look nice," he said. "Seems every time I lay eyes on you, you've transformed yourself."

"Oh, thank you. You, too!" I bounced on my heels as a shot of sheer embarrassment shot across my face. I'd meant he looked nice, too. Not that he'd transformed himself. Though maybe he *had*. I was liking casual Allen.

"Did you want some coffee?" Allen asked, his lips pinching as he seemed to fight a smirk. He pulled a hand out of his pocket to gesture behind him. Some distance away was his blue jeep. "It's from home. But I brought two Thermoses in case you..."

"Oh, uh, thank you, but I'm trying to wean off of it. At least for the foreseeable future." We made our way to the thrift shop's front door. There was a fair amount of shoppers making their way in and out of the store every few moments. Around the back, cars lined up so that people in the midst of spring cleaning could offer up donations.

"Are you overworking yourself?" Allen asked slyly as we reached the door.

"Um, something like that." Perfect segue into talking about how I'd been on a book binge of his *client's* novels. But as I went to grab for the handle, he got there first, holding it open—first for the two old ladies leaving the store with their arms loaded up with reusable tote bags stuffed to the gills, and then for me to step inside. He kept holding it for a harried mother holding the hands of two toddlers as they plodded quickly on either side of her.

It wasn't just me imagining the old women *and* the harried mother doing a double take when they thanked him. He had that kind of effect on people.

I stood by the shopping baskets the thrift shop offered for eager shoppers and just stared at him.

"So," he said, clapping his hands together as he approached me. "Show me the way?"

Drat. The moment to talk about Breedlove had passed.

"Take a basket, please," I said. "Two if you want to get started on the stock for your own box."

"Oh? Do you think the box will be put together so quickly? How disappointing." His eyes shimmered as he took two baskets.

I grabbed one of my own, biting back the comment about how me finishing the job quickly would save him a lot of money if I was charging by the hour. "Well, we have a lot to go over. Not first of which is permission to install one. You said you lived in a condo building, right? So you don't have land of your own to put it on."

"My mother owns the building. Well, her real estate company does."

Oh. Deep pockets indeed. "Then you'll need her

permission, I suppose. Is there a nice spot for the box? By the mailboxes, perhaps, like by my place?"

"Well, the mailboxes are indoors. But there's a rather nice patch of grass out front, surrounded by some flowers in the warmer months." Allen stopped as we passed by a collection of knickknacks, shifting his second basket to the other hand and picking up a rather hideous glass statue of a melted-mud-like creature I supposed was supposed to resemble a cat. Its eyes were painted crookedly, skewed off from where the porcelain had left recesses for them. "One man's trash…"

"Is certainly *nobody's* treasure." I laughed. "And I love cats, but that *thing*? Not so much."

"It's a cat?" he asked. "I thought it was a seal."

"The ears," I pointed out. They were triangular.

"I thought those were tusks."

I snorted. "A seal with tusks on the top of its head?"

He put the cursed object down, his eyes widening exaggeratedly. "Does it *look* like whoever made that had any idea what any animal looks like?"

"Touché."

"You like cats?" Allen asked. "I thought I might have seen Bodhi holding one in front of your place the other day, but all I really saw was a quick blur."

I laughed. "That was Darcy. He's eight years old and gray-striped. I got him as a kitten my senior year of high school and my parents kept him while I was in college, but now he lives permanently with me."

"Kittens are the best." Allen's sculpted cheekbones became even more pronounced as happiness invaded his expression.

An incredibly attractive man who was into cats?

My lungs practically forgot how to breathe, my brain scrambling. Did I want to get a good paycheck from this guy? Sleuth around and make him admit the truth about his sister and my favorite author being one and the same?

Or did I want to rip that light-blue shirt off him and jump him, right here in the store?

A kid's squeal one aisle over splashed some cold water onto *that* thought.

"Do you have any kittens?" I asked.

"I *did*."

I gasped, pulling to an abrupt stop, picturing kittens hit by cars, coming down with fatal diseases, falling off trees they'd boldly climbed up. The basket in my hand swung wildly, smacking up against a crystalline vase.

Despite the two baskets he carried, Allen scrambled to stop my basket from swinging, saving me the trouble of buying a collection of crystalline vase pieces. He smirked. "I only meant they grew up. I have two cats. Poe and Raven, a black-furred boy and girl."

"Oh! *Oh*." I'd been foolish to let my imagination run off with me. "Literary kitties."

"Mr. Darcy, too, I take it?"

"Yes." I held tightly to the basket handle with both

hands and scuffed a toe in the rather worn, thin, brown carpet beneath our feet.

"Val always teases me for being more into cats than dogs. She has a Pekingese, and the cats hate her, so we don't often do playdates. If you come to my place to help me plan, I'll let you meet—"

"Val? Vally? Is that you?"

Allen's eyes snapped up and I turned around to follow his gaze.

The *clomp, clomp* of heels made it clear the woman was speeding up her pace. She was beautiful, impossible to look away from, all curves in a pale green spring dress, waves of auburn hair spilling over her shoulders.

And she greeted Allen by kissing him—right on the cheek.

Chapter Eight

"What in the world are you doing here, dear?" The woman came up for air after kissing the slightly bearded face of my client.

Client. He *was* just a client.

She pulled back, leaving Allen's wary expression evident, the smile on his lips more forced than usual. "I'm here—"

But the woman didn't even let him speak.

She turned around, her bright green eyes blinking rapidly as she took me in. "My goodness! But who might you be, dear?"

She was as beautiful as a romantic heroine—*more* beautiful, maybe.

The kind of girlfriend far more in Allen Cox's league.

But then again...

She took hold of me by the shoulders and leaned forward and kissed me, one time on each cheek.

"*Mother*!" Allen shouted.

Everyone's heads turned our way—though half of them had been turned to gaze at her to begin with.

Mother. Of course. There were just the slightest hints of wrinkles around her eyes, an unnatural plump to her lips and cheeks that might have involved cosmetic treatments.

Not that I was judging her, of course. Whatever she was doing was working.

"Oh, all right," said Allen's mother. At a thrift shop on a Saturday morning. I'd never run into anyone I'd met here and yet the first time I'd come with someone…

"I'm embarrassing you, I can tell." She waved her hands and finally let go of my shoulders. "Can you blame me? For *years*, you've stayed holed up in that condo, bringing me no closer to any grandchildren, and then I finally catch you red-handed with a beautiful woman!"

My eyelids fluttered as my toes curled up inside my shoes.

Allen's voice practically cracked. "*Mother*, this is someone I'm hiring for a job."

I couldn't bring myself to look at him. Would I find disgust at the idea of dating me there?

Surely not. I couldn't have been imagining his flirtations. But if he hadn't dated *anyone* in years, then what hope did I have?

Maybe he wasn't even into women or dating or romance.

"*Hiring her*?" The woman—whose name I still didn't know—wrinkled her nose. "Dammit, Vallen, if you let *this one* slip through your fingers..."

Vallen?

"Oh my god..." Allen let out a deep sigh.

"Be *serious*, dear." She looked at me, her gaze zeroing in on my left hand clutching the basket handle. "Darling, are you married?"

"Huh? Oh. No."

"Seeing someone? *Exclusively*," she added.

Allen actually slapped his palm across his forehead.

"Um, no, not at the present time." My voice was squeaking now, words failing me.

"There? You see?" Allen's mother looked over her shoulder at him tellingly. "Oh! But of course I forgot to ask if you'd prefer to bang women—"

Allen let out a mixture of a grunt and a yelp and a few feet away, a woman gasped, slapping her feet to get farther away from us. An old man kept leering, though, chuckling under his breath.

"Oh, please," said Allen's mother. "Heaven knows none of we Coxes are prudes." She snorted. "And we believe love is love, as I'm expecting your sister to finally get started on her wedding plans and for her and/or Maya to give me some grandbabies any day now."

"They've been engaged only a few *months*," Allen said. "Give them some space." Then he cocked his head and shook it. "Never mind. That's not even... Can you *please* keep your voice down and stop bothering Quinn—"

"Is that your name, dear?" She spun to me.

"Um, yes," I sputtered. "Quinn Simmons."

"Hmm, haven't heard of the Simmonses…" She tapped a manicured finger against her lips.

Heard of us? Were we supposed to be famous?

Allen dropped his two baskets to the floor and put his hands on both of her shoulders, directing her down the aisle. "Not everyone runs in your charity and real estate circles."

"Oh, I don't mind *that*," she said, not even commenting on the fact that her son was currently directing her down the aisle and perhaps in the direction of the door. "I was just curious is all." She managed to wiggle out of his grip and turn around. "You snatch that catch." She pinched his bicep playfully. "Once you make sure she sleeps with men." She ignored Allen's gaping mouth and waved over his shoulder at me. "So nice to meet you, Quinn! I'm Vera, by the way! Toodles!"

I'd never met anyone who'd actually said *toodles* before. "Toodles," I said back, stupidly, weakly wriggling my fingers at her.

My eyes caught the leering old man's and he snickered, shuffling down the aisle.

"There, I'm done embarrassing you. Are you happy now?" Vera said stiffly, tugging on her dress. "I just need to pick up a gift for your father—you know how he likes antiques." She leaned forward toward his ear, but she still spoke rather loudly. "It's the anniversary of the first night we made love."

"*Oh*-kay! That's enough of that." Allen spun around, quickly bending to pick up his baskets. His tanned skin was flushed darker at the neck as he gestured for me to pass him by.

"Bye!" Vera called from behind us. "You better text me! I don't care how *busy* you are with that work of yours. And, Quinn, I hope you'll come over for dinner soon!"

Allen let out a deep, exasperated breath but didn't say anything more to her.

We reached the end of the aisle, and he stopped, his neck still red and his lips in a thin line. He took a breath and offered me a wary smile. "Shall we?"

Taken off guard, I nodded and let him follow me to where they stocked the books and movies.

"So... Um..." I said as we went down the aisle stacked high with books—I could always count on this thrift store to have a bunch of them. I looked left and right. Fortunately, no one had followed us—not his mother, not a random onlooker, not that old man with the lecherous grin. "Books." I gestured to the books in front of us.

An awkward silence hung between us.

"I'm *so* sorry," he said, putting both baskets down. "I can't *begin* to apologize. I never would expose someone to my mother unawares like that. I had no idea she shopped at these types of places. 'Antiquing' doesn't conjure to mind"—he gestured in front of him—"books. These types of books, anyway."

At twenty-five cents a pop for most of them, yeah, it wasn't like there were classic first editions of anything a hundred years old.

"That's... uh... We all have embarrassing family members, right?" I chuckled, though it came out a bit forced. "I mean, my parents created and designed the Ooh-La-La Box, and they can hardly keep their hands off each other whenever we're out together. We have a healthy relationship with romance in my household, too."

What was I even *talking* about? I took a deep breath. It was a bit early in this relationship—strictly professional or acquaintance level at best—to be spilling all of my parents' quirks out at him.

Or to be talking about my *healthy relationship* with romance.

"A healthy relationship with romance?" Allen's eyebrow quirked.

Shit. How to pivot out of that topic real quick?

"Um, so one thing that did make me curious—she called *you* 'Val'? 'Vallen'?"

Allen—Vallen?—let out a heavy sigh. "Yeah, they thought it was cute. Twins: Vallen and Valerie. But for *both* of us to go by 'Val' was confusing, to say the least. I asked my friends to call me 'Allen' almost as soon as I was aware of my parents' ridiculous idea. I legally changed it as soon as I was eighteen. Both parents refuse to recognize that."

"Gotcha." I chewed my lip. *Vallen* was a rather unique, dare I say *romantic hero*-like name. But I wasn't about to disrespect the name of his choosing. "Why keep the 'Allen' part?" I wondered out loud. Oops. Probably should have kept my mouth shut.

"Well, I'm named after my two grandfathers," he explained. "First and middle name. And I *did* like my grandfather, but just the fact that they took my grandmother from the other side's name to name my sister and they happened to match up so closely—nah." He shrugged, then rolled his eyes. "My mom *loves* how they matched up, though. Practically planned to name two kids this since before we were conceived—us being twins making it almost seem like destiny to her."

That *was* a weird coincidence. I could almost see why his mother refused to acknowledge any name change after all of that to-do. *Almost.* Allen's feelings about the matter mattered more.

"Val didn't change her name?" I asked, remembering her dislike of it.

"She's all right with 'Val,' just not 'Valerie.' So she doesn't much care about chopping off the last few letters when she only uses them for legal matters." His Adam's apple bobbed. "But anyway, as you can tell, I don't run my love life past my mother too often. And maybe not for the reasons you think."

The chuckle I let out went on for far too long to seem natural. "I'm thinking because she'd be all over you about marriage and demanding grandbabies." At least my parents weren't like that.

"That, too." He leaned closer, his breath like a warm balm to my suddenly shivering soul. "But mostly it's because my love life is far too taboo."

Well, *that* was more information than I'd signed up for this morning.

"Oh," I said, trying not to think about how and why his love life would be taboo. I had *too good* of an imagination, thanks to my years as a bookworm. "I see." I put my own basket down beside his and clapped my hands together once. "So, um, what you want to look for, since all of the prices are good here, are books in decent condition."

Allen slipped both hands into his pockets and shook his head just slightly, clamping his lips together but failing to stop the twinkle that reached his eye.

He was drawing unnecessary attention to his soft, captivating lips.

Nope. No. Not going to think those thoughts here.

I did a quick perusal of the shelf at eye height and picked out a book. It was several decades old at least, its spine cracked almost into non-existence, the corners of the front cover gone entirely. "This is an example of a book I'd throw away if it showed up in my Mini Libraries." I flipped through it to show him. The pages were warped. Yellow, sure, but that was unavoidable when looking through old books.

"Throw it out?" Allen took the book from me. His nose wrinkled, but he dropped the book into his basket. "Isn't that sacrilegious for a booklover?"

"*No.*" I bent down and snagged the book out of his

basket and put it back on the shelf. "Some readers might get a little *rabid* about it, but really, there comes a time when books have lived a lifetime. There are plenty more books to be saved still worth saving. You want a good Mini Donation Library, you have to be tough about these things."

"You're the boss," he said, doing a closer perusal of the shelf. "At least when it comes to this."

My eyes bugged out before I carefully schooled my expression. *Why* had my first thoughts gone to him being the boss in the bedroom?

Probably because *he'd* been the one filling my head with naughty ideas.

"I'm just lending you my years of experience in the matter." I jutted out my chin. "Okay, so I have two boxes to shop for, one half filled with things for kids, and half with general adult fiction. It's called the 'All-Ages Box,' but sometimes some generic action thrillers might get in there with iffy content. Really, it's just a way to separate the box from the romance exclusive one."

"The tantalizing one." Allen picked a series of Harlequins off the shelf, all in pretty good condition. The white covers and painted models helped me pinpoint their origins to sometime in the '90s. "How about these?"

"Perfect," I said. "I'll take them for the Ooh-La-La Box, unless you want them for yours?"

"By all means." Allen dropped them in the middle basket. My eyes lingered a moment too long on the tight package that was his ass, and I felt myself slowly running a hand down my thigh.

Allen smirked as he stood, hitting me with a direct, probing gaze, so I quickly turned back to the shelf and grabbed a few chapter books, clearing my throat. "Have you thought about what kind of box you want? All genres? A lot of parents like the box for their kids, so you really can't leave kids' books off the table." V.L. Breedlove had said she'd wanted an all-romance box in her newsletter. But how much of that was fact, and how much fiction?

Only Allen and Val seemed to know.

"There's no way I'm not including a healthy dose of romance." He reached across the top of my head to grab a book, his scent—like sandalwood and the tantalizing musk of old books—lingering behind me. His chest rubbed my scalp, just for a moment, and despite my best efforts to hold it in, I let out a gasp.

Allen leaned back, offering me a bemused smile. "Romance is the most popular book genre in the world for a reason."

"So it is." I tugged at my plaid shirt a few times, suddenly overwhelmingly warm in this place. They probably had the furnace set too high for it being this late in the season. "Yup. Looks like a good one." I gave the romance book in his hand a quick onceover. Good condition.

"Have you read it?" he asked, flipping through the pages. The cover, which I'd glossed over, really, in a quick assessment of the book's state, revealed a woman in lingerie with a blindfold on, her wrists tied together with a tie. She was flipped over, dangling her arms, head, and upper torso off of a bed.

I squeaked. "Nope. Haven't read that one."

"Pity. I was hoping you could tell me if the sex scenes are as good as the cover promises."

"Can't judge books by their covers. Maybe a bit too much for a box with all-ages books," I said, reaching over and slamming the book in his hands closed. "But I'll take it for my Ooh-La-La Box, thank you." I tossed it into my basket.

"Maybe I'll put up two boxes, too. That way, I can fill it with *all the hot romance* to my heart's content."

I pointedly decided not to look at him as he purred those words and grabbed a few more books off the shelf, flipping through them to assess their conditions.

It was as good a segue as any to get to what *really* mattered here. "V.L. Breedlove mentioned she wants to make an all-romance Mini Donation Library for her neighborhood. In her newsletter."

"You're a subscriber." It wasn't a question, though his voice grew a bit clipped.

"And you're her PA. How, again, did you book that gig? Inquiring minds have to know."

He didn't take his eyes off the shelf. "What did you think? About 'The Terrible Twos'?"

He was trying to confuse me again. Wait a second, though—the title of the free short I'd gotten for preordering *Riding My Baby* was about Gideon,

Bianca, and their two-year-old daughter. "You know I got the preorder bonus?"

"I *send* out all of Breedlove's preorder bonuses."

And I'd sent the email from my QuinnSimmons-Freelancer email account. Duh.

Fine. Yes. I needn't act surprised. "I adored it," I said simply.

He clicked his tongue. "You don't think it was a tad cliché?"

I gasped, and the book I'd been holding fell straight down into one of the baskets on the floor. "You're criticizing. My favorite author. Your *client*? Do you actually read all of the books you promote?"

"I do." Allen pursed his lips as he studied me up and down. "Favorite author, huh?"

"Yes." I crossed my arms. "Admittedly, I just started reading her books a week ago, but it's the plain and simple truth."

"Hmm, and not just part of a ploy to get me to reveal Breedlove's identity?"

Damn. He wasn't wrong, but he wasn't totally right, either.

"I mean it! I really do." I let out a deep breath. "Breedlove's writing... It changed me." I shivered. "It makes me so happy. It bulldozed its way through the reality of my everyday life and just... took over." Clutching my hand to my chest, I stared down at the pile of books we were accumulating in our baskets. "Books leave an impact on me all the time, but not many carve such a deep and lasting mark on my heart."

Allen was quiet for a moment. "Guess my idea to put a bunch of signed copies in your Ooh-La-La Box worked well." He threaded his hand through his thick locks. "Now *that's* an effective PA."

Flattery would get me everywhere, apparently.

"An *amazing* PA. So good, I'm surprised more authors don't hire you," I said coyly. "Are you open to doing marketing for other authors?"

"No, just the one." Allen grabbed another book off the shelf and flipped through it. "One is plenty."

I wondered how *that* had happened. Probably because he'd shared a womb with that one author he worked for? "And you're paid well?"

"Yeah." His chest rumbled with a throaty chuckle. "Breedlove has a rabid fanbase. They helped take the books to heights most authors can only dream of."

"That's good," I said. "Since I'll overlook your comment about the short being *cliché*, can I ask if you're a fan, too? Do *you* like romance?"

"I do." He put the book back—the back cover was cracked, I noted, and I was glad my lesson had sunk in with him already. "Though I don't have a lot of time to read. I'm more a fan of the *real-life* variety."

There was that sparkle in his eye again. I wasn't going down that route.

Focus. Focus on the task at hand.

"So who's your favorite author? Other than Edgar Allan Poe, judging by the names of your cats. Oh!" *Allen.*

He tapped the side of his head with his finger. "Poe

is my favorite. And yes, I partially decided on changing my name because of him, though I might have changed the spelling if that were the entire reason."

"What about your favorite romance author, though?" Poe had written some romantic prose, but it certainly didn't have happily-ever-afters.

"I can't say V.L. Breedlove," he said.

"Why not?" I tossed a handful of books into my basket.

"Because I'm *intimately familiar* with Breedlove's books."

Was *everything* an entendre with this man?

Still. That was a hint, right? He was too close to the books because they were his sister's.

I took a quick glance at the book he held now. The cover depicted a pair of pink, fuzzy handcuffs against a black backdrop. "You know, you *can* put some sweet romance in your box, too. Not everything has to be dirty."

"But the best things are." He tossed the pink-hand-cuff book down into his basket and winked.

I rolled my eyes. I was getting somewhere. He wasn't going to derail me.

"You know, 'V.L.' isn't the most common combination of initials." My nose stuck into the air, I pretended to focus on the open book I had in my hands, but the words kind of blurred in and out of clarity.

"It's a pen name," he said. "Breedlove prefers privacy, as I've told you."

"I figured, it's just... I know a lot of authors have reasons for choosing their pen names."

"And you want to know Breedlove's?"

"It's just, well, seeing those books in my Ooh-La-La Box, the picture on Breedlove's Instagram..."

"That was me." Allen dropped a book in the middle basket and raised both hands up in surrender. "I run the author's social media. Part of a PA's work."

I clutched the stack of books I'd gathered against my chest, almost as if for comfort. "But why *you*? Why, of all the people in the world, did V.L. Breedlove choose you as her PA?"

Allen put both hands on his hips. "I have a degree in marketing."

"You do?" I'd failed to ask exactly what else he marketed for besides V.L. Breedlove, if he had no other author clients. Although at the rate she put out books, it could almost be a full-time job.

"I do." He scratched the back of his head. "I worked for my dad for a few years after college—he runs a security agency—but it wasn't for me. So I saved up and took a risk and launched my own business. Suffice it to say, it worked out for me." He scratched his thin beard, his gaze flicking quickly to the shelf of books. He grabbed another book off the shelf. "You're a freelancer, too. How'd you go down that route?"

"Well, I had trouble getting an office job out of college." I tossed the books in my hands one by one into the middle basket. Mine was overflowing already. "I had an English degree, and I wanted to do copyediting. Couldn't find anything suitable, so I started doing it from home. Then it just… took on its own life from there. I love working from home."

"Flexible schedule." Allen nodded.

"Cozy work atmosphere," I added.

"Cats," we both said as one, our eyes meeting.

I giggled and broke eye contact. "Although the hours can get kind of unmanageable when I'm not officially clocking in and out every day."

"Tell me about it."

"I often work weekends."

"Same."

I sighed. "But I mean, I *can* take off work on almost any day. If I'm not behind with a deadline."

"Which is almost never for me." Allen took out a middle grade book with a boy fighting a giant rat of some sort on the cover and nodded approvingly at it, tossing it into his basket.

So he wasn't going to just grab the sauciest books for the debut of his neighborhood box. Thank goodness.

He's distracting me again, I reminded myself.

"I don't doubt you deserve to be Breedlove's PA—if she owes any ounce of her success to your marketing efforts, you've more than proven yourself worthy. But what I'm asking is… is…" My mouth was dry, and I swallowed, waiting for Allen to look my way.

I got straight to the point, no more dropping hints he'd deflect with bulls-eye accuracy. "Is V.L. Breedlove your sister?"

Chapter Nine

Allen's jaw twitched almost imperceptibly. "If V.L. Breedlove *were* my sister, do you really think I'd just admit it?" He leaned forward, his voice lowering. "Breedlove prefers privacy, as you recall."

He had me there.

I guess it was really early in our relationship—friendship—acquaintanceship for him to divulge secrets.

"Okay, how about this?" I asked. "You talk it over with her, and if you're both really impressed by the Mini Donation Library I help build at your apartment complex, you *consider* letting me gush to your sister about Breedlove's books."

Allen's lips pinched together—damn, his almost-smiles were sexier than his actual smiles, and those alone could blow me away—and he bent down to pick up both of his baskets with one hand. "I don't think you need my permission to gush to her about books. *Especially* Breedlove's books."

Was that a confirmation of my theory? Dammit, why was this man so intent on teasing me?

I snatched my own basket up and flicked a strand of hair behind my ear. "Hmm? Is that so? Any particular reason why Breedlove's books make for a good topic to broach with her?"

"Well, she's not much of a reader, to be honest." Allen didn't seem to be joking as we made our way down the aisle. "But she's read every one of Breedlove's books at least. It's about all she has time for."

Hmm... Hmm, hmm, hmm. Well, at the rate Breedlove put out books, it made sense that she might not have time to read anything else. And *of course* she read them as she wrote them and revised them.

I knew all the best authors loved the genre they wrote in and read and supported other authors, but there was only so much time in the day. Still, I doubted she wasn't "much of a reader." How many writers didn't first love reading, long before they picked up a pen? Metaphorically speaking, of course. Long before they started mashing letters on a keyboard?

"I'll keep that in mind," I tried to say smoothly.

Allen reached out quickly to grab me by the arm just as we were about to approach the checkout.

His mother's laughter hit my ears before I zeroed in on what had stopped him. She was at the checkout counter talking, the cashier wrapping a rather large, delicate vase in newspaper.

Allen tugged me down the nearest aisle and hunched over behind a pile of stuffed animals, all looking a little *too* loved but still groomed and cleaned to put their best paws forward. He put down his baskets and pushed aside a sparkly, furry dragon butt in order to peek through the pile in the direction of the cashier.

"That bad, huh?" I whispered as I hunched down, gently scooching aside a lion's maw to make room for me beside him.

Before I thrust my head into the pile, I caught a glance of the little boy I'd seen entering the store with his sister and their harried mother, a giant toy race car in his hands, but his attention unabashedly focused on the two of us.

I wriggled fingers at him and smiled, then stuck my face beside Allen's.

"If she sees us again, she'll make me have lunch with her," Allen explained. In our little fort of plush, our cheeks were so close that I could almost feel the warmth of his breath.

"That's a bad thing?" I asked.

He turned to me, his mouth open slightly, as if to wonder how I could be so clueless.

"She's... eccentric," I offered.

Allen grumbled and looked straight ahead. "Don't get me wrong. I dine with my parents at least once a month. But that's *plenty*."

I watched as Vera, all smiles, accepted the large newspaper-wrapped package from the cashier and headed toward the door. She struggled a bit at the entryway and I stepped back in order to get over there and hold the door for her, but Allen caught me by the wrist.

His grip was firm but not too strong. His hand was large, and I had a wild flash of him pinning me down with that firm grip in a very different kind of situation.

Someone coming in held the door for Vera and she was gone.

Allen let out a visible sigh and stood straight. His hand was still on my wrist. His gaze held mine, and for a second—just a second—I had the wild thought of getting on my tiptoes and pressing my lips to his.

But then somewhere behind me, an electronic siren wailed, the sound too flat to be anything but a toy, and Allen dropped hold of me.

"Timmy! There you are!"

Both Allen and I jumped and turned around. The harried mother had the little girl against her chest, and the girl cradled a doll. She grabbed for her boy's hand. "Don't walk away from Mommy, okay?"

"So, we can head up now." Allen snatched both of his baskets, one in each hand this time, and led the way, straight to the cashier.

He put both baskets on the counter, and I lunged for the handle of the one he'd carried for me. "Oh, that one's mine."

Allen took the third basket I'd carried and—not expecting it—I let the thing slip from my fingers.

"All of these, please," he told the cashier, a middle-aged woman with her hair in tightly coiled braids.

"All together?" she asked, looking between both Allen and me, as if waiting for an objection or forever hold one's peace.

"You don't have to. These are for my boxes," I sputtered.

"Consider it a donation," he said, already pulling out his wallet.

"Okay, well, thank you." I bit my lip and nodded at the cashier. She offered me a slight smile and an arched brow but got to work counting the books in each basket. I cleared my throat. "The condo community will appreciate it. I mean, they won't know who you are or anything, and it's not like I talk to all of them. But *if* they knew." I gasped, my mouth running faster than my lungs could keep up with. "You know, I can tell Evangeline. She'll put it in the newsletter—"

"Please." Allen flicked out a black credit card with gold writing on it. "I don't need you to tell anyone. I'm doing it for *you*."

"Right." I gripped the counter with both hands. "Since, uh, I'm teaching you what I do today. Without charging."

"You *really* need to negotiate your rates better." Allen kept looking forward as the cashier opened some paper bags. "Here, let me," he offered, taking the stack of books she'd already counted and sliding them gently inside the first bag.

"What a gentleman," the cashier said, looking

straight at me, as if willing me to understand some secret message.

That she was jealous he was with me?

No need to be. This was strictly business. I started stacking books she hadn't gotten to yet within the nearest basket better so it'd be less of a mess for her to get through.

Working as a team, the three of us got through the books fairly quickly. There were miniature mountains of them spread into four paper grocery bags.

"Ten fifty," the cashier said.

Allen did a double-take but handed over his card. He looked down at me as she finished the transaction. "You were going to fight me over ten fifty? Less than, if you were willing to at least let me buy my own basket?"

"I wasn't going to *fight* you," I said. "But yes. Thrift stores are a great place to buy books when working on a tight budget." I smiled at the cashier as she passed back the card and I grabbed for two bags. "Though I have a pretty good idea just how *tight* that budgie of yours is." I blinked, my brain catching up to what I'd said. "Bugel. Bulget. Bulgie. *Bulge*... et..." I said, loud enough for the whole store to hear me.

The cashier's jaw dropped, and the little boy I hadn't noticed waiting with his mom and sister from behind me looked up at his mom and asked, "Mommy? What's that man's bulge?"

Allen snorted, gripping the counter with both hands as if he were about to fall over.

"Budget," I said softly, my voice cracking. "How

tight that budget of yours is. Since... you offered me... so much. It must not... be tight." Every word I spoke was slower, quieter, my heartbeat drowning out any sound.

"A budgie's a bird," I said to no one in particular.

Allen burst out laughing. The sound sent a tingle down my spine, and I looked over. The cashier joined him in some nervous laughter of her own and the mom was busy hushing her son.

Time to go.

I snatched the two bags, my arms straining just a little, and turned to leave.

"Let me," Allen insisted.

"Get the other two," I shot back, my feet carrying me away from him so fast, he had no hope of taking the bags from me.

By the time I was slamming my back into the front door, keen to open it myself and melt into my car, never to be seen by any of these human eyes again, Allen was jogging to catch up to me.

"Here," he said, shifting his second bag beside his first in the crook of one arm. "You need someone to hold them while you get your keys out at least?"

"I'm fine," I said, my voice monotone, my insides numb. "I usually work alone." As was my routine, I set the books down on the parking lot pavement in front of my trunk before I fished around in my purse for my keys.

The bags still in Allen's hands crinkled as he adjusted them in his grip. "Are you blushing, Quinn?"

Being asked that just made my cheeks burn even hotter. I popped open the trunk and heaved the first paper bag up into it with a grunt. "I spend a lot of time at home," I explained. "With just my cat. Sometimes my brain-to-mouth words are out of practice."

"Your... brain-to-mouth words?" He sounded amused.

I gripped the second bag, foolishly by the top instead of the bottom, and the bag ripped, sort of collapsing into the trunk, spilling the contents everywhere, but fortunately not onto the parking lot.

I sighed and put both hands on my hips, just the slightest pressure of tears building behind my eyes. "My brain-to-hand coordination, too."

"It's all right." Allen put both of his bags on the ground and scrambled to right the remainder of the broken bag, shoveling books back into it. "Hey," he said, turning over his shoulder to look at me. His expression was serious, though his face seemed to shine. "You're talking to someone who also works from home."

I flicked my hands in the air, conducting an invisible symphony with each point. "And lives next door to his sister and sees his parents once a month and goes out for fabulous dinners with friends." I was babbling, I knew it.

Allen stood and took my flailing hands in his. They were warm, secure. They made my rapid heartbeat slow, and the flutter in my chest stopped threatening to make me hyperventilate. I stared up into his eyes.

"You met my mother and you didn't immediately run for the hills," he said. "I would say she's far more embarrassing than a slip of the tongue."

"Yeah..." My gaze flicked downward. Then I jumped in place when I realized what I'd said, a lock of my hair dangling down in front of my eye. "I don't mean—"

He chuckled. "You did. And rightfully so." He reached over to move the errant lock of hair over my shoulder and away from my face, his other hand still gently holding mine.

My knees shook.

He let go of my hands and brought a fist to his mouth, clearing his throat, then turned his attention to the trunk and shifted aside the broken bag. "You make me sound like a social butterfly, but I'm not," he said. "I prefer being home with Poe and Raven—more than anything."

"*Anything*?" I asked.

He smirked as he set first one and then the other bag inside my trunk. "Well, having a date over *might* be an improvement."

"Just *might*, huh?" I threaded my fingers together and bounced on my heels.

"Well, the cats sure tend to sleep a lot. And I find I work best when *someone's* in my lap." He leaned on the open trunk door with one hand, moving slightly toward me.

I yelped, picturing myself on his lap as he wrapped his arms around me to type on a computer keyboard.

He ran a hand through his hair. "But the cats seem to prefer each other for cuddling—most of the time."

"Right... Cats... Yeah, it's comforting when Darcy's snuggling on my lap, too." I laughed nervously. Then I looked beyond him to the books in the trunk. "Oh, but what about your books? For your box? I mean, once we get it built—"

"The books we picked out got all mixed up when we were bagging them," Allen explained. We? He'd been the only one bagging them... "Besides, I thought you were going to show me how you curate a collection. Thought I could observe and then pick the books to take home with me."

"Oh, uh, sure." I gestured wildly with my hands, my thumbs pointing toward the driver's side of my car. "Shouldn't keep them waiting. I skipped a fill-up day this week, and ravenous readers are going to revolt."

"They sure do rely on you there, it seems," Allen said. He leaned back and shut the trunk to my car.

"Yes, I wanted to warn you about that. Once you put up a Mini Donation Library, if you don't keep it stocked, you're going to get complaints."

He nodded at me like an eager student. "I'll make sure it stays stocked."

"I'm serious. You can't create a Mini Donation Library on a whim."

He put a hand over his heart and spoke ceremoniously. "I swear, on my honor, to never let the shelves go empty, even if it means never moving, apparently, for the rest of my life."

I shook my head just slightly, but it was hard not to laugh. "I'll settle for you appointing a successor curator in the event that you do."

"I will not fail you, my lady." There was levity in his voice, but the promise made my heart skip a beat. If this were one of Breedlove's books, he'd grab my hand and whisper those words...

Taking a deep breath, I tried to keep the tremor out of my voice as I spoke again. "And wait until you run into your own Mrs. Whithouse."

He quirked an eyebrow.

"Head of the Anti-Mini Donation Library Committee," I explained, giving the nosy neighbor a proper title. "Though I've seen her taking some books from the All-Ages Box, despite her disgust for my other box."

"The *fun* box," he said.

"Yeah, that's one way of putting it. So, um, meet me there?"

Allen nodded. "And then I can take you out for lunch."

Take me out? Was he asking me... on a date?

"To discuss the box for my neighborhood. Naturally." He winked at me.

Wait. Winking meant his words were just a cover, right?

Right?

I did little finger-bang motions at him, shaking my index fingers at him like a complete and utter moron.

"Lunch date. I mean... Work date. Work work." My mouth dropped as I tried to figure out how to fix this. Allen's grin grew wider. "I'm gonna... go now..."

Though it was only a few feet away, I *ran* for the driver's side door.

Chapter Ten

"At this point, you're basically looking for the same things you look for when buying books for the library." My cheeks were flushing at Allen's proximity. He leaned against the Ooh-La-La Box, watching me stock the Mini Donation Library carefully. Almost *too* carefully. I was having a hard time even looking in his direction.

When I did, I found his dark eyes positively glued to my every movement. A more rapt student I couldn't ask for.

I cleared my throat. "Today's not the best example since everything looks great—or maybe it is, since it would be ideal that we all share decent-condition books—but usually, someone will add some books, and sometimes, they're just... garbage."

Allen chuckled, and I wondered if I'd ever get tired of his deep, throaty laugh. "Books are sometimes garbage. Got it. You've emphasized that point quite often."

"You know what I mean." I dug into the nearest paper bag, found I was holding a middle grade book, and set it down on the bench between the two boxes. "But yes. To curate a library, no matter how big or how small, you have to have the stomach to recognize that."

"And you can't recycle them?"

I shook my head. "There's glue in the bindings, mixed materials... Most books just aren't recyclable."

Allen *tsked* and stood straighter, snatching up the MG book I'd set down and walking over to the All-Ages Box. "What a waste."

I watched him open the second library and slide the MG book in neatly against one side of the box. Nodding my approval, I riffled through a bag for some Harlequins. "I look at it this way. Chances are, if it got *that bad*, it served its purpose. Time for new books to get a chance to be that loved, too. Well, *newer*." I held up a book from the bag with a 1970s-style cover design. A Gothic romance, with a woman in a flowing gown running away from a dark, eerie castle.

He arched a brow as he started riffling through the few books already in the All-Ages Box. "Looks like she's *running from* a chance to be loved."

My nose wrinkled and I shelved the book. "Oh, she'll run *to* it by the end. They always do. That's what makes it a happily ever after. I'm sure the hero is all dark and brooding but will turn out to have a soft spot for puppies or something."

Allen snorted as he took casual steps back toward the bench between us. "Is that all it takes? A love for canines?"

I purposely gave him a long, lingering look from head to toe. "The hero being hot as hell doesn't hurt, either."

Allen fished out another stack of books. "No wonder real-life men can't compete."

"Hmm?" My cheeks flushing, I grabbed for another book in the bag nearest Allen, just as he did. Our hands brushed as we both brought out one of the sexy BDSM titles he'd chosen. "I wouldn't have thought *you'd* have that problem," I whispered.

I let him have the book and snatched the others in a stack in his arms before he could respond.

"Despite what my mother said, I do date." He put down his book and grabbed some more. These, too, he sorted through, stacking some to take to his own box—whenever that actually existed. "Or *hook up*, I should say, more often than not. I'm just busy... It can be hard to find the time."

"You found the time for this today."

He stared at me, a couple of books up against his chest, then he looked away. "It's partly work for me, too. As you surmised from the newsletter, Breedlove intends to chronicle the story of the neighborhood box."

"Oh, of *your* neighborhood box, huh? Not one in her own neighborhood?" I fluffed my hair and batted my eyes, purposely playing dumb. "Will the reclusive

V.L. Breedlove even come to see your Mini Donation Library in person, despite acting in her newsletter like it's all her idea?"

Allen blinked, then quickly looked back down, sorting through the very last of the books in one of the two remaining bags.

"Another job of the PA, huh? I should thank you." My hand curled into a fist, and I knocked my knuckles against his shoulder playfully. "If you hadn't filled this box last week with a bunch of signed copies, who knows how long it would have taken Bodhi to recommend her books to me?"

"But you would have read the books eventually," he said, not looking up. "If Bodhi remembered to recommend them to you." He offered me a short glance. "He likes them, but I'm not sure he's *quite* as dogged as you are about outing my client's identity."

"But he *is* curious, then?" I stuck my fingers in my jeans pockets and rocked on my heels, as casual as could be. "What's his theory?"

"I'd rather not say." Allen started picking the stack of books from the bench and putting them all in one bag. "I tried keeping all the all-ages books in this bag." He nodded at the bag we'd yet to tackle. "Though, obviously, some still got mixed in."

There he went, dodging my questions again. Damn, he was wily.

"I can ask him myself," I said, not willing to let it go, even as I grabbed a stack from the last bag and strode over to the All-Ages Box.

"Yay! Quinn!"

I'd recognize that high-pitched voice anywhere. Still sorting through the stack in my hand—there was a YA series in there, and I wanted to make sure to shelve them in the right order—I glanced over my shoulder to see Benjamin running down the sidewalk, his sister, Penelope, a few steps behind them, holding the leash to their dog. The corgi sort of waddle-walked, her tongue wagging out of her mouth.

Evangeline and her husband, Lucas, were a few steps behind them, arm in arm.

"Puppy alert," said Allen, though I was pretty sure that corgi was grown. "Now all I have to do is demonstrate a love for canines, and I can brood all I want."

"I prefer the idea of you with cats." I pursed my lips at him, looking him up and down. "But brood away."

"New books!" Benjamin screeched, interrupting us. He darted up beside me and brushed his head against my arms as he crawled under me to pop up between me and the All-Ages Box. There was very little room in that space.

"Uh, *hello*!" I said, holding the books still in my hands above his head. "I'm still filling it, buddy."

"You didn't fill up the box on Wednesday," said Penelope. Her dog's panting grew louder as they neared. Allen, amusingly, kind of flinched out of the way as the dog headed straight for his ankles. So much for his "love for canines." Penelope tugged on the leash, drawing her dog back. "Mom had to take Benjamin and me to the bookstore downtown." She had two books under her arm, which she handed to me, but her eyes flicked to Allen behind me, still moving slowly away from her friendly—and stationary, I might add—pooch. "She said we had to donate these when we were done, though."

I quickly put the books I'd been holding on the top shelf of the All-Ages Box as Benjamin launched himself at the bottom shelf, picking out some Dav Pilkey graphic novels. I took the books Penelope was offering me. Brand-spankin' new, a middle grade book and a chapter book, one about a fairy tale academy and the other about dinosaurs.

"You just got these Wednesday? You two read fast," I said, shelving the new additions. "Some other kids are going to be really happy. Thank you." I patted Benjamin's head and smiled at Penelope.

She was staring unabashedly at Allen, though.

"I know you," she said.

Allen cocked his head. "You do? I think I'd remember a kid—"

"My mom knows you." She looked over her shoulder as her parents reached the end of the block. "She *saw* you. You're Mr. Hottie."

Oh, I couldn't wait to see how Evangeline handled this.

"Hey," said Evangeline as she and her husband, Lucas, got close enough to talk to all of us.

Fortunately, she seemed to have just missed Penelope letting Allen know her mother referred to him as "Mr. Hottie."

"Mom, it's Mr. Hottie!" Penelope cried, looking over her shoulder at her parents and pointing straight at Allen.

I went to smack my forehead, then thought better of it, instead clapping my hands together.

Lucas—a somewhat short and handsome man, with rosy-peach skin and a buzzcut haircut—looked from his daughter to his wife to Allen and back, his mouth agape. "Mr.—?"

"*Cox*," Allen said, chuckling as he stepped around Penelope and her dog to grab for Lucas's hand. Lucas shook it limply, then Allen extended his handshake toward Evangeline.

"Cox" was not doing Lucas's imagination any favors, clearly. From "Mr. Hottie" to "Mr. Cocks"?

"C-O-X," I said softly. In case anyone's mind jumped to dirty places like mine did.

Evangeline fidgeted in place, but Benjamin and Penelope lost interest. Penelope started browsing through the All-Ages Box, her dog panting eagerly beside her, and Benjamin slid beside our last paper bag on the bench to start flipping through his possible selections.

"Oh, uh, nice to meet you. Evangeline. And Lucas. Vanderberg. Those rather forward children are ours, Benjamin and Penelope." Evangeline's voice croaked as she brushed a chunk of her bob behind her ear and then took Allen's proffered hand. She glanced at her husband, who quirked an eyebrow—not angrily, necessarily, but with clear curiosity.

"So…" I clapped my hands together again, drawing everyone's attention. "Looks like you were right, after all, Evangeline. I do have a new helper for the Mini Donation Libraries. Temporarily, of course." I waved my hand at Allen, lest he think I was roping him in for life.

Roping… Why did my first thought dart to that woman bound by a tie on the book Allen had selected? He'd worn a tie the night I'd met him…

Evangeline giggled nervously. "Ah, I see. Um, as far as that, uh, *nickname* goes… I just observed you pulling up to the libraries last week and donating books. Thank you, by the way. I'm the head of the Condo Association. We appreciate it. The books in these libraries are much-loved."

"Ah." Lucas's chest puffed out. "The gorgeous guy who donated those books you were so obsessed with last week. I heard you talking about them with Joanna."

Joanna was another neighbor I knew liked my pick of romance novels for the Ooh-La-La Box, although we'd only chatted a few times.

Evangeline's cheeks flushed, her lips pursed together.

Allen chuckled, and I was caught—suddenly—by a burning sensation in my chest. Evangeline was married—happily—and I couldn't begrudge her the right to *look*. It was more the fact that Allen, running a hand through his thick, wavy hair, was just as charming toward Evangeline as he was toward me.

Of course he could turn on the charm for any fan of V.L. Breedlove. He was her PA, for Pete's sake.

"Glad to be of service," Allen purred.

My muscles tightened as I jumped back in a pathetic attempt at relevancy. "Allen is V.L. Breedlove's PA," I told her.

I wasn't about to spout my theory that he was also the author's brother, though. I would keep that much for myself—at least until I wrung a confession out of one or both of them.

"Are you?" Evangeline gasped. "Well, tell her my friends and I *adore* her books. Oh my god, Quinn, I haven't checked in with you since you started reading them. What did you think?"

I squealed. Actually *squealed*, grabbing her hands and bouncing in place like a teenager at a boy band concert.

Allen stumbled backward, his eyes widened.

Lucas wasn't fazed. "I know when it's my cue to exit." Lucas nodded at Allen and me, then patted his wife's arm. "Hey, kids, did you pick your books for the week yet?"

"Daddy!" Benjamin cried, rushing up to him and handing him one of the books. Ever so carefully, he stood on his tiptoes beside his sister and put the other ones back. "Can we bring our books to the park?"

"Sure," Lucas said. "But let's not get them dirty." He took the leash from Penelope's hand as Penelope finished browsing the new books, then Penelope shut the door, one of the middle grade books Allen had selected in her hands, and the three took off down the sidewalk.

"She picked one of your selections, did you notice?" I asked Allen.

He looked after the retreating Vanderbergs. "Guess I'm a good student, after all."

I tapped a finger to my bottom lip. "You're doing quite well so far, I must say. We'll see what the final grade is, though."

"Student?" Evangeline asked.

"Never mind that—V.L. Breedlove!" I shouted at her.

Allen cleared his throat and went to grab that last bag, pulling the books out one by one and organizing them on the bench—something I thought he'd basically already done. "Don't mind me," he said.

Evangeline giggled. "So, did you read the whole series?"

"Of *course*." I rolled my eyes. "You were right that I wouldn't be able to do anything else until I did. I was so behind with work until just yesterday."

Evangeline gasped, then laughed. "Now *that's* a book binge."

I rolled my shoulders. "And I'm paying for it—but it was worth the price."

Allen snickered behind me, his chest rumbling.

I ignored him. "What's your favorite Maxwell Security couple?" I asked her.

We spoke at the same time.

"Leah and Sterling!" Evangeline shouted, as I said, "Gideon and Bianca!"

Then we both laughed.

"I *do* love Leah and Sterling," I said. "Sterling is just so... take-charge."

"That's one way of putting it." Evangeline made a little whip motion, complete with the cracking sound effect. "And *of course* I love Gideon and Bianca. Gideon's past is so sad, but he's so sweet. And his overbearing, self-absorbed mother? Ugh. My heart broke for him."

"Until Bianca gave him his happy ending, of course. I love how he asked her out when she told his mother to stop embarrassing herself." I could never have Bianca's gumption. "Oh my god, did you sign up for Breedlove's newsletter? And get the bonus story about them from the *Riding My Baby* preorder?"

"I am subscribed, but I didn't preorder that book yet."

I swayed suddenly, having to grab on to Evangeline's arm to steady myself. "Why not?"

She winced. "I haven't read her MC series yet."

"How? *How* were you able to stop yourself?"

Evangeline wrinkled her nose. "That good, huh? I thought I'd need to clear my schedule before I dove into one of her series again. Looks like I was right."

"Get *on* that!"

Evangeline peered over my shoulder. I followed her gaze, but Allen still had his back to us as he shifted books from one pile to another across the bench.

She lowered her voice. "So spill. Who is V.L. Breedlove? Is she local?"

Opening my mouth, I quickly shut it and checked over my shoulder again. Allen wasn't looking. "I'm working on it," I whispered. We could discuss details later—especially if I got more details out of him today. At our work lunch.

"Hmm..." Evangeline leaned back. "Well, so another book out next week. Are you ready?"

"*So* ready. I need to make sure I'm caught up with work at midnight Monday night. Getting no sleep until morning."

Allen laughed again.

Evangeline gasped. "Do e-books drop at midnight? Dammit, that gives me just two days to get caught up."

"Well, you probably *do* need sleep, right?" I grinned.

"Yes, unfortunately, I do."

Allen stepped over, his job sorting through the remaining books apparently over, as they were all back in the bag. "Ladies, you've won me over. I don't know if you were just putting on a show to pretend you liked Breedlove's books *that* much—"

"We weren't," I said emphatically.

Evangeline nodded.

Allen's Adam's apple bobbed perceptibly. He clapped his hands together. "Then I have a proposition for you."

Chapter Eleven

This was it! He was going to admit his sister was V.L. Breedlove and arrange for a signing or just a meet-and-greet. I took hold of Evangeline's hand and bounced on my feet, practically salivating.

Allen beamed as he took in the pair of us. Even Evangeline was getting in on the bouncing.

"I was just going to say..." Allen cocked his head. "Man, this is going to be a letdown for you."

"Oh, just *out with it*, Allen!" I said.

His eyebrows shot upward, but he couldn't help but laugh. "I just thought I could chronicle the story of leaving the books here, and how you and Evangeline and this Joanna your husband mentioned liked them—"

"Not just us," said Evangeline. "The *whole neigh-borhood* is in a tizzy." She let go of my hand and fanned herself. "Well, all the romance readers here, anyway."

"Even better." Allen's gorgeous face was practically

rosy. "Maybe I could post it on Breedlove's social media, in the newsletter. However many of you want to appear in a picture with your books, then I'll write the story..."

"*You'll* write it?" My lip curled. "So you're admitting you write Breedlove's newsletter for her?" I gasped. "Is that why she wrote about your Mini Donation Library? Because *you're* going to chronicle the building of it?"

Evangeline looked to me for clarification, but I'd have to explain later. She'd know what I was talking about, though, if she got Breedlove's newsletter.

Allen shrugged. "A PA's job is marketing."

"Please tell me you at least discuss what the newsletter is going to say!" I cried. Why did it bother me to hear the words coming direct from my favorite author weren't her words at all?

Because the newsletter had seemed like one little glimpse into her life, one tidbit she was willing to share with us. But apparently, it was just another bit of "marketing."

"Breedlove makes *all* the decisions regarding the newsletter's content," Allen said firmly.

Hmm. Well, that made me feel a little better.

And I supposed with all the writing she did, she might not have had time to write newsletters. But still...

"Let me talk to everyone, but yes, that sounds like a great idea!" Evangeline didn't seem as bothered by Allen's revelation as I was. She started walking backward, slowly, in the direction her family had gone. "But if I don't catch up to Lucas and the kids, they're going to wonder if I got lost in a book binge again. Shall I contact you about the posts?" Evangeline asked me.

"Oh, uh, I guess I'll let Allen take charge of that—"

"Yes, that would be fine," Allen said, interrupting. "Quinn can be my point of contact."

I could?

Evangeline smiled. "I always thought we should start a neighborhood book club. Just didn't think we'd start out as the V.L.-Breedlove-Only Club."

Allen chuckled. "Start out, but then branch out, I'm sure. Breedlove can only write so many books."

"And ravenous readers can read them at the speed of light," I pointed out.

"Looks like I know what I'm doing for the rest of the weekend, then." Evangeline waved and turned to go. "A motorcycle club awaits!" She shouted that last bit.

If only Mrs. Whithouse were here to wag her finger at her.

"You about ready to go?" Allen asked once Evangeline had left us to ourselves.

"Go?" I cocked my head. Then I gasped. "Right! Lunch!"

Allen arched a brow. "I can honestly say I've never had someone forget about lunch plans with me before."

My chest puffed out. "I didn't forget." My shoulders slouched. "I don't generally forget these things. Not that I... have a lot of lunch plans."

"Hmm?" Allen offered, grabbing for the last bag of books. He cradled it to his side. "Want a ride or do you want to meet me there?"

"Where?"

"Well, I was going to suggest a café near my place—"

"That's fine."

"But then I thought, if you're free this afternoon, we could get started. With the paid work. You teaching me what setting up one or two of those Mini Donation Libraries entails."

It wasn't like I actually had any plans this afternoon. Other than napping to recover from this week's horrid sleeping schedule.

"Sure," I said. "We can talk at the café—"

"What about my place?" Allen asked. "We can order in, I can show you where I want to build the box, and you can take a look at my wood and tell me if it's going to work for you."

"Your... wood?" My brain wasn't so frazzled as to assume he was talking about the morning variety. But my dirty thoughts *did* go there, no denying that.

Allen's lascivious grin made it clear his thoughts were circling around the dirty drain of something similar. "For the box. These *are* made of wood, right? I had some time last night, so I went to the hardware store to buy some materials."

"Getting ahead of yourself, aren't you?" I said. "What if you picked the entirely wrong thing?"

"Then I'll return it." Allen leaned closer. "And

make sure you're there to tell me *everything* you want me to do."

I shivered, but in a good way. A start-bouncing-on-my-heels-and-get-moving-before-I-jump-him sort of way.

"Besides," he said, "I thought you might like to meet my cats."

"Cats!" I squealed, almost as excited about that as I had been about V.L. Breedlove's books. "You have a deal."

"Guess I'm lucky you're a cat lover."

"You mean, and not a dog lover? I saw you with the Vanderbergs' corgi. Not a fan?"

Allen used his one free hand to scratch his chiseled jaw. "Let's just say I haven't earned my right to brood just yet."

"Hmm..." Picturing him as the brooding lord of some Gothic castle did all sorts of things to the lower half of my body. I shook my head to clear it. "I'll meet you there. Text me your address, and I'll head there in a few minutes?"

Better to have my own method of escape if I was going to spend an afternoon at Allen's apartment.

An excuse to leave early if I got too close to jumping his bones.

Not that that would be a *bad* thing, per se...

But I had a job to do here. I was a professional.

Taking a deep breath, I straightened my back.

The corner of Allen's mouth twitched, but he

fished his car keys out of his pocket and nodded my way. "It's a date," he promised.

Then he turned and headed toward his jeep parked on the street before I could ask him to clarify that.

My GPS deposited me downtown out front of a brick building I remembered had once housed some kind of textile factory like a hundred years ago but had sat vacant and decaying for most of my childhood. If I remembered right, a real estate company had bought it about a decade ago and refurbished it, turning it into condominiums.

This was the building Allen and his sister lived in. I rolled into the guest parking lot, only just managing to find a space. The parking lot was cramped—not really conducive to drive-bys looking for books. Sliding my crossbody purse over my head, I got out of the car and looked around. There was the courtyard he'd mentioned, a nice strip of grass leading back, an array of condo doors in three sides around the place. Rows of hedges lined the borders between the lawn and cobblestone sidewalk, gaps between the hedges every so often to allow access to the lawn, yellow and red tulips blooming along the outside of the hedges.

I held both hands out in front of me, to frame the area in my sights, thinking hard and barely even noticing the sound of a nearby door opening.

The gap between the two bushes in the front here

left the perfect amount of space for a Mini Donation Library or two—but that was just it. It was clearly there to allow access to the grass. Putting Allen's boxes there would cause issues, even if his mother was the owner of the building.

"I'm thinking of proposing she pull out the hedges from here to there."

I jumped in place and turned around to find Allen, shielding his eyes from the sun with one hand, an open Thermos in the other. He took a sip from what might have been the coffee he'd offered me earlier.

"That'll ruin the design," I said, pointing to the hedges traveling around the courtyard.

"Maybe, but it'll make kids and dogs trying to get through to use the courtyard a hell of a lot happier." He winked.

"Oh? And do you count yourself among them?"

"Among the kids or the dogs?" He cocked his head.

I threaded my hands behind my back and winced. "A dog lover, I mean, I guess? Someone who'd care if dogs had easy access? Or kids if... If..."

"I don't have any kids." He gave me a onceover, and I caught just a hint of a smile as he took another sip of his drink. "Are you kidding? My mother would have mentioned it when you met her if I had, believe me. And you know how I feel about dogs."

"You need them to brood, though," I teased.

"I'll brood with my cats, thank you."

"Like a Bond villain stroking a cat on his lap?"

"I was hoping you'd see me more as James Bond himself."

"Well, you did mention an *active* love life..." I bit down on my bottom lip. "And... he's a playboy."

"Old-school Bond, maybe." He took a step closer and leaned in.

"The sleep-with-them-and-leave-them type."

"Hey, his relationships lasted, like, a whole movie. Or maybe half of one."

I nodded thoughtfully. "And is that why your mother claims you haven't been in a relationship in a while?"

He blinked rapidly. "My mother is coming up far too much in this conversation for my liking—"

A door opened, followed immediately by a series of shrill barks wrapped up in a tiny, furry package.

"That's our cue—" said Allen, using his free hand to grab mine. His hand was warm, just a tad rough, and it encircled mine easily.

He tugged and stopped. A little Pekingese on a leash waddled up to his shins and jumped up, barking incessantly. "Pearl," he said through clenched teeth. "Get down!"

The dog did and moved on toward me, sniffing at me eagerly. Allen yanked me and put me securely behind him, shifting as the dog did in order to act as a shield between us. I had to laugh. Allen's jaw clenched visibly, and he was clearly more afraid of the dog than I was, even if I had to agree the canine was a bit unwieldly.

"Pearl!" A recognizable voice drew my attention over Allen's broad shoulder. Val was pulling a condo door closed with one hand, the end of a retractable leash connected to the little Pekingese in the other.

Pearl's tongue lolled out of her mouth and she trotted on little stubby feet across the cobblestones to Val, who picked her up and cradled her against her chest, giving her a kiss. Val looked gorgeous today, as she had the other night, even with her dark hair pulled back into a messy bun behind her head and wearing what clearly qualified as a threadbare pajama sweatshirt along with a pair of plaid flannel pajama pants.

Flannel pajama pants.

Just like the ones V.L. Breedlove had written about relaxing in yesterday in her newsletter.

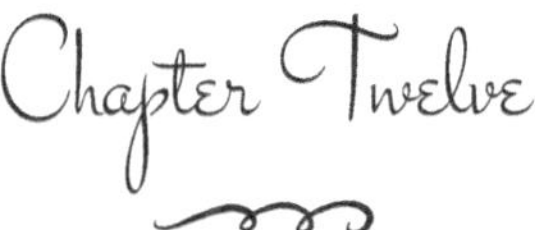

Chapter Twelve

"What have I told you about the retractable leash?" Allen said to his sister as she approached, the panting dog in the crux of her arm.

Val rolled her eyes. "It's easier for me. She doesn't tug as hard."

"She's ten pounds!" Allen shouted.

"*You* try walking her more than once in a blue moon and tell me if my little queenie is strong enough to pull a man over. Aren't you, baby? Aren't you?" She cooed to her dog and bounced her. The dog lapped up the attention, just lolling her pink tongue out of her black muzzle as she looked from Val to Allen to me and back.

"You have less control with a retractable leash," Allen said, waving his Thermos around as he spoke. "She could twist around and get caught in the bushes or something—she could go up to a kid and bite them before you even notice!"

"Yes, Mother." Val made a gagging face.

"I'm serious. I bought you that leather leash for a reason. It's safer for both the animal and those around it—"

"Hi. Almost didn't see you there." Val leaned around her brother, ignoring his tirade, and used Pearl's paw to wave at me. "Quinn, right? One of Bodhi's friends?"

"Right." I leaned around Allen, my long hair dangling downward. "Val."

"You can come on out from behind my lug of a brother. Whatever the stick up Allen's ass might make him say, my dog does not hurt people."

Wasn't that how Bodhi had described Allen? I wondered if he'd gotten the idea from Allen's sister.

"Oh, I wasn't scared. Allen was just..." I looked up at him from where I was leaning. His face was flushed. I stood straighter and stepped beside him. "Protecting me. And I appreciate that."

Allen did a double-take, but a light invaded his dark eyes as he gazed down at me. I smiled back up at him.

"Okay, well, I can see I'm interrupting something..." Val brushed past Allen and whispered something in his ear. I couldn't entirely hear her—not that I was listening *too* hard—but I did make out the words, "Don't make it weird" and "Bodhi's friend."

Pearl chose that moment to yip rather harshly and lunge toward Allen.

He leaped back, but again, shielded me with his body.

"Oh, come on, hush now," Val said, stroking her dog, who wasn't in any danger of escaping her arms, I supposed. She set her down at the open spot between the hedges, then let the retractable leash go wild as Pearl ran out into the grass, stopping to sniff and urinate every few steps.

"Not dangerous, huh?" Allen grumbled.

"She just sniffs cat on you," said Val.

"And that makes it okay somehow?"

Val put her free hand on her flannel pajama pants hip, and I opened my mouth, trying to figure out how to ask if that was the pair of pants she'd mentioned in the newsletter. Then again, hadn't Allen said he'd written her newsletters? Had he added flourish to what she'd wanted put in the newsletter by describing her pants?

Was I thinking about this way too hard? Yes.

I leaned around Allen again, shuffling closer to Val, then cleared my throat. "I'm here to help Allen. With the Mini Donation Libraries?" *The ones you're supposedly chronicling the construction of for your mailing list?*

"Oh, right, yes, yes, of course." Val sized me up over one shoulder. "And how's it going?"

Allen tapped his fingers across the hollow metal of his Thermos. "Great. Except... we bumped into Mother at a thrift store this morning."

Val winced. "Ouch. So when's the wedding?"

I flinched. "Pardon?"

Val chuckled. Even her chuckle was like a romance heroine's, deep and lustful. "I assume our mother arranged for the two of you to get married within the first thirty seconds of introduction."

"Not too far off," said Allen. Then he looked at me. My face must have expressed some kind of horror —though I hadn't meant it to. "She's only teasing you. The women in my family are brutal like that."

"Oh, like you and Daddy are such angels." Val tapped the side of her nose with a dark red manicured fingernail. "The stick up that butt of yours goes deep and yet... *Who* tells *whom* to tone it down a bit in the racy parts when—"

"Okay, that's enough of that. We have a busy afternoon planned." Allen took hold of my hand and tugged me gently toward the line of condo entrances opposite of the door Val had exited from. I stumbled after him, half-wondering how "busy" this afternoon could be.

But I kept looking over my shoulder. Val had used "whom"—and correctly, to boot. Who besides a writer often did that?

But what else had she mentioned? Toning down racy parts?

What, in her books?

Why the hell would Allen tell *the* V.L. Breedlove to tone down anything racy in her books? Did he *understand* just what those books did to eager readers like me?

They blew my mind and rocked my world, that was what they did.

"Allen," I started, about to ask. He was at the door to one of the condos and he dropped my hand in order to open it. It was unlocked. Perhaps he'd seen me from the condo and strolled out for just a moment to meet me in the courtyard. "What did she mean, 'racy parts'?"

But Allen didn't answer that. He gestured for me to go inside, and I did, one last, forlorn look over my shoulder at the woman I suspected to be my favorite author standing at the edge of the courtyard. A white, furry blob was frolicking among the bright green grass.

"Just watch the steps," Allen said. "You can take off your shoes at the top."

The condo opened straight to a staircase, no mudroom of sorts like at Bodhi and Rory's and my places. I grabbed hold of the railing and walked up the wooden steps, moving through shadows and into a bright, flooding light.

Allen's condo was huge. A floor-to-ceiling window basically took the place of one wall. There were thick window treatments off to one side, but I still shuddered to think of the heating bill in the winter.

There were no room divisions—aside from a couple of small doors, which I assumed led to things like closets and a bathroom. But the spacious kitchen against one wall was separated from a dining table—easily able to fit ten— by a shiny black island complete with sink and stovetop.

There was a large-screen TV and a sectional as well

as a recliner in one corner of the condo. And then there were a set of stairs—just a few—that led to a loft of sorts housing a dresser and a giant, king-sized bed.

And I thought *I'd* lucked out with the parents'-help lottery. His mom owned this building?

"It's a bit messy," Allen said as he came to the top of the stairs behind me.

I caught sight of a tablet on a glass coffee table that may have been, arguably, slightly askew.

I shot him a skeptical arch of my brow. "If this is messy, you really need to avoid seeing my place."

Allen frowned slightly. "And here I thought you'd be introducing me to Mr. Darcy."

Almost as if hearing about their kindred feline, two black-furred heads popped up from an elaborate brown-carpeted cat tree over in the corner near the glass window-wall and the drawn-back curtain. There was a chorus of chirps proceeded by the clunk, clunk of padded feet jumping down the levels of the tree and to the hardwood floor. Allen kicked off his shoes and then met them halfway, dropping off his Thermos on the kitchen island so that he could bend down and give each identical cat chin scritches.

"Hello, boy. Hello, girl. Did you miss me?" Both cats rubbed Allen's knees, his thighs, his back, dancing around his crouched form as if the two had practiced this grand gesture of welcome. "You're not getting dinner early," Allen insisted.

One of them—I wondered how Allen even knew which was which—stopped rubbing Allen to look up at me as I cautiously approached after carefully setting my shoes on a mat near the top of the stairs. The other followed suit, only it was the second one who came over skipping on their feet. The first one retreated behind Allen as he stood up.

"That's Poe," he said. "The boy." He scooped up the yellow-eyed cat I presumed to be Raven in his arms. "He's friendlier."

Well, that was one way of telling them apart.

"Hello, Poe," I said, crouching and holding out a bent finger for him to sniff.

He did so without hesitation, pronouncing me acceptable within half a second and slamming his head against my hand, my arm, and then my side, with such force and such loud trills that I fell over on my ass before I could even attempt to gain my balance.

"He thinks you might have treats," Allen added.

I scrambled to sit on my calves and pet Poe's cheeks and the top of his head. "No treats, buddy. Sorry."

That didn't stop him from sniffing eagerly at my purse, which I supposed smelled of Darcy.

Raven leaped from Allen's arms to the floor and more slowly headed our way. It was as if she'd waited for her brother to check me out first.

Or maybe she didn't want to miss out on any treats they imagined to be in my purse.

"I should have brought a host and hostess gift," I said, allowing Raven to sniff my finger and accept a cautious pet on the head before she walked around my back and started sniffing the purse from behind me.

"They're never this engaged with new guests," Allen said, padding over on socked feet.

"I think they smell my cat," I explained.

"Hmm, that might do it. I bet their little noses are getting tired of smelling dog on everyone else."

"You have a lot of guests?" I asked, my eyes darting to the giant dining table as Poe gave up on the purse and settled for kneading at my legs. One paw kept sliding into the ripped hole over my knee, but luckily, he kept his claws retracted.

"My sister and Maya mostly. Maya doesn't have a dog, but she spends so much time with Val and Pearl that the cats know she's clearly a part of that dog household."

I laughed. "You sound bitter."

"You met that little rascal! She's *so* hyper. And my sister spoils her."

Just then, Poe trotted over to Allen's ankles, and Raven followed suit, the two of them in their weaving dance around him again. "All right, all right. You can have your dinner a smidge early."

I chuckled. "Spoiled, huh?"

Allen's eyes sparkled as he looked over his shoulder at me while he pulled some canned food out of a nearby cupboard. "It's different when I spoil my babies."

"Oh?" Removing my purse from over my shoulder and setting it near my shoes, I stood up and strolled over to him, keeping my hands clutched tightly behind my back. "How's that?"

"I make sure *my* spoiled darlings are *very* well-behaved." He spoke huskily, a thrill of excitement floating up my body from my core out to my fingers and my toes. Yeah, Bodhi was right.

I needed to get laid.

Actually, I needed to finish this job so I wouldn't feel guilty maybe asking *this guy* if he wouldn't mind helping me get laid.

Only I'd phrase it better. That would sound like I wanted him to hook me up with a friend or something.

I stuck out my tongue at my own mixed-up thoughts as the cats meowed and carried on, one of them standing against Allen's thigh as he scooped half of the can in one fish-shaped bowl on the ground and then another.

"What's wrong?" Allen asked, rinsing out the can in the sink. "Don't like the smell of cat food?"

Composing myself, I took a deep breath. *Mind out of the gutter, Quinn*, I reminded myself. *Then hurry up and get to work*, my head snapped right back at me.

"Nothing's wrong. Um, where's your wood?" I asked, glancing around and making a point of not looking straight ahead at him. My brain was in no shape for repartee just now.

"Closet," he said, tossing the can into a bin under his sink and gesturing with his shoulder toward one of the few doors I'd spotted. He turned on his sink and began to wash his hands.

"I'll check it out," I said quickly, my mind wholly —*wholly*—focused on the task at hand.

"Wait, Quinn. Just a second. I'll get—"

But I was already at the closet, and I opened it up. There were planks of wood in there, all right, propped up against the walls of the spacious storage area.

There were a couple of coats and some other various odds and ends, too.

But more importantly than any of that, there was a shelf just *full* from side to side with what could only be described as sex toys—and quite a few of the *ker-snap*, whip-crack variety.

The running water from the kitchen turned off.

I kept staring straight ahead of me at that shelf.

"And here I thought I might just spoil you if you were well-behaved," came Allen's voice from behind me.

Chapter Thirteen

"Sorry, sorry!" I backed up, only to jump my ass straight into Allen's thighs, which made me yelp even more and stumble sideways. "I shouldn't have opened your closet like that without asking, I was just..." My face grew flush as I stared back inside, my eyes widening. "I wanted to get to work," I squeaked out.

Yes. To work. To distract me from dirty thoughts at least as long as this *well-paying*, I might remind myself, job was in progress.

So much for that idea.

Allen gauged my reaction and then snickered, slipping beside me without another comment and pulling out the planks of wood one at a time. I watched sheepishly out of the corner of my eye, my head hung down whenever Allen might have caught me looking, and slapped a hand to my mouth when the last bit of wood bumped up against a lady's purple personal massager with all the bells and whistles.

The corner of Allen's mouth quirked up as he shut the door.

"I suppose you wouldn't believe me if I said I mostly use all of that for research?"

I did a double-take. "I would question both the 'research' and the 'mostly' in that statement."

"Touché," he added, spreading the wood out along the wall as one of the cats came over to see what we were up to, licking their paw and then wiping the leg across their maw and repeating the motion.

Clearing my throat, I made a great show of inspecting the wood—like I even knew what I was looking for. "Seems solid." I knocked on it. That made the cat stop their bath partway, a little pink tongue hanging out from their mouth as they cocked their head. "Yup. Looks good."

"You have no idea what you're looking for," Allen said, a touch of mirth in his voice.

"I have no idea what I'm looking for," I admitted, letting it out with a breath. "My dad built the boxes at my place. But it looks good. Solid." After heading back to my purse, I reached in and fished out my phone, unlocking it as I made my way back to Allen and doing a Google search for the Mini Donation Library Organization's official registration and tip page. "There are multiple blueprints for boxes here." I navigated through the website and brought up some PDF files.

Allen leaned over my shoulder, and I could just *feel* him there, hovering. It sent a racy thrill down my spine.

The cat went back to their bath, joined now by the

feline's practical clone who mirrored their sibling's movements, rubbing their face with their wet paw.

"There's a website for these things?"

"A registry and everything, so people can travel to your library's location and keep the chain of giving and borrowing going."

I took a deep breath as my stomach growled. "Let's say I'm on the clock now?" It was 2:10. Somehow, hours had flown by.

Allen looked at me askance. "I've been counting you as being on the clock since we met up this morning."

I whirled around. "But that was just when you were shadowing me doing what I'd normally be doing—"

"And teaching me how to run a Mini Library. Like I hired you to do."

"But I would have gone anyway—"

Allen took my phone from my hand and set it gently down on the counter beside a double-stacked oven. "Quinn, please don't sell yourself short."

I bit back my retort. I felt guilty taking his ridiculously generous money, despite looking around...

But did him having plenty of money mean *I* deserved to be overpaid? "I forgot to say: You have a really nice place."

One of the cats—friendlier Poe, presumably—came up and rubbed my ankles. "And even nicer kitties." I bent down to give him some pets.

"I appreciate that, as does Poe, clearly," Allen said,

confirming my guess. "But don't change the subject. What time did you go on the clock with me today?"

"2:10," I said, standing straight and sticking my nose slightly into the air.

Allen took a step closer, his full lips sliding into a slight frown. "*Quinn...*"

"2:00?" I suggested, my voice quavering.

"You are most certainly *not* well-behaved." He closed the distance between us now, his hand hovering in the air over my cheek as a furball wove around and between our ankles in a figure eight.

I leaned up on my tiptoes just slightly, my body *begging* me to go in for a kiss.

Then my phone rang.

"I should get that." Tapping my fingers against my thighs, I stepped back and checked out my phone screen.

Spam, of course. If it were anyone else, I'd actually worry about why they were calling instead of texting.

Still, the interruption might have been just the splash of metaphorical cold water I needed.

"Do you have a printer?" I asked without turning around. My gaze darted over the open space. There wasn't a desktop computer or office desk anywhere, which was a little weird for someone who worked at home.

Then again, I often worked in my pajamas with a laptop on my outstretched legs on the couch, so who was I to judge?

"Uh, no," he said. "Val does, though. Do I need to

go and ask her if we can use it?" He winced as he came into view. He clearly didn't want to go ask his sister anything right now.

But a printer, huh? Did she prefer to print out her manuscripts for revising? That made sense.

"Well, you can bring up the PDFs for the box blueprints on a tablet if you prefer." I headed toward the coffee table, where I'd seen a tablet, but perhaps—justifiably, considering the toys-in-the-closet incident—thinking I'd pick it up and start scrolling through his tablet without his permission, he swept in front of me and picked it up.

I put a hand on my hip and sent him a bemused look.

"Let me bring up the site," he said gruffly, but not unkindly. As he tapped away at the screen, both Poe and Raven trotted past him in front of the TV, jumping up to the TV stand and using that to leap directly to the middle of the cat tree.

One of them reached the very top level first and continued bathing. The other took a slightly longer route around and through a few condo portions of the tree and then joined their sibling—licking the other cat's cheek.

"Inseparable, aren't they? So cute," I remarked.

Allen stopped tapping at the tablet to look at his cats. His shoulders loosened, a tightness I hadn't noticed relaxing. "They're twins. Only two in their litter."

"Like you and Val?" I teased.

Allen rolled his eyes and turned his attention to the screen again. "If you ever find me licking my sister's ear, please send help."

Chuckling, I let the silence descend between us as Allen zoomed in on, presumably, the PDF on the screen.

"Maya said the two of you work together."

"Hmm?" Allen didn't look up. "Maya's my accountant. I introduced her to Val."

Huh. Interesting. Relevant to my plan to "gotcha" him about his sister being V.L. Breedlove? Maybe not?

"No, I mean, you and your sister."

"Uh-huh... Yeah, I like this one. Simple enough I think I could build it. Though I might have to borrow my dad's tools and their garage..."

"And *you* work as V.L. Breedlove's PA," I pointed out.

That got him to look up. "As we've established." He smirked.

I lifted both hands out, as if to say, "Well?"

He chuckled again and crossed the room, his face glued to the screen as he tapped away. "I said Breedlove was my only author client."

I followed him. He climbed up the short set of stairs leading to the loft, and there, behind another cluster of drawn-back curtains, was a small laptop desk on wheels on which sat a silver laptop. One-handed, he futzed around with some kind of contraption that extended the laptop up to a height better suited for him standing. Ah. One of those healthy, standing office workers. Setting the tablet down on the desk, he opened the lid of the laptop and a password screen popped up.

"I think... You forgot you were talking to me there," I pointed out.

His fingers stopped moving across the keyboard of his laptop and he turned around. "Never. Sorry." He gestured at his head. "People tell me I can get too focused on what I'm doing sometimes. What were you saying?"

"Er, no, I didn't say anything. It's just you said Breedlove was your only author client."

"Oh, yes. But I didn't say the only thing I did was act as Breedlove's PA." Behind him, on the laptop screen, the wallpaper came into focus. It was the cover for *Riding My Baby*. Breedlove's next book.

My eyes popped and I swooped in. "You must have advanced copies, right? Right?"

Allen jumped as I appeared like a ninja beside him in front of the screen. He slapped the laptop screen closed. "You are one wily woman, aren't you?"

Wily or simply lacking in social decorum after far too long trapped inside working all alone?

I took a deep breath. *Professionalism.*

"Sorry. I did pre-order it."

"I remember." He smirked. Right. We'd talked about me getting the pre-order bonus.

"It's just... I didn't see anything about a Street Team or how to get ARCs, and you better *believe* I would have jumped all over that if I had."

"I coordinated a Street Team in the early days," he said. He took a sharp breath. "That's a PA's job."

"Can you let me join? Please? Pretty please?" I was probably blowing my chances of this handsome man ever seeing me as sexual partner material by acting like a simpering toddler, but I couldn't help it. This was *V.L. Breedlove.* This was the stuff my dreams were made of.

Real-life love never worked out quite so wonderfully for me. I could give up on that if it meant holding even tighter to the books that were my escape.

Allen searched my face, probably filing my pouty face away as "too immature" for him and all those sex toys in the closet.

But I couldn't stop myself.

"The Street Team and beta readers are locked in," he said. "Too many cooks in the kitchen interferes with the writing process. And Breedlove has *a lot* of books to write and release."

"I won't give feedback!" I said. "Other than to say I love it! I'll worship the ground she walks on! I won't tell a soul I'm reading it early!"

Allen rubbed a hand over his face, pinching his chin as he stared down at me. There was a slight color to his cheeks. "You don't have to go that far."

"I won't if you don't want me to." I pantomimed zipping my lips. "I'll be as quiet as a mouse. I'll do anything you say." I went up on my toes and whispered the next part. "*Anything.*"

My face reddened as I set back on my heels and realized what I'd just said. I hadn't meant it *that* way. Or... had I?

Professionalism? Out the window.

I was technically on the clock for this job. We'd established that much.

Allen picked up his tablet and started tapping away at it. "I'll hold you to that."

My insides turned to jelly as my heart beat harder and harder. He couldn't have been... Was he bringing up the book?

I grew tongue-tied as Allen turned the screen around, a white page with words and a sleek, stylized "Chapter One: Aaron" near the top of the page.

"Is that... Is that... *Riding My Baby*?" The words cracked as they left my lips, my hands reaching for the tablet.

He yanked it higher, out of grasp, and leaned forward, his voice growing husky. "Somebody promised she'd follow my orders first."

Chapter Fourteen

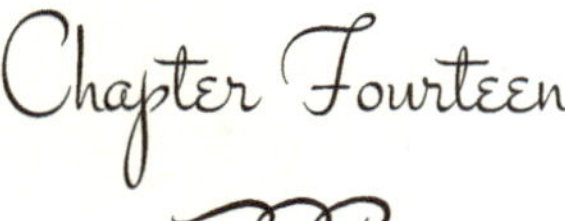

Okay, enough dancing around the topic. I wasn't imagining things, right?

Allen laughed, and the rumble in his chest drove the pleasure center of my brain—and the area between my legs, if I'm being honest—wild.

He handed the tablet to me. "I only want willing women in my bed. You don't have to sleep with me to read it, though the offer is most definitely there. Until then... My only order is: This book doesn't leave this room until Tuesday."

My limbs were weak as I accepted the tablet, my thoughts going wild inside my head. Which was more important? The book? Sleeping with this hot, handsome man?

My brain did not compute.

I plopped down right where I was on the steps leading up to the loft, my back to him, steadying the tablet screen across my knees with shaky hands.

Brain did not compute reality. Brain computed only books. Beloved books.

Safe and sexy and safe and safe and safe books.

I'd gotten three lines into *Riding My Baby* and realized I hadn't said a word. "Thank... Thank you."

I had to re-read those lines. I wasn't focused on *the* next V.L. Breedlove book. What was wrong with me?

Allen sat down on the step above me, looking over my shoulder at the tablet. "You're welcome. You're so enthusiastic. You make me nervous."

I made *him* nervous?

"I promised to be quiet," I said meekly.

I re-read the first few lines again, my heartbeat echoing wildly in my head.

"I forgot to order delivery," he said, out of the blue.

"Shh," I snapped without meaning to. My stomach rumbling revealed what it thought about not jumping on that. "I'm reading," I said, as much to my stomach as to him.

"I can take care of it while you're reading," he said softly. When I didn't respond, he leaned closer, his musky fragrance sending wild tingles all along my core. He pointed to the tablet, and for a second, I thought he'd point something out in the book, so I lifted it up so he could reach it. "Let me bring up the menu—"

"Don't you dare!" I said—loudly. Too loudly.

I gasped and locked eyes with him. He was already beaming, though. "You really love Breedlove's books?"

"I do," I whispered. It came out rather huskily.

"You have to be the first woman I've ever invited to

my bed who picked a book over me." His lips were close, too close as he spoke. "I'm at war with myself. I *want* to be flattered…" He left the rest unsaid.

"I'm, um, not sure I'm ready for that," I whispered. He preferred when women flattered him by jumping to it when invited, did he?

"Then I'll wait for you to tell me when you are."

My head was light, my insides swirling. My body was at war with everything it wanted—*needed* right now. Sustenance was so far down the list when this book was in my hand, when his lips were so close to mine.

I set the tablet down on my thighs and leaned up, closing my eyelids.

"You have to ask." His voice was so stern. It did wild, buzzing things to my clit.

"Kiss me," I said softly, the words catching on my breath.

His hands reached out to grab either side of my cheeks, and lips pressed against my mouth—gently at first, then rougher, hungrier, his tongue pushing through to entangle with mine.

Leaning up into the kiss, I took hold of his fore-arms, gasping for breath.

I opened my eyes. He stared *into* me, his dark irises searching mine. His palms were warm on my cheeks.

My stomach rumbled.

He laughed, his hands falling down. "I have to feed you. I promised."

Suddenly shy, I looked down at my lap. The tablet

had a screensaver up. "And I'm supposed to be talking to you about Mini Donation Libraries."

"Oh?" He shifted back, his dark hair shaking slightly. "Is that what you want to focus on now? Huh."

"Build the boxes." I tucked my hair behind one ear, my voice catching on my throat. "Maybe have your friend Jake make them stand out a bit with art. Talk to your mom about rearranging the hedges—oh, but I wanted to tell you. Your parking lot isn't that conducive to drive-bys. I mean, you can focus on just the neighborhood exchanging books—and it largely will be them—but I don't know. If you go that route, you could even put the boxes inside, wherever the mailboxes are."

"Quinn?"

My chest thumped at the sound of my name on his breath. "Yes?" I stared up at him.

"You've taught me well. Bill me for the day—an eight-hour day—and I'll let you know if I have any more questions."

"But I—"

His finger moved to trace along one of my cheeks. "Let me feed you, and then let's pick up where we left off."

One of my hands went to my stomach to suppress another rumble. "Okay," I squeaked.

"Let me bring up the menu—"

I snatched the tablet and held it to the other side, far out of his reach. "Order me anything. I'll eat sandpaper if you'll just let me read this book in peace."

He arched a brow. "Still focused on the book?"

I nodded, my cheeks flushing. "Still focused on the book." I swiped at the screen to dismiss the screensaver.

"Well, you're lucky the author has a bit of an ego," he said, standing and stretching. "Because I'm willing to put a pin in this to hear what you have to say—and I promise I won't feed you sandpaper."

"You might if I give it a bad review," I teased. The author had an ego, huh? So would he run across the courtyard to tell his sister I was about to devour this sucker in no time flat?

"What happened to worshipping at the altar of Breedlove?"

"Not quite what I said, but I'm only teasing." I smiled and caught his eye as he reached the bottom of the steps. "But I'm not kidding when I say, just leave me be. Until I finish, I'm going to be lost in another reality."

He shook his head, but it was hard to miss the light dancing over his irises. "You are something, Quinn Simmons. I'm not sure quite what yet, but *something*."

I'd take that. If it got me advanced copies of Breedlove's books and someone to hand me some food I could wolf down so I didn't have to look up from the screen until I reached the last page, I'd take that.

I just hoped he still saw me as a woman he'd like to bang even after witnessing my messy, hopeless book-worm side in action.

I was about a quarter through *Riding My Baby* when the aroma of something mouth-watering drew my attention upward.

"You're going to get a sore back there. Why not move to the table for now—and a more comfortable chair after lunch?"

Allen held a plate out toward me on the stairs leading up to his loft. It was black on the bottom and red on top—nice and stark and more interesting than the typical white plate—but more importantly, there was a panini on top and some potato chips arranged nicely along one side, as well as a whole dill pickle.

My stomach rumbled.

"The pesto chicken is my favorite," he said, offering me a playful wink. "But if you would have preferred the sandpaper, I apologize."

"Chicken sounds great. Smells great." I looked at the extended plate and then back down at the tablet on my knees. The plate and then the tablet. The plate and the tablet.

"Follow your nose," he said, waving the plate closer to my face and then pulling it away when I went to snatch half of the panini with one hand. He walked backward, never taking his eyes off me, headed toward the table, where another plate was already set up.

I didn't seem to have registered him leaving, return-ing, or setting that all up.

"Did you even notice I left?" he asked, my thoughts perhaps too easy to read.

"No...?" I admitted, though it came out as more of a question.

He put one hand over his heart as he set the plate across from the other on the table. "Ouch."

"It's nothing personal," I assured him. "I'm reading." I gestured at the tablet on my lap with both hands, as if that explained it all.

"I hadn't noticed," he said sarcastically, crossing his arms over his chest. "You only chomped at me like a hungry dog anytime I threatened to pull that thing away from you."

"I did not *chomp* at you." I thought back. At least I *hoped* I hadn't.

I stretched, my eyes darting back down to the screen. Aaron and Lola were coasting down the highway on his bike, the Appalachian Mountains off in the distance. Only a few more lines until the end of the chapter.

"I'd hate to think what would have happened if a fire alarm had gone off when I was gone," Allen said.

"I'd have noticed *that*," I said sheepishly. Wincing, I took hold of the tablet and stood. My bones cracked, my neck ached. But my adrenaline had yet to crash. "I noticed the cats when they came over and rubbed me at one point."

Allen looked over my head as I headed down the stairs. "Yes, I see they tried to lead you to a more comfortable location."

I turned around to see what he was looking at and found both black, furry lumps curled up at the end of his king-sized bed.

"They must have given up," I said. "I didn't realize how much time had passed." I cracked my neck to either side and took a seat at the table, putting the tablet beside my plate.

Allen grabbed for the tablet.

My hand reached out to cover it.

We locked eyes.

Grimacing, I let my hand fall to my lap and nodded for him to take his own tablet.

"Not like a hungry dog, huh?" he said. He pushed the tablet to the edge of the table, then walked around and took a seat across from me.

There was a glass of iced tea in front of each of our plates.

He pushed a dispenser full of sugar toward me. "I hope you like tea. I'd have asked what you wanted to drink, but you didn't respond to me the few times I called your name. But you can add sugar as you like."

My eyes blinked rapidly as I thought back, trying to remember the hottest man I'd ever spoken to at length calling my name a few times and getting no response.

Nope. Didn't remember.

"I love tea," I said. "No sweetener, thank you. Unless it's hot tea and honey."

"Can't go wrong with that," he said, smiling and picking up his sandwich. The same one he'd gotten me.

The sandwich was like a warm, cozy night spent in

my reading socks before a flickering fireplace-simulating space heater. In other words: It was happiness in my mouth.

I moaned.

Like, *really* moaned. *Riding My Baby* was still fresh on my mind, as were all the things Aaron had promised to do to Lola. I'd have been arrested for public indecency if Allen hadn't gotten us takeout.

Chapter Fifteen

Allen chuckled at the orgasmic sound leaving my mouth. "I take it you like the sandwich."

My lips pressed together tightly for a moment in hot shame. "I do. Thank you. And I apologize for being a terrible guest. I'm supposed to be *working* with you—"

He held up a hand to stop me. "We settled that. But if you want to instruct me in any more things about the Mini Libraries, I'm all ears."

I waited until I was halfway finished with my sandwich before I picked up some chips and got back to talking between bites and sips. "Did you give any thought to whether you'd like the box inside or outside?"

Allen finished up his pickle. "Well, if we register the box with the Mini Donation Libraries Organization website, we can't expect visitors to come inside the lobby where the mailboxes are, right?"

"That might make it hard for them to find. But you don't have to register it. Make it just for the condo residents and you won't have to worry about weather-proofing your box like my dad did. That also requires occasional maintenance. Is there room by your mailboxes?"

Allen cocked his head. "No, not really. I'm still partial to my moving-the-hedges idea. They've bothered me for ages. Anytime I have to dog-sit for that little monster, she gets tangled up in the plant life before she reaches the lawn."

"Do you dog-sit often?" I asked. "You'd think you'd be more comfortable around dogs by now."

"You've *met* the little creature! How can you even *say* that?"

I laughed at Allen's slack jaw. He grinned back and picked up the rest of his sandwich. "And yes, I suppose I do. Both Val and I work from home, but Val gets out more. And yet *she* chose the pet that can't be left alone for more than a few minutes without destruction and piss everywhere."

I almost choked on my tea.

"I apologize for my language," he said roughly.

"It's not that." I tittered. "I'm just picturing someone trying to get work done with this dog tearing up the place."

"It's not easy, believe me. But she settles down if she's not alone."

"How come she never appears in the newsletter?" I asked. "Most readers love hearing about pets."

"Cats more than dogs, I'd wager." Allen's chest puffed out proudly.

"Well, dogs are popular, too," I said, though I agreed that I liked hearing about writerly assistant cats just a smidge more than dogs in author newsletters. They were so precocious. "Especially cute little dogs. Besides"—I looked over my shoulder to check on his cats up on the bed—"you could have her 'borrow' *your* cats, couldn't you?"

"Hmm..." Allen thought about it as he examined a rather misshapen potato chip. "I've been reluctant to feature my babies in the newsletter."

His *babies*? Heaven help me, I wanted to jump this guy's bones.

"What's wrong with letting Val pretend she owns your cats? Or she could admit they're her brother's and claim she often visits them."

He shrugged. "I don't want the newsletters to get too personal. Besides, what other than books would Breedlove even write about?"

"You just said Val had an active social life."

Allen grimaced and bit down on the misshapen chip.

"And you have *some* experience to draw on. More than I do, I'd wager. You went to Bodhi and Rory's the other day. Dressed to the nines, I might add."

He perked up at that compliment. What a little ego. "My sister encourages me to get out of the house every so often." He leaned back in his chair. "And while I usually protest, I have to really thank her this time. To tell the truth, though, it was that Mini Donation Libraries idea that sparked my desire to come. I saw them when picking up their mail—"

"And started chronicling them for V.L. Breedlove's social media," I added.

"Right. Bodhi told me he'd introduce you to me, and you'd give me the whole story behind the Ooh-La-La Box in particular. But I couldn't have known the woman behind the boxes would be so..."

"Bizarre?" I finished for him, picking up the pickle. "Hopeless?"

Allen cocked an eyebrow. "Sexy," he finished.

I dropped the pickle back down to the plate.

"You work fast," I muttered, though not angrily in the least.

"I do," he said. "Usually, it's because I'm a busy man and I want what I want when I want it, but now..."

"Now?"

"I'm willing to wait."

I wiped my hands on the cloth napkin he'd provided for me and stood, taking hold of the tablet once more.

"Guess I'll be waiting some more?" he asked.

"Try me when I finish this book," I said, rather boldly. My hands ached, this strange desire to toss aside the book and start exploring every line and muscle of his body overtaking me.

I headed toward his couch in search of a more

comfortable reading nook. The sun was growing lower over the horizon, but the tablet was backlit.

"There's a lamp by my bed," he offered. "And two cats."

I froze, spun around, and headed up the loft stairs.

"No funny business," I warned him, shaking a finger in his direction as I reached the top.

"You won't hear a peep out of me." He zipped his fingers across his lips.

I threw myself on his bed, getting one open eye each from both of the black cats for daring to disturb them. I offered them both a pet and then fluffed the pillows, stacking them behind me against the headboard, flicking on the lamp beside me, and losing myself once more in the sexy, Southern motorcycle clubhouse to which Lola had found herself dragged kicking and screaming—literally.

It was dark by the time my bleary eyes got the rest they so desperately craved.

I leaned back on the pillow, cradling the tablet against my chest, visions of Aaron and Lola on his motorcycle still dancing in my head.

Visions of her bent over his club's pool table, Aaron cradling her ass, which had been popping out of the miniskirt she'd tried on just for him as he danced his fingers between her legs and rocked her to her very core.

That was a hard scene to forget.

I let out a dreamy sigh and took a deep breath to gear up for another. The scent of something rich and hearty—like stew, maybe—lured my eyes open. I sat up on an elbow and peered down the loft. From the bed, I got a good look at the kitchen.

Allen was there, stirring something at the burners on the kitchen island.

He was cooking? We'd just eaten! And when had he started that? I hadn't noticed at all.

The cats were gone from the bed, too. I spotted them both staring relentlessly in Allen's direction from atop the nearby couch and a recliner, respectively, their feet curled up under them as they sat in little loaf formations.

I brought the tablet back up off my chest and tapped at the top to bring up the time. It was seven o'clock. Oh, no. Poor Darcy would be eager for his evening meal.

We'd eaten hours ago.

I'd been reading and reading and not noticing a single thing going on around here.

"Ah. You finally taking a break?" Allen's voice carried across the space between us. He thumbed over his shoulder. "Sorry, the bathroom is a bit of a walk. I love the loft design, but there isn't room for a master bath up there."

"I, uh..." I swung my legs off the bed and gave my head a moment to stop swimming. "I finished it," I said as I made my way down the steps, the tablet clutched to my side.

"Oh?" Allen swallowed noticeably as I neared, reaching into a little jar of green garnishes and sprinkling it into the stew or whatever it was he was working on. "What did you think?" His voice caught in his throat as he cleared it.

I set the tablet down on his dining table and just stood there a second, in need of time to gather my thoughts. And, apparently, nature was calling, after all. I'd just ignored it for hours in order to get through the book.

"Can you give me a second?" I said, rushing for the door he'd indicated to be the bathroom, snatching my phone off his kitchen counter as I went.

"That bad, huh?" His voice carried behind me and it took me until I was on the other side of the door to realize he'd meant the book, not my urge to go.

I *had* left at an inopportune moment. I'd just been... overwhelmed.

I barely had time to register the sleek, black marble of his sink or freestanding tub, and the shower stall with all the trimmings opposite the toilet in this overly large bathroom. Even as I did my business, phone in hand, my fingers itched to tell Mom, Milly, Evangeline —anyone who would listen about how great V.L. Breedlove's next book was.

But as I moved to compose a message, first to Evangeline, I froze. I'd promised not to tell anyone I'd gotten to read it early. Oh my *god*, how I wished I hadn't made that promise. But I'd have sold my soul if it meant reading that book early, so it was a price I'd have to pay.

Instead, I texted Evangeline to ask if she was home and if she minded running over to my place to give Darcy his half can of wet food, since he was likely out of kibble by now. She had a key to my place in case of emergencies, just as I had one for hers. More often than not, I'd been the one running over to let her dog out while she'd been out and around town with her family. Quinn Simmons was always home. Except when she wasn't, apparently.

She texted back as I was washing my hands.

Sure. On my way now. What are you up to tonight?

Once I'd dried my hands, I scooped the phone back up and leaned my butt against the edge of the sink. *Currently in the bathroom of Mr. Hottie.*

Evangeline sent back several exclamation points and sly faces.

Okay, I'm in your place and your little mister is insistent I put this phone down and feed him, but you owe me details.

I'll tell you them when I can, I wrote back. *It's not what you're thinking...* Only my finger hovered over the *send* button. *Was* this going to be what I was thinking?

Allen and I had flirted. That hadn't been a hallucination, right? Some kind of mix-up my brain had made between the book and reality?

I set the phone down, not sending that last line, and stared into the mirror.

Okay. I only looked half-bad. But that meant I didn't look half-bad. Somehow. It made sense to me in that moment, anyway.

I'd done my makeup and nails this morning, trying to look cute for the hot guy I'd been about to spend a few hours with. And now "a few hours" had turned into a whole day and—*ohmygod*, I'd spent more time ignoring him and reading than talking to the man! To the *extremely good-looking* man cooking me a meal—presumably—right outside that door.

And I'd left him alone out there without gushing about the book like I'd promised to.

What was wrong with me?

I took a bit of water and splashed it over my eyes, knowing my eyeshadow and concealer were in danger of smudging, but needing that intense sense of cold to wake up now more than ever.

Leaning on the sink and looking back into the mirror, I wished I'd thought to wear something cuter. True, this was me—casual and maybe just a little bit of a slob—but who managed to get into the bed of a person way out of their league without putting in more effort than a little at-home manicure and a dab of concealer?

"Get out there and *try* to be human," I told the Quinn reflected in the mirror.

I stood up and flicked my hair over both shoulders, straightening my checkered shirt. It was wrinkled because I'd been lying down so long—on the poor man's bed. Without him in it.

"Get out there and do this," I repeated under my breath like a mantra.

Snatching up my phone, I strode for the door, channeling all of the best romantic heroines I could think of.

Chapter Sixteen

"Stew's ready," Allen said without looking my way as he ladled some of the meal into a black-and-red bowl. "I hope you like beef stew. I didn't want to bother you to ask you—and there was the fact that the only thing you've asked me to get you to eat is sandpaper. So I figured anything a step up from that might be okay."

"Ha ha." I set my phone back on the counter and spoke the words teasingly, not unkindly, as I stepped closer. The aroma was divine, practically stopping me in my tracks. "It sounds—and smells—amazing. Thank you." We exchanged a look and my breath caught in my throat. Never in a million years would I have thought that seeing a fine-ass man in the kitchen could be so sexy. Cooking had *never* been something I'd thought of as attractive in the slightest.

"You cook?" I asked, accepting the plate and bowl he handed me.

"On occasion. I don't often really have the time.

It's easier to order out." He began scooping the stew in a second bowl and I walked around the island to sit down. "But there's a supermarket down the street, so I ran over there to get ingredients for one of the few meals I can make."

He'd gone grocery shopping while I'd read? I *had* been out of it.

One of the cats—Poe, I'd presume—jumped off the couch and sat beside my dining table chair on the floor. He sat straight, as tall as he could, and just stared at me with wide, yellow eyes.

"Don't give him any scraps," Allen said as he walked around the island to slide his plate across the table from me.

"I wouldn't without asking," I said, staring down at the kitty and feeling those little sweet eyes working their magic on me. Still, it wasn't *my* cat. "But I take it *someone* does or he wouldn't be asking."

"Oh, I wouldn't be so sure." Allen walked back into the kitchen and grabbed the salt and pepper shakers, bringing them to the table and sprinkling some of each in his bowl. "I think he's just attracted to the scent."

"Huh," I said, picking up the spoon Allen had tucked on the plate beside the bowl. "*This* cat isn't spoiled or anything, right?"

As if on cue, Poe reached up and tapped the side of my knee with his paw, claws sheathed.

"Aw," I said, looking down at him.

"Don't fall for it." Allen was back in the kitchen.

"He already got his supper. What about dashing Mr. Darcy?" he asked over his shoulder as he opened a cupboard and brought out two wineglasses.

"I texted Evangeline and asked her to feed him for me," I said. "Once I realized how late it was." I gave Poe's head a little tap. He was standing against my thigh now, sniffing the air in the direction of my steaming stew.

"Oh, good. I was worried about the little guy. Even if I haven't met him yet."

Yet? My stomach did flip-flops and Poe sat back down. That was a sign Allen wanted to hang out again, right? And come over to my place?

"Wait, do you drink?" Allen asked, holding a bottle of wine he'd brought down from a rack over the fridge. "I remember you just had water at Bodhi and Rory's."

"Not often," I admitted. "But I'm not opposed to a small glass."

Allen popped the cork and started pouring, a little more in one glass than the other.

I blew on the hot stew on my spoon and Poe started purring from beside me.

Raven let out a little mew and skipped over into the kitchen toward Allen.

"No cork to bat around," he told her, putting the cork back in the bottle. "The bottle isn't empty."

I giggled. What was with cats and trash they found more exciting than cat toys? I finally tried the stew and it was *so* good. I had to cover my mouth to stop myself from emitting another one of those easily construed moans.

"Want some water, too?" he asked, coming around the island and sliding a glass of red wine toward me.

"Yes, please." I could get used to this. Eating fine food, being waited on hand and foot.

Poe tapped my thigh again.

Allen sure knew how to pamper.

"This is so good, Allen," I said, suddenly coming back to my senses. "Thank you. Oh my god, I can't believe how rude I've been all day, and here you are just spoiling and spoiling me—"

"I like spoiling a beautiful woman," Allen said. The clink of ice against a glass echoed out into the room.

I nearly choked on my next bite of stew. I hadn't been imagining things, huh?

"I was glad to give you time to yourself to read Breedlove's next book," he said, coming back with the glass of water. He sat across from me at last, Raven coming out from the kitchen area in order to sit beside him. "Only it's too bad you didn't like it." He gazed down at his stew and blew on his first spoonful.

His lips were so distracting curled into a perfect little "O" like that.

I shook my head, and Poe trotted over to join his sister at Allen's ankle. I peeked under the table to find them both staring up at him, just as Poe had done to me.

Straightening up, I took a deep breath. How to

gather my thoughts? How to express how I felt? What were words? Words be how used?

"I loved it," I said at last. I was choking up as emotions overwhelmed me. A tear spilled first from one eye and then the other and I laughed, a crazy-sounding giggle, as I wiped my tears away.

Allen's spoon clanked down into his stew and he stared straight at me, his jaw dropped slightly. "Are you okay? You don't have to lie if you think the truth will hurt my feelings. We got some good feedback from the Street Team, so I think we'll still go ahead with the release anyway, but no book can please every reader—"

"I. *Loved*. It," I reiterated. And then I burst into tears.

Allen's jaw went slack.

"It was so romantic," I gushed, giving my all to convincing him. If he truly understood how much V.L. Breedlove's books meant to me, maybe I'd be lucky to get my hands on advanced copies more often. "The danger Lola and Aaron were in had my heart pumping —and it never seemed ridiculous or over-the-top like some books I've read do. I mean, those are fun and they have their place, but..." I put my spoon down and held my hand over my heart. "I've known Aaron since Book 1 in the series—he was always kind of on the side there, but I knew he'd have his time in the spotlight—and then Lola showed up and it was just like... She was *made* for him, you know? I know that's silly since yes, the author literally wrote her into existence for that man, but they bring out each other's strengths and make up for each other's weaknesses. Despite the wild lives they lead, it feels so *snug* and cozy, being able to lose myself in their relationship." I grabbed a cloth napkin Allen had provided on the table and dabbed at my eyes. "That's why I love romance books, you know? When they work, they're just so moving."

"Oh," said Allen softly, his voice taking on a wistful tone.

"And there's the banter, too. Gotta love a feisty heroine and a man who can make me laugh."

"If only repartee were easy to come up with on the fly," Allen said.

I blushed. "You're not so bad at it yourself."

"I don't know. I don't usually do so well in a crowded room."

I thought about how Bodhi had told me Allen had a stick up his ass. He didn't seem that way to me. Not outside of a social gathering. "Neither do I. But one on one—you know just what to say to make a girl smile."

Allen beamed at that, then cleared his throat and tapped his spoon against his bowl. "Well, I'm glad you liked it. I should have guessed by how quiet you got while you finished it. I'll, uh, be sure the author knows."

"Because of her big ego?" I teased.

"Because compliments do an author good—and really, it never stops feeling fake." He gestured in the air with his spoon and I noticed Poe standing on two feet against Allen's thigh, reaching in vain with one paw for the hovering utensil. "This whole successful-indie-author thing."

"'Successful' is an understatement. The books gave *you* a job, too," I pointed out.

He quirked an eyebrow.

"I just mean... Well, what other kinds of clients do you have? I'm genuinely interested." I blew on another spoonful of stew before taking a bite.

"I started with a number of local businesses," he said. "Like my mom's real estate company, my dad's security agency..."

"Keeping it in the family?" I asked. As if I had room to criticize, getting the condo as a graduation gift of sorts. I mean, it wasn't as stylish as *this* downtown piece of prime real estate, but I was genuinely happy there.

"My sister and I both have genuinely benefited from nepotism." Allen took a cloth napkin off his lap and dabbed at his mouth.

"Except for the writing," I pointed out. "Both of you—finishing even just one book is something to be proud of."

Allen's eyes twinkled. "'Even just one book,' huh?"

I nodded and scraped the last of my stew out of the bowl. "I love reading, but I don't really want to write anything myself."

"You *are* a writer, though."

"For business clients. Charities, non-profits, small businesses—anything I can find online."

"Finding clients sounds like a hustle in and of itself."

"It is." I sighed. "Though some of my favorites do hire me again." I glanced over toward the, uh, "toy" closet, and the planks of wood Allen had stacked at some point beside the door. "Though I guess some of the best jobs are limited."

"You're welcome to help me build and paint the boxes." Allen pet one of the cats beside him as he pushed his bowl and plate to the side.

"Oh, my dad did that part, so I don't know how much help I'd be." I leaned back in my chair, watching as first one and then the other cat trotted over toward their cat tree beside the large-screen TV. They must have given up all hope of getting any treats.

"You can help me when I fill them up with all the books we picked out," he offered, leaning his elbow on the table and threading his fingers together.

"I'd like that," I said. "I want to see them set up—see you take pictures for Breedlove's newsletter and social media accounts, too."

"Do you want to appear in the newsletter?" he offered. "As the architect of sorts?"

My heart jumped into my throat. "Oh, I couldn't. And besides, Breedlove's 'rockstars' wouldn't care about me." I fluffed a hand in the air, referring to how Breedlove addressed her readers in the newsletters.

"*I* think you're a rockstar," he said. "You're so full of passion when talking about the things you like."

"Well, um, thank you." I tucked a stray strand of

hair behind my ear, my longer-than-usual nails getting a bit caught up in a knot. I grimaced. "I'm so... *so* awkward, though. I know that."

Allen leaned back in his seat. "I would call it more 'charming.'"

"You'd be generous, then, to put it mildly." I let out a little chuckle that got caught in my throat.

My gaze flicked back to the closet full of "toys."

Allen turned over his shoulder as if to follow my gaze. "Are you curious?" He leaned back over the table toward me. "I'd be happy to satisfy."

I did a double-take. "See, that's, um... My flirtation game is *way* too rusty to figure out if you're serious or to throw something *charming* back at you." My knee bounced steadily under the table. "Awkward is all I have to offer."

"I thought you were a romance reader," he purred.

"Yeah, not a romance *experiencer*. Not since college, really. Not much, anyway. And even then, it was awkward and clunky and just about *the last thing* from romantic." I kept rambling, my eyes growing wider and wider as Allen stood up and walked around the table, tapping a single index finger across my lips.

"I was going to ask if you wanted dessert," he said, his voice going huskier, if possible. "Or if you'd rather skip dessert and spend the rest of the evening *playing* in my bed?"

His finger dropped away, his eyes locked on mine, waiting for my answer.

"Yes, please," I squeaked, stiffening.

"Yes what?"

"Yes, please, sir?" I offered.

He chuckled. "Charming, Quinn. Your adorableness is utterly charming." He took a step back. "Dessert it is."

Dessert? My breath hitched. But I'd thought…

Oh.

Like an idiot, I'd just answered in the affirmative when he'd asked which option I preferred. Twice. Instead of specifying what I was saying *yes* to.

Chapter Seventeen

"I've got a box mix for brownies," Allen said, rummaging through a kitchen cupboard. "Or I can have something delivered. A chocolate-chip pizza? Sorry. I'm not much of a baker."

His words landed like hollow *thud*s in my brain, my chest squeezing tightly. I stood quickly, sending the chair scraping against the hardwood floor behind me.

Both cat heads popped up from where they'd been resting on two different tiers of the cat tree.

"Allen, will you show me?" I asked. "What it's like..." My voice grew reverent, hushed, even. "To have sex like they did in the book."

"Hmm?" Allen slowly shut the cupboard, a grin broad on his face as he leaned back against the counter and crossed his arms. "Which book?"

"The one I just... You know... *Riding My Baby*, of course! You said you read it, right?"

"I read every one of Breedlove's books."

"Right. So I, uh..." I winced. "Actually, would that be awkward, considering who wrote them? For you to act anything out from them, I mean?"

He quirked an eyebrow as he slowly, purposefully, made his way over to me, like a cat stalking its prey. "Not especially, no. There's nothing of that nature in those books I haven't tried myself." His gaze flicked to the "toy" closet.

I wondered, briefly, if part of Allen's PA job was to empirically experience a few ideas for Val so she could write about them in her books. Was Val bisexual? Had she been with men before? Was it all just the product of her vivacious imagination? There were lesbians in her books, but they were never the main focus. Maybe Val relied on her brother to... help fill in the details.

I shuddered. I was an only child, but *those kinds* of scenes weren't what I talked about with my mom in detail when gushing about romance books.

"Quinn, you're getting that glazed look on your face." Allen's voice rumbled deep in his chest as he stepped back toward the table. "The one where you're lost in your thoughts. I thought it was just when you were reading, but—"

I opened my mouth, shut it, and took a deep breath.

Then I looked down at what I was wearing and my jaw dropped. "Oh my god. I was *not* expecting to try to seduce you today—"

"Seduce me?" he purred, finally reaching my side. His finger brushed up my arm and I shivered. But that just made it worse. I was in ripped jeans and a plaid shirt—not exactly in the running for "Sexiest Woman of the Year."

I mean, I'd *tried*. The nail polish. The makeup. The cute-but-not-*too*-cute attire. I hadn't expected to go from potentially being up to bat to hitting a home run in a few hours flat.

But that damn *book*. This gorgeous man. My skin was heated from head to toe. That book had put me in a mood, dammit, and here he was just in front of me, practically serving himself up to me on a platter.

Who was I to refuse?

"I have condoms," Allen said. "All sorts of kinds. Ribbed for your pleasure, cherry-flavored—"

"*Cherry*-flavored?" I squeaked, my eyelids fluttering like butterflies.

He smirked. "Would you prefer I stock up on grape next time?"

"*Next time*?" I peeped even softer. Then I let out a deep breath. "Um, no. I mean, thank you for thinking ahead. And I'm on birth control—for medical reasons, not because I'm getting laid... Because I'm not. Which is probably not really making me prime sexing material in your eyes, but, um, I just needed to explain I'm not worried about that, though I certainly wasn't *expecting* this—"

"'Prime sexing material,' huh?" Allen's finger landed under my chin this time, and he gently directed my gaze to meet his. "Have you looked at yourself lately?"

"*Yes.*" Sighing, I took a step back. "That's the problem. I'm not dressed up. I mean, you've seen me at my worst—this is certainly no match for my sopping-wet-hair-and-baggy-sweats first impression, but if I could go home and change and try again—"

"Quinn," Allen said sharply. "The goal, generally, for a man interested in a woman, is to get her clothes *off*. Not to have her put other clothes on."

I went quiet.

He stepped closer again, taking me gently by the arms.

"You were beautiful the first moment I saw you, and you're beautiful now."

I fought the urge to tell him he was being kind, particularly during that *first meeting*, but even the urge was swallowed up soon enough by the hitch in my breath at the sight of him so near, his grip growing more intense, more *possessive* without ever hurting me.

The pressure of his hands on my arms felt good. I wanted that touch everywhere. I wanted, at least for this night, to be *his*, like a romance heroine and her gorgeous, sexy suitor—the kind who wouldn't be satisfied until she was his and his alone.

"Look at me," said Allen.

There was nowhere else I'd rather look. "I am," I whispered hoarsely.

"Do I look dressed up?"

"No," I squeaked. In fact, he looked just as casual as I did. "But you look sexy."

"So do you," he whispered, leaning forward. His breath tickled the top of my head.

My knees weakened, the area between my thighs throbbing with salacious promise.

"Let me fuck you as if you were the romantic heroine in your favorite book," he said.

More magic words—at least in my sorry excuse for a love life, and to this unapologetic bookworm—had never been spoken.

Allen stepped back and took my hand in his, lifting it up into the air as if I were a model he wanted to escort down a runway.

I sashayed a bit, a grin broad on my face, as we made our way toward the stairs leading to his bedroom loft.

When we got to the bottom stair, he surprised me by bending down and picking me up in his arms, carrying me princess-style up those few steps. I screamed giddily and hung on to his neck as he pounced up the stairs, then leaped up onto the bed, setting me down so we were both standing atop the plush comforter.

"Whoa!" I said, grabbing hold of both of his hands as I tried to get my balance.

Our eyes met, and our smiles matched. I was one step away from bouncing on the bed and dancing, our hands clasped together.

Then I was hit with an irrational desire to flee.

"I need to freshen up," I said, my face falling as I

wondered just how sweaty I might have gotten with all the running around we'd done today.

Also wondering if fantasizing about Aaron and Lola *tearing up* their bed had soaked my already-unsexy boy-short panties into total turn-offs should he get these jeans off my legs. "I could really use a shower."

Allen leaned over and smelled me, his nose rubbing against my temple and my cheek and down to my neck. "You smell just fine to me."

"Even so," I said, my heart thumping. I put both hands against his chest, pushing him slightly away. The bed was unsteady beneath my feet and I tumbled a bit, so he took my hands back in his and spun me around, as if we *were* dancing.

I laughed and fell back into him, my cheek against his shirt, the warmth of his chest so welcoming, so cozy.

Leaning back after a beat, I locked eyes with him again.

The corner of his lip twitched and he bent down over my ear, taking one of my hands to his lips. "Don't take long." His voice, rough and commanding, the soft press of his lips to my fingers, had nearly all worries flying out of my head. Nearly.

"I'll leave a robe," he said. "Just let me get in there first."

He jumped off the bed, then held his hand back up to me, helping me down without me tumbling into him this time.

I squeezed my palms together and tried to count

my breaths—in and out, in and out—as Allen rummaged around a dresser drawer nearby, then, his arms covered in black terrycloth, he headed down the steps again and across the condo to the bathroom. "I'll be just a minute." He winked back at me.

I followed down the steps slower, softer, as if afraid thundering too fast would make this dream dissolve into a somber reality, then I paced back and forth, trying not to disturb the kitties fast asleep far across the room, shaking out my hands and tilting my neck side to side.

You can do this, I told myself. "Don't chicken out."

Chickening out was the *last* thing I wanted. I didn't care if Allen and I had only known each other less than a week, if he'd hinted at a rough-and-tumble-type of sex life with women his mother certainly didn't know about.

I wanted him. I *needed* him, if just for tonight at least.

V.L. Breedlove had revved me up, and I wasn't about to regret this.

Besides... I *liked* him. That was enough for now. And he was so freaking gorgeous.

Allen didn't take long, and he was still wearing the same outfit when he exited the bathroom, leaving the door wide open behind him. "You're free to use anything in there. Towels are on the rack."

I shuffled past him, too embarrassed to even look up, when he caught me by the wrist as I neared the bathroom door.

"What scene?" he asked.

"Pardon?" My tongue darted out to lick my lips.

"You said you wanted me to teach you something out of that book. There's a shower scene—"

My eyebrows just about shot up off my head. "No, not that scene. Um, not ready for that..." I coughed.

He laughed, the skin around his eyes endearingly wrinkling as he let go of my wrist.

And then he stared at me. Waiting.

"The-The riding crop," I whispered. My hand went to my buttock, just remembering the way Lola had buckled at the feeling of Aaron's steady, firm hot-as-hell playfully-punishing smack against her ass.

Allen cocked his head. "Interesting."

I gasped. "I, uh... I've never done anything like that before, and it just, uh, it..." I lowered my voice. "It turned my groin into jelly."

Allen's lips clamped together, and he shook his head slightly, the amusement evident in his eyes.

"You don't have to do it," I said, surprised to find the disappointment lining my voice.

"But I'd *love* to." He moved closer. "I want to see that fine, naked ass of yours as you pretend you're a very naughty girl."

I squeaked.

"If you're *sure*," he said.

"I am." I nodded, biting my lip.

"We need a safe word," he said. "Say it and I'll stop immediately."

I frowned.

He leaned forward, touching his forehead to mine. "Only to nurse your little sore ass. And we can do so much more than that."

I shivered, the area between my legs growing wetter just at the brief contact of our heads.

"Lo-ron," I said, my breath hot.

He leaned back, sputtering just a little. "Excuse me?"

"Lo-ron," I repeated. "The Lola and Aaron ship name I gave them in my head. I don't think I'll say that word unless I mean to."

"All right." The corner of his mouth quirked. "'Lo-ron' it is, my little bookworm."

He spoke the word "bookworm" as if he meant "minx."

He took hold of me by the waist and pressed a kiss to my temple.

The moan that escaped my lips would have been loud enough to wake the dead.

"I've gotta go," I said, pulling away and ducking inside the bathroom. "Or I'll have cum before we've even started."

Allen hugged the outside of the doorframe as I slowly went to shut it, his forearm against the top. "I wouldn't let that be the end of it," he promised, leaning in and tilting his head toward me.

It was all I could do to shut the door and lock it, too.

Not because I thought he'd come join my shower

despite my insistence that I wasn't ready for that kind of intimacy.

But because I wasn't sure I could stop myself from ripping the door back open and pouncing on him before I took another breath.

Chapter Eighteen

Freshly showered and just about losing myself in the luxuriousness of the oversized black robe, I flicked my blow-dried hair behind my back and checked myself in the mirror one more time.

The makeup had washed off for the most part, and I'd forgotten to bring any extra for touch-ups, but there was a rosiness to my cheeks and even a sort of plumpness to my lips that gave me a glowing effect.

There were floral-scented lotions, extra tooth-brushes Allen had set out on the counter, and even the hair dryer, which made me think, not for the first time, that Allen was used to female guests.

It didn't matter.

Even if, judging by Allen's good looks, they were likely hotter than I was and could probably also string two words together without tripping over their tongues.

I had fun with Allen, and he actually seemed to

find my bookworm side amusing. His work was related to some of my favorite things in the world.

He meant something to me. We hadn't known each other long, and there was no promise of something like this another day, but tonight, I would let him show me. Show me what it was like to be a romance heroine.

With a soft *click*, I cracked open the door and opened it slowly, as if afraid to disturb Allen in whatever it was he was doing.

The condo was darker now, awash in a warm, yellowish glow. I stepped out from the bathroom, my bare feet cushioned by foam slippers he'd provided.

"Take your place, my naughty girl."

Allen's voice echoed out across the vast space, and I jumped. The curtains had been drawn everywhere across the giant, wall-sized windows, except for near the cat tree, where two black lumps of fur were still softly curled up and fast asleep. I tiptoed past them and toward the stairs leading to the loft, eager not to disturb them.

The loft was glowing, not with candlelight as I'd first thought, but with dangling warm, white lights draped across the brick walls like more sophisticated Christmas lights.

Allen stood at the foot of the bed, holding a black riding crop in one hand, its end against the other palm, and wearing nothing but tight black boxer-briefs.

My footsteps halted, my mouth falling open.

He was gorgeous. I'd known that, but... Wow.

Sculpted muscles, a fine, dark coating of hair. Unblemished skin that practically glistened in the soft light. His lips were firm, his face all seriousness, as he smacked the crop against his open palm.

"Naughty girl, are you reporting for your punishment?" His voice was like fire, warming my skin.

I shuddered as I neared, softly, slowly, my hand reaching out, begging to touch.

Those were the words Aaron had spoken to Lola after he'd rescued her from being kidnapped by a rival motorcycle gang—*after* she'd gone against his wishes that she stay safe inside his club's compound. All because she hadn't wanted to be told what to do, and she hadn't wanted to miss her shift at work.

Even though he'd promised to take care of her for the rest of his days.

"No touching," Allen said harshly as my fingers were about to wrap around his corded bicep. "Only *I* touch."

I bit my lip.

He lifted his chin, exposing his thick neck, a look of haughtiness spread across his features. "You left the compound."

Oh, right. I giggled, covering my lips with my fist. He was in character as Aaron right now. He really *had* read that scene in fine detail.

"It isn't *funny*," he said sharply. "You almost got yourself raped and killed!"

"Sorry," I said quickly, though it was hard to stop

myself from snorting. Which Lola definitely *had not* done in this scene.

"That's it," said Allen. He pointed to the bed with his riding crop. "I told you if you disobeyed me, you'd get punished."

"Ye-Yes," I said, shuffling over to the bed.

I stood in front of it. Glanced over my shoulder, unsure what to do next.

Even though the scene was practically *emblazoned* into my brain. My groin grew swollen, tingly just at the thought of it.

But I couldn't be as bold as Lola. I wouldn't throw myself down, ready for my "punishment."

"Strip," said Allen, brooking no argument.

"I—" I bit my lip.

"*Strip*," he said again. "One more spanking for your further disobedience."

That hadn't been in the book because Lola had thrown herself all into it.

With trembling fingers, the area between my legs throbbing and growing engorged, I untied the robe's sash and then let the terrycloth slip down my shoulders.

I paused, checking over my shoulder again.

Allen gasped, the seriousness of his expression briefly replaced by a softness. But he grew stern again, drawing his brows together as he caught my eyes.

"All the way," he purred.

Taking a deep breath, I let the robe fall to the ground.

I jumped when the leather tip of the riding crop landed softly on my shoulder, tracing down the curve of my back and to my rear end.

"Gorgeous," he said softly.

I checked over my shoulder again, feeling my face flush, unable to meet his eyes.

At this point in the book, Aaron and Lola had already had sex, had already explored each other intimately.

I felt more naked than she had, more exposed, even vulnerable.

"On your knees, on the bed," he said, his voice hardening as the whip cracked against his palm.

My heart thundered, wincing at the sound. Was I afraid? Did I say the safe word now?

I may have felt exposed, but with Allen... With the real Allen just a single made-up shipping word away, I knew I could retreat into the softness of his embrace at any point.

I steeled myself.

I wanted this.

I would push myself.

I wouldn't hide away, living the same old life, the same introverted existence every day.

This was the romance I craved. The type of experience I longed for.

Kicking off the slippers, I crawled onto the bed, getting on my hands and knees as Lola had in this scene.

"Good girl," Allen purred, pacing back and forth at

the end of the bed. The riding crop traced the curvature of one of my buttocks and then the other, sliding down the crack between them.

He leaned closer, putting a warm, tender hand on the small of my back. "Are you ready?" he whispered.

I nodded, and he leaned back.

With a crack, the crop smacked against my ass. I cried out, the sting shocking—but the slight pain quickly faded to numbness, my knees growing shaky as my pussy grew wetter.

"That was for leaving the compound," Allen said, still in character. "And what say you?"

"Sorry," I mumbled, my voice caught in my throat.

"What was that?" he asked, louder.

"I'm sorry, *master*," I added, trembling with excitement at the word. Lola had agreed to be Aaron's captive in bed—but only in bed.

"That's more like it. And again." He hesitated, as if to give me time to cry out, but instead, I dug my moistening palms against the comforter, arching my back and bearing my buttocks to him.

He cracked the whip on the other cheek and I cried out, moaning.

"And that was for your sass," he said, and I let out another chuckle. Lola had sassed Aaron, sure, but I wasn't sure if I had any of her stubborn feistiness in me.

I took a deep breath as Allen paced back and forth, slapping the crop against his palm again and again.

"One more for you stripping too slowly," he added, then paused and whacked the crop down again.

My head went back and I let out a moan, my back arching. Allen traced the riding crop softly along my spine, moving closer and gripping my left thigh with his other hand.

I just about exploded, my right knee spreading out on the bed, my legs growing wobbly, my arms unable to keep supporting this weight.

Allen dropped the crop beside me on the bed, the fingers of his left hand moving up my thigh and toward my core. "Permission, naughty girl, to use my hand?" he whispered.

For what, I wasn't sure. Another spanking? An exploratory mission along my back end?

I was breathless and I was ready for any of it.

I nodded, heaving, nearly buckling until Allen climbed up behind me, kneeling on the bed and lining up just behind me, gripping my hips on either side and roughly yanking me toward him.

Through his boxer-shorts, his hardness slammed between the crack of my ass.

"I've got you," he whispered roughly into my ear, then he nibbled on the earlobe and I closed my eyes, falling back against his broad, bare chest.

His right hand wrapped around to the front of me, trailing downward, downward, nestling between the coarse, flaxen curls glistening with moisture.

I was about to learn just how he planned to use that hand.

"Don't stop." My voice was throaty, primal, spoken through heaving breaths. The years I'd spent losing myself in books—happily, mind you—and here I was, *feeling* a handsome man's touch. *Living* my fantasies. Maybe Bodhi hadn't been so wrong when he'd told me I'd been overdue for this kind of intimate touch.

Allen's finger slipped between my folds, circling the point of pleasure with such firm, kneading strokes that almost sent me tumbling forward on the bed. His other hand shot out to catch me by the abdomen, but I rested my palms flat against the comforter regardless, breathing in and out. The more his hand worked, the more his stiffness grinded against my backside, even through his boxer-shorts, and the more the rush of blood to my head wanted me to fall flat on my face. My fingers stretched out against the plush comforter, clutching the material for need of *something* to grip. Then I found the riding crop and my hand shifted over, seizing the leather grip, my palm positively soaking.

Allen's finger stopped just shy of sliding into my entrance. "Naughty girl. Stealing my toy." He leaned forward, his warm chest colliding with my back, cradling me in his unyielding grip. "As soon as I got it back, you'd earn more punishment."

My hand let go of the crop, spreading out against the comforter again. My ass ground up higher against him, as if *begging* for retribution.

A chuckle escaped Allen's lips and he leaned back, one hand still on my belly, the other sliding up and down through the sleekness between my curls. I collapsed back against him, my head falling comfortably against the crook of his neck.

"You really don't want to be naughty," he said softly, his voice grinding through my core in tandem with his touch. "Do you?" His hand came up from between my thighs and he licked the moisture off his two fingers. Then his hand hovered back over my core, as if waiting for an answer before he'd move again.

"No," I squeaked, knowing Lola in *Riding My Baby* would have come up with something more intelligent, sassier, if Aaron had been the one asking. "But I want... I want..."

Allen's hand slipped back between my folds, gliding down over my clit and sending tingles shooting out to every corner of my body.

His finger teased at my entrance, sliding just the tip inside and facing no resistance as the whole area grew sleek with moisture. "What do you want?" He growled.

"I want... you," I finished. "Inside."

He slid up higher without an ounce of hesitation.

Gasping, I nearly buckled, but he caught me by the stomach, pulling me back against him as a second finger pushed inside. "But, my little bookworm, do you really want *me*?"

"Yes." My eyes closed, my head rolled as his thumb worked my clit, his two fingers maneuvering their way up and down inside me. "I want you. I want Allen."

Gently, taking their time traveling up along my core, his fingers slipped away.

"Permission to end the roleplay?" he teased.

I'd almost forgotten about that. How we'd been acting out a sexy Aaron and Lola love scene. It had gone on longer in the book, but things were already hot and heavy between us and I couldn't keep pretending.

Not when I had this real, tangible man within reach.

Shifting upright, I crawled forward on the bed, turning around and nodding.

Allen's breaths were as heavy as mine, our mouths open, his eyes flicking down my naked body and then locking with my own.

Lola wasn't allowed to touch Aaron in this scene.

My nails dug into my palms. I wanted to touch him. I *needed* to.

I reached out and grabbed his upper arms, firm and thick in my grip, my fingers not quite making it all the way round.

He didn't stop me.

"Quinn," he said softly.

Then he wrapped his arms around me and pulled me toward him, kissing me.

After what he'd been doing between my thighs, the feel of his lips on mine shouldn't have been responsible for the pleasurable aches spreading out to every ligament and bone in my body. But I wanted more, more. There would never be enough of his mouth exploring mine.

Chapter Nineteen

Allen's kisses were hungry, his tongue dancing inside my mouth, brushing against me with feather-soft touches.

"Quinn." The sound of my name on his lips was almost melancholy.

His hand flicked my hair behind my shoulder, cradling my ear as his kisses moved along my jawline. My head tilted back, bringing my cheek up into the touch.

My hands gripped his back to steady myself, being careful not to dig too deep with these long, manicured nails but finding it hard not to want to squeeze his body and grind myself against him.

My eyes flickered to his groin as his kisses danced up along my temple.

"Your shorts." My touch slid down his back and tucked inside the elastic at his waist. I caught my breath at the sharp relief that was his hip bone. As defined as a sculpture.

Kissing my lips one more time, Allen slid back and out of my grip. My hands flailed at air as he stepped off the bed.

He grinned, running a hand through his waves of dark hair. "Shall we skip the cherry for tonight?"

It took me a second to realize what he was referring to. Cherry condoms. I swallowed. It'd been quite some time since I'd filled my mouth with that salty, feverish flavor, condom or not.

"I—"

"Maybe next time," he purred, bending down to slide out of his boxer-shorts.

He was already talking about a next time. Even if we'd gotten this all mixed up. In every romance book I'd read, it was *clear* the couple were endgame before they even wound up in bed together.

At least to me, the reader.

Here, I...

I didn't want to think about it.

I *couldn't* think about it.

He stood up again, kicking his boxer-shorts aside, and there was only that thick, stiff girth I wanted exploring inside me.

I couldn't *read* this story like I could read any of V.L. Breedlove's. But dammit if I was going to let the mood her words had put me in—this *man* had put me in—go to waste.

I wanted him now. He wanted me, as evident by the fully erected cock my fingers reached out to stroke.

That was all that mattered in this moment.

Allen gripped my hand as it touched his most intimate part, guiding it back and forth. The sensation drove me wild. He chuckled. "I don't really need more encouragement."

I nodded, my hand trembling as I let it fall. Squeezing my hands between my thighs, I sat on my shins at the edge of the bed. I had to bite my bottom lip just to keep myself together. My breasts heaved between my forearms. I was a trembling mess of excitement.

He leaned forward, grabbing my chin and leaning it upward before capturing my mouth with a kiss. "I can't wait another second," he whispered.

Our eyes held each other, but then, with some considerable effort, he ripped himself away, shuffling over to the stand beside his bed and pulling out a condom.

He didn't ask me to put it on with him, tearing through the wrapper with his teeth and rolling the contents onto his member in record time.

It was for the best, considering with each heavy breath I took, my entire body throbbed. A sudden shudder of ecstasy took hold of me and I toppled backward onto the bed.

Allen seized the opportunity to slide over me, his hands flat on the bed on either side of my head.

"Are you ready?" he asked, teasing me with the rippled latex dancing across my clit, sliding up and down along my slit.

"Yes," I said, breathy, my hands gripping his back, my back arching. And my legs spreading as my groin sought more, more contact with the length of him.

As wet as I was, as fired up as he had me, he didn't need to hesitate any longer.

Lining up at my entrance, his cock plunged inside, my pussy widening to accommodate him and squeezing with spasms of delight. He didn't stop once he'd filled me with the length of him, pulling backward, the ribs in the condom yanking at my interior walls with indelible speed. Then he thrust in again, our skin slapping together, my thighs pressing hard against the sides of his torso, each movement building, building, my heart thudding so quickly, I wasn't sure I'd ever be able to catch my breath.

"Allen," I screamed, my head tossing back against the mattress. My body quivered, my core pulsing with unquenchable *need*.

"Quinn," he murmured, his breaths as heavy as my own as he kept up the unrelenting thrusting, moving hard, harder, as if he could never merge with me enough.

Trembling, I writhed beneath him as he let out a deep groan and stopped his movements, his cock erupting inside me.

My vision went black, spots dancing before my eyes as I let out a blissful squeal.

Our breaths echoed out in tandem, decelerating as Allen slowly slipped out of me.

He collapsed beside me, running a hand through his hair and smiling broadly at me. His forehead was dotted with sweat.

"Roleplay is fun, but there's nothing quite like the real thing," he said.

I curled up beside him, resting a cheek against his pec. "I could say the same thing about books."

He wrapped one arm around me and we lay there a bit, clutching on to each other's flesh, letting our breaths even out in the comforting grip of one another's arms.

It was still chilly enough that once the warming effects of our tumble in the bed had worn off, it was easy to drag myself off the mattress and make a quick stop to his bathroom to mop up, returning to his bed with the robe he'd offered me and climbing under the covers to wait for Allen to clean up and join me.

I didn't check what time it was when Allen emerged from the bathroom, wearing nothing but a pair of red flannel pajama pants, making a quick stop by the cat tree and cooing indistinguishable words to his kitties. Feeling my cheeks darken, I tucked my head under the cover, considering the cats had probably at least been aware of the *noise* we'd been making. Did I feel a bit like I'd been caught doing something naughty? I hadn't brought anyone home to my place, and besides, I had a bedroom door. This place was wide open, exposed.

Beautiful, but so exposed.

Padding footfalls echoed out against the hardwood.

"Hey." The comforter jostled and Allen's deep voice greeted me as my coverings flew back. He smirked in the warm glow of a bedside table he'd turned on. "You cold? You sure you don't want to borrow a pair of pajamas?"

My gaze flicked to his crotch, taking in the flannel pajamas I wondered if he often lounged in when working from home. "I'm fine," I said, squirming and burying myself in his robe even further. "This is comfortable."

Allen slid in beside me and pulled the comforter back on, though it took some doing for him to avoid covering my head again, considering my scalp was lower than the pillow. "Do you mind sleeping with cats?"

As if on cue, one of the shadowy felines jumped up on the bottom of the bed, the other going straight for Allen's pillow.

I giggled. "Mine usually sleeps by my feet—unless it's too hot out. Then he sleeps *under* my bed."

One of Allen's cats waited for him to put his head down and then curled up between his scalp and the headboard, their tail hanging down behind his head.

We both chuckled.

"She usually hangs her tail *between* me and my guest. I think she likes you."

My face fell, but I tried to cover it by clearing my throat and scooching back up to lay my head on the pillow beside Allen's.

Of course he'd had other "guests." He'd said as much—and he hadn't bought all those toys in the closet just to roleplay solo.

"I'm glad," I said, pasting a smile on my face.

Poe got comfortable somewhere between our legs, a little lump stretching across my ankles.

"What do you do if she doesn't like cats?" I asked, trying to be cool. To keep it casual, like I'd told myself —*warned* myself—this would be.

"Meet up elsewhere," he said. He gestured around, one arm exiting the comforter. "Not like there's a lot of room here to hide from my pets." He clicked the bedside light off.

"A lot of room, but not a lot of room to hide," I agreed into the darkness.

For a moment, there was only the soft, audible snore of the cat at our feet, the lulling, steady purr of the cat on the pillow above Allen's head. My eyes adjusted to the dark, the condo courtyard lamplight and moonlight piercing through small gaps in the wide curtains.

Allen looked positively *gorgeous*, even with the cat tail dangling down the back of his head. I snickered. Maybe *because* of it. I couldn't imagine him with a woman who didn't like or was allergic to cats. They seemed to complete the full picture of him, adding some softness to an already dazzling personality.

His hand stroked my cheek in the dark. "Are you all right?"

I frowned. I'd just been laughing, so what had clued him in to these gnawing feelings of insecurity?

"I'm... better than all right." It wasn't a lie. The green monster rearing her head aside, this had been one of the most amazing days of my life in... in *ever*, really. For a second there, I'd been mixing up all the incredible lives I'd lived through books with my own.

My own was... mostly just filled with memories of all the glorious fictional lives I'd slipped into through the written word.

This here—not to dismiss the happiness my books had brought me—this was different.

My arm threaded under and around his and I cradled his cheek against my palm. It was rough with his light beard, and I loved how it tickled my skin. "Thank you," I said.

"Thank *you*." He leaned forward and kissed me.

My breath caught. One kiss, and my groin started to tingle.

Raven's tail whapped down against our cheeks. Over and over again.

We both laughed and settled for leaning our foreheads against one another's instead. Raven's tail went back behind Allen's head.

"I just mean..." I whispered into the darkness. "Just a week ago, I never would have imagined this. If you hadn't put those V.L. Breedlove books in my Mini Donation Library, I never would have discovered my new favorite author, never would have met you, maybe, or if we had, it wouldn't have been more than a brief encounter at a mutual friend's dinner party."

"I don't know about that," he said. "It's true I asked Bodhi and Rory about those libraries and wanted to add one to my own neighborhood the more they told me about them, but I think... The moment I saw you, I would have wanted you in my bed. No matter what."

I snorted. "You *do* remember what I looked like the moment you saw me, right?"

"Beautiful," he said softly. He kissed the top of my forehead, something his cat apparently allowed. "Real. And just like me."

"You were wearing a *suit*," I protested, my heart still thumping at the thought of him finding me beautiful.

"For a dinner party!" He pulled back and smirked at me. "I normally dress like this."

My gaze flicked down to his bare shoulders, remembering his fine, fit chest and his flannel pajamas.

My smile could have rivaled the Grinch's when he had particularly wicked thoughts.

"Well, I dress a little warmer when it's cold out," he admitted. He playfully pinched my cheek to wipe off my salacious grin.

"So you're just like me, huh?" I said. "At home alone with a cat—or two—in your most comfortable clothing."

"That's most of my days, yes." He shrugged. "Not

that I'm complaining. Despite what Val thinks, I get out enough."

I bit my lip, trying to stave away the idea of him hanging out at bars or wherever he picked up ladies in our town. To distract myself, it was my turn to play-fully pinch him, reaching for his bicep under the cover and squeezing it. If I'd done the same to *my* arm, it would have been soft, spongy.

"That's one difference between us apparent home-bodies," I said. "You clearly get a good workout."

"Whatever *you're* doing is working just fine for you."

I dropped his bicep and he tugged me against him again, our foreheads touching.

I'd refrain from telling him the most exercise I got was lifting loads of books in and out of my car for the mini libraries.

Instead, I'd just bask in the compliment. Tonight, I was a romance novel heroine. In the arms of her romance hero.

The heroine always wound up with the hero. Only HEAs—*happily ever afters*—allowed in this genre.

"Quinn, I think you should know—"

"Hmm?" I asked, fatigue taking over my brain. For someone who rarely worked out, I'd just had the workout of my life. It could have just been eight o'clock for all I knew, but I was *bone tired*.

"Never mind." He leaned back to give me one more forehead kiss.

After that, I must have fallen asleep, that heady musk of his, so much like the comfort of old books, filling my senses as I drifted off into my dreams.

Chapter Twenty

"Good morning."

I *really* must have been tired. Sunlight streamed in broadly around me through exposed windows, the sizzle of something on the stove across the large condo catching my attention.

The large condo. The insanely bright light.

I shot up.

I was in a robe on Allen's bed.

That hadn't been a dream.

"I wanted to let you sleep in." Allen was at the foot of the bed, wearing those flannel pajama pants still, but he'd added a gray sweatshirt with a faded college team logo across the front. "But the food is almost ready, and I figured you wanted to get home, too."

One of the cats jumped up onto the bed at my feet, meowing.

"To see Mr. Darcy." Allen winked. "Otherwise, you'd be welcome to stay all day."

"Darcy." I flicked the comforter off, careful not to hit the cat, who was busy meowing up at Allen and didn't seem to notice the blanket's movement.

Could I ask Evangeline to feed him again this morning?

No. She and her family usually were out Sunday mornings. Besides, the little guy was probably worried about me.

Since I worked from home, he wasn't one of those cats who was left home alone for long periods.

My body ached, but in a good way as I sat at the edge of the bed. Allen reached a hand down and I took it to help me stand, my lips curling. Leaning over, he pressed a kiss to my mouth as the furry, black feline wove between both of our ankles, purring.

"Good morning," Allen said again, softer this time.

"Good morning." I stepped back and stretched. My body ached *all over*, but particularly in those well-used places last night. "What time is it?"

"Eight," he said as I slipped my feet into the slippers I'd kicked off the night before and we headed down the stairs—careful not to let the little, weaving cat trip us. I chuckled because it was clear he was a cat owner, the way he stared down at the steps with me, making slow, careful movements because that furry feline was sure to dart right where we were about to step.

"Eight is way earlier than I usually get up," I admitted with a wince as we reached the bottom step.

"Life as a writer, right?" He winked.

The other cat meowed and jumped off the cat tree to join their sibling, the two weaving around Allen's legs in motion as we passed the kitchen. "All right, all right, I'll feed you," he said.

"I'm just going to get dressed," I told him, heading for the bathroom, where I'd left my things.

It felt weird looking at myself in the mirror a short while later, dressed just as I had been the day before, minus the makeup. I smoothed out my hair, brushed my teeth, just watching myself, looking for that subtle difference I knew I recognized.

It was a sort of glow.

Allen knocked on the other side of the door. "Quinn? It's ready."

I spit into the sink. "Coming!" It took just another few seconds to rinse and finish getting ready.

Passing by my phone on the counter, I wondered if I should check it, but the moment I saw Allen, two plates in his hands piled full of eggs, toast, and bacon, I walked right by it, headed for my seat at the table.

My seat. As if eating three meals in a row here made me some sort of regular fixture.

"Thank you," I said as he slipped the food in front of me.

"Coffee?" he asked.

"Please. A little cream." A little coffee with breakfast didn't count against my vow to "cut back."

Allen's plate of food steamed across from me as he worked his Keurig. He gave me my choice of coffee flavors and I opted for mocha. He had a variety of creamer flavors, too.

"You know, you need to be careful," I said as he sat down, sliding a mug my way and cradling his own. "A woman could get spoiled."

His eyes twinkled as he took a sip of his coffee. "That's sort of the idea."

"Hmm?" I glanced across the kitchen to where Raven and Poe were munching down on kibble, first one, and then the other seeming to pick up on the scent of bacon in the air and abandoning the dried food they'd been so insistent upon receiving in order to sit stiffly at Allen's feet.

I laughed. "I think spoiling is just a habit with you."

Allen's jaw dropped, but case in point, he was already breaking off little bits of his bacon and handing it downward.

He dropped the rest of his bacon on his plate and arched a brow in my direction, his expression probably the closest thing in real life I'd seen to a smolder.

"I'm very particular about who gets spoiled," he said, and his gruff voice was making me squirm in my seat.

"Well..." I cleared my throat and took a drink, trying not to get trapped in his eyes. "It just leads to begging." My cheeks flushed. I'd meant the cats, but thinking about it, I could have meant me too.

"Oh, I *adore* a bit of begging."

There he went again. I nearly choked on my coffee.

"Too hot?" he asked, smirking as he took another sip of his steaming drink.

"You know exactly what you're saying at all times, don't you?" What was he, some sort of master of entendre?

"If only," he said, putting his mug down and picking up his fork.

A flash of something dark crossed over his face as he focused on his food, and I wondered what I'd said to dampen the mood.

I ate, too, watching as first one and then the other cat jumped up on the back of the couch, still within sight if Allen were to hand them more table scraps, but more comfortable observing us from afar.

Allen broke the silence, his plate nearly cleaned.

"So, um, I'm actually going to be a bit busy the next couple of days." He looked up, his expression back to being cheery. "But I'd love to see you again."

A lump grew in my throat, my chest tightening. "Me-Me, too."

Me, on the other hand, I clearly did *not* know how to suavely steer any conversation.

Allen didn't seem to mind. "Good. Invoice me, and I'll pay, and then we'll be done with our business transaction."

My gut tightened, the fork slipping from my fingers. "Um, right. Yes, of course."

Allen reached across the table and covered my hand. "I only meant, I'm a man of my word, and I'm going to pay you for your instruction yesterday. Once that's taken care of, we can see each other again. Without the client-freelancer thing hanging between us. Right?"

A relieved breath escaped my lips. "Right."

He still wanted to *pay* me?

Well, it wasn't like I couldn't use the money.

"I have invoicing software," I said. "Text me an email address and I'll send it off today."

"Eight hours," he said. "$200 per hour."

"I, uh, don't think I was teaching you a full eight hours."

"Quinn." He looked at me sternly.

I slouched a bit in my seat. "$1600 it is," I squeaked.

"That's better." He smirked.

I finished up the last of my meal as Allen watched me. I could barely meet his eyes, but I could *feel* him studying me and I tried not to eat like the last clown out of the car to get to an about-to-close buffet. However, exactly, that would look.

Even in my head, my thoughts were not those of a wordsmith.

I gripped the napkin on my lap tightly, trying to fight the urge to hide under the table.

"Quinn, do you really not know—"

Before Allen could finish what he'd been about to say, both cats lifted their heads in tandem, looking toward the staircase leading downstairs to the front door.

One's ears went back, then the other let out a rumbly growl. The first one hissed.

Allen sighed.

Then from far below, an incessant string of barking echoed out, followed by the sound of the doorbell.

The cats jumped down from the couch and ran up to the loft, scurrying under the bed.

"My sister," Allen said with a groan as he stood from the table. The doorbell rang again. "Excuse me." He nodded at me as he passed to go get the door.

My hand unclenched the napkin I'd been gripping, my mouth growing dry.

V.L. Breedlove was here. And I'd just read an ARC of her newest release.

Murmured voices carried up from down below, but overpowering whatever they were saying was the incessant yip-yipping of Pearl, who burst to the top of the staircase on her own.

Either Raven or Poe offered one more gallant effort, hissing and arching their back from the top of the loft while the other cat scrambled back under the bed. But then the dog's eyes grew wide and she charged up the stairs, yipping excitedly, her long coat swinging wildly, and the cat retreated along with their sibling.

"Pearl!" shouted Allen as he reached the top of the stairs. He charged after the little fawn-colored dog, who was climbing the short set of steps to the loft.

"She just wants to play," Val said as she came into view. She was a bit more dressed up today, a sort of glamorous casual with tight, glittering red yoga pants and an off-the-shoulder pink sweater, her hair held off her face by a red headband. She kicked off loafers beside my own shoes at the top of the staircase leading down.

"Yeah, and her idea of *playing* terrifies my cats." Allen swooped down and missed grabbing the little dog as she yelped back and forth at the space under the bed, her little nose pointed downward and her butt wagging in the air. He stumbled but recovered smoothly, getting hold of her the second time and carrying her down the steps. She tried climbing over his shoulder and kept barking toward the bed until the bed was no longer in sight.

"Hi."

I jumped. I'd been so focused on the sight of Allen wrestling with the little dog, a grimace on his face as the dog kept squirming and almost getting the best of him, that I almost forgot about the fact that I wasn't a reader witnessing a scene in a book—I was here to be remarked upon. Part of the plot, if you would.

"Hi." I stood up from the table and tucked a strand of hair behind my ear. "Nice to see you again."

"Hmm?" Val looked from me to her brother and back again. "So you spent the night?" She tapped her toes against the floor, her eyes sparkling.

My cheeks were on fire.

"Leave her alone," Allen said. Almost as if on cue, Pearl leaped from his arms and did the exact opposite of what he'd asked—running straight for me. She jumped up and leaned on my shins, doing a yipping, leaping dance.

"H-Hi," I said to the dog. I bent down in an attempt to pet her head, but she was so hyper, I panicked and pulled back up.

"Pearl, leave her alone." Sighing, Allen made his way to stand beside me, trying his best to run interference, but the little canine was determined to make it to me, weaving through Allen's legs and back around us to come at me from the other side.

"Pearl, *sit*." Val put a hand on her hip and pointed to the couch.

Pearl kept yipping for a bit, though some of the spring in her step was dampened.

"*Sit*!" Val repeated, wagging her hand again at the couch.

If I didn't know better, I'd have thought the little dog let out a sigh and trotted over toward the couch, leaping up onto the middle cushion. She nearly drowned in the vastness of the couch on either side of her. She put her chin down on the cushion and looked depressed, only to pop up with more energy a second later and roll around, managing to dig her nose into the crack at the back of the cushion and pull out a worn knot rope toy.

Val laughed as the dog went to town munching first one and then the other end of the rope. But then her smile vanished as she turned to her brother. "I know you were going to take the whole weekend off, but I assume that means you haven't checked your email since last night."

Allen frowned. "I hadn't gotten around to it yet today."

A tightness blossomed in my chest at the thought that I'd kept him from something important.

It must have shown on my face as Allen crossed the room and headed back up to the loft, shifting aside some curtains and letting more light in over his desk.

"You don't have to look so guilty," Val said, bumping her elbow against my arm. "I can't blame him if you were the reason he's been unreachable."

"You live across the courtyard," Allen mumbled. His desktop screen booted up. "I figured if anything really *important* came up, you'd know how to get my attention."

"And that's why I came over personally. I'll save you the time it takes to log in. *Riding My Baby*'s cover was rejected for the paperback edition."

Allen cursed.

I found myself holding my breath. What did that mean for the publication? I mean, thank god I'd been able to read it. But I couldn't stand the idea of Breedlove's other fans being unable to do the same.

Chapter Twenty-One

"The cover was rejected? *Again*?" Allen ran a hand through his hair, the color draining from his face. "What now?"

Butterflies pattered up from my stomach to my chest. They were talking shop. Talking V.L. Breedlove shop right in front of me. "Too sexy?" I ventured, remembering the cover, with Lola's arms wrapped around Aaron's chest from behind, kissing his stubble, her hair dangling down. Both of them naked from the torso up. Only Aaron's full torso visible, of course.

Val chuckled and walked into Allen's kitchen, turning on his coffee maker. "It *is* that. But no, that's not the issue. It only affects the paperback. Spine text needs to be moved .15 centimeters or something—you'll have to see the email." She helped herself to a mug in the cupboard as if it were old hat, and for wont of something useful to do amidst this situation that didn't involve me, I stacked Allen's and my breakfast plates.

Allen cursed again, sitting in front of his desktop and running a hand down his face as his leg bounced. "Reba moved the text already once!"

"Cover designer," Val explained as I brought the stack of dishes over to the sink across from her. Our eyes met and I nodded, as if this kind of talk all made sense to me.

"I already emailed her. *For* you, I might add. Normally, you handle these things." Val selected a coffee pod and loaded it into the coffee maker, choosing a size as the water heated up, the rumbling sound growing louder. "He's such a control freak about all the details."

Chewing my lip, I nodded. Wouldn't it be his job as her PA to see to all the details? Then again, if she'd emailed the cover designer herself, it didn't seem like she did *nothing* outside of the actual writing.

"But she's not going to be able to fix it this fast!" Allen shouted across the room.

The tension in the air was starting to prick at me, so I seized on the opportunity of my phone being nearby on the counter and picked it up.

"She will," Val assured him. "She knows to watch her inbox for any extra issues. She's always been good like that."

"But we launch in two days!"

"So the paperback edition might be a little late." Val fluffed her hand as the coffee maker filled up with her coffee. "But we still have time. Maybe the next revision will pass before then. You know the e-books sell far better either way."

"But this is going to mess with our strategy—how are we going to get the audiobook releases to sync up with publication days if we can't even get the *paperbacks* to do so?!"

I hadn't actually *looked* at my phone screen yet. Digging my nails into my palm, I'd been too fascinated by the siblings' exchange. Speaking of siblings, the two black cats appeared again, jumping up onto the bed. I could just make their tails out atop the mattress.

The coffee maker finished brewing and Val helped herself to a bit of cream from the fridge. "We can't even *think* of simultaneous audiobook releases until you okay a freaking *slow down* in the schedule. We need these books locked and loaded *months* in advance, not the week before!"

Allen was wholly invested in his computer screen, practically hunched over as he clicked his mouse. "Slow down and readers forget you."

Val shook her head and took a sip. "Traditional authors often go a full year—or more—between releases."

"Indie authors don't!" Allen's deep voice practically squeaked. "Consistent output is crucial. There's so much else readers might be interested in—"

There was a text message from my mom, another from Milly, and a third from Evangeline waiting for me. I glanced at Evangeline's first, in case it was about

Darcy, but it was about the Romance Book Club at the condos—specifically the V.L. Breedlove Club to start.

"I don't think you need to worry about that," I said, clearing my throat so my voice grew louder. "V.L. Breedlove's fans are for life." My skin grew flush as I glanced out of the corner of my eye at Val. She took a sip of her drink, but her full lips were curled into a stifled smile behind the mug. "In fact, I'm going to talk to Evangeline about the V.L. Breedlove Book Club today." I straightened up.

"What do you mean?" Val put her mug down on the counter and arched a brow at me. "Well, this is news to me."

"Yeah, it's—well, yesterday, Allen was in my neighborhood helping me with my Mini Donation Libraries and my friend there and I got to talking about Breedlove's books—"

"They're starting a Romance Book Club and I thought if they focused on Breedlove books to start at least, it'd make for a nice entry in the newsletter. But one thing at a time. We have a *crisis* on our hands!" His leg bounced at the desk, his stare pinned to the computer screen.

"You'll have to excuse my brother," she said. "Perfectionist *and* control freak." She frowned. "I'm not exactly doing a good job making him seem dateable, am I?"

Flinching, I clutched my phone harder but didn't look at the screen. I *did* feel a little hurt by the way Allen had dismissed discussion of the Book Club out of hand like that. I'd only been trying to tell his sister about it. And hadn't he been fully for the idea less than a day ago?

"Um, no, it's okay..." I held my phone out and jiggled it, as if it offered an excuse for me. "I need to get going anyway."

Who was I kidding? Allen had made it so clear that he had *frequent* guests over. I'd told myself it had all been a bit of fun. And it certainly had been.

Val grabbed my arm to stop me from heading over to the stairs leading down. "He *is* a catch. It'll just take a special woman to put up with his introversion—and the way he focuses on his career."

I tapped my thigh with my free hand and stared at him. I didn't think of introversion as something to "put up with" at all. And I thought it was so cool the two of them were basically running this indie author business together.

But maybe he didn't even *want* a "special woman" to take up too much of his time.

I offered Val a faltering smile. "I loved *Riding My Baby*. Allen let me read an early copy yesterday."

"Oh, he did, huh?" Val laughed. "And here I thought you'd have wanted to spend the day doing something other than *reading* yesterday." She said that as if it were silly to even consider reading in such a situation. I supposed to most people, that *would* be a strange idea of a date.

But to a bookworm—and to be pampered so as I'd read—that had been paradise.

Didn't V.L. Breedlove herself feel the same way?

"Um, well, anyway... I just wanted to let you know. And we *are* forming that Book Club, whatever he says."

She walked me toward the top of the stairs. "Oh, he'll *love* it. I think it's a great idea for the newsletter—and it's sweet of you and your friends to offer to do it. Just let him calm down from this crisis." Her voice rose. "*Perceived* crisis, I should say. Nothing worth freaking out over!"

Allen's head whipped around from the computer. His jaw dropped a bit. "Quinn, are you leaving?"

He looked so disturbed at the idea—though we'd already discussed me leaving to feed my cat—that I nearly fell over as I tried to slip my shoes on. "Uh, yeah. Darcy and—"

"I'll walk you to your car." Allen leaped up from the computer and headed down the short set of stairs.

"No, don't worry about it." I scooped my purse off the floor and slipped my phone inside. "You have this issue to deal with—I'm fine. I'll see you later."

I couldn't bring myself to look at him. Couldn't bring myself to even wait for him to meet me at the top of the stairs leading to the front door. I just scattered down those steps.

"Quinn?" Allen called from upstairs.

I waved meekly back up at him, a broad smile plastered on my face. "Thank you so much. I'll-I'll be in touch. About that Book Club. And the invoice."

He started heading down the stairs after me, but I

was out the door and down the sidewalk toward the parking lot before he said another word.

Darcy was sticking to me like glue ever since I'd come back. To be fair, I hadn't spent the night away since college, I was pretty sure. It'd certainly been a while. "Down!" I told him as he jumped up on the kitchen counter for the fourteenth time already today.

He normally behaved better.

"We *just* finished playing!" I told him as he leaped back down to my feet with a chirp and a *thud*. He was fed, brushed, played with—the little guy should have had his fill of me for the next ten years, but here he was, trying to get my attention while I got ready to make dinner and set my phone down on the stand beside the sink. Mom and I often had video chats on Sundays. It was one of the few days I forced myself to cook a proper meal because I tried to be caught up with work and take some time off. "Tried" being the operative word, of course. But this weekend, I had nothing urgent waiting for me.

Darcy's purrs grew more thunderous as his forehead rammed into my shins. I shook my head but smiled as I grabbed the kitchen spray and cleaned the counter *yet again* from his dirty little paws before I got ready to chop up some potatoes. It was only about noon, but Slow Cooker Sundays was the name of the game. Best to prep dinner at lunchtime and then spend the rest of the afternoon relaxing while my little Crockpot did the rest of the work.

"You're going to make me feel guilty for ever leaving at all," I told him.

Darcy rammed his head into my shins again.

"That's your aim, isn't it?" I bent down and gave him cheek and chin scratches, then escorted him around the kitchen counter and to the open space with the TV and couch. "Here, have your guitar."

I fished his catnip-laced cloth guitar toy out of his toy box and his eyes widened as he batted it out of my grip.

I yanked my hand back against my chest, cradling it. He hadn't clawed it, but only just. "You're welcome," I said. "Sheesh."

Darcy was too busy bunny-thumping the guitar and alligator-rolling it to "death."

I brought up a video call with Mom, and she accepted it before I moved to wash my hands. "Hey, Mom."

"Hi, honey!" It was even earlier in the morning in New Mexico, but Mom was the one who'd taught me about Slow Cooker Sundays in the first place, so she was getting her ingredients ready, too. "Oh!" She lifted a potato up to the screen as I wiped my hands dry on a kitchen towel. "I see a lot of potatoes there. Beef stew?"

"Close," I told her. Was this too similar to last night's meal? "Beef curry."

She smiled and nodded, her tanned face lighting

up. "Still, great minds think alike." She held up a carrot and then an onion. "Almost the same ingredients."

I chuckled, a lightness permeating my chest and driving out this hard knot that had worked its way there.

A notification of a text from Allen popped up, again apologizing for his attitude when I'd left, telling me he'd paid the invoice. I dismissed the text with the tip of my pinky and picked up a potato, turning on the sink.

"What's wrong?" Mom asked. I looked over at her as I scrubbed first one and then another potato under the sink with a brush. She'd been about to do the same, but her dark irises peered through her glasses at me, the wrinkles at the corners of her eyes growing more visible as her brow drew down.

"Nothing," I lied. "It's just... been a week."

"Can't say I miss that. You work too hard." Mom went back to scrubbing potatoes, using her upper arm to itch her cheek. Her pixie-short gray hair—which had once been blonde, like mine—made her seem almost cherubic as she hummed and scrubbed. Her humming, coming to me across all those miles, soothed me, kicking in some old natural instinct.

"So how's my grandcat?" Mom asked after we'd both scrubbed quite a few of our vegetables.

"Fine," I said. "Better than fine. He's been very clingy because I left him home alone last ni—" I cut myself short.

Mom froze and shut off her faucet. "Oh? Home alone last night, did you say?"

I shut my own faucet off as I felt the heat rising on my cheeks. "Last evening," I said quickly, not wanting to lie, but not really wanting to get into it. I *had* left him alone last evening. And then some. "I had a job. Sort of."

"What does that mean?" Mom asked, picking up her peeler and getting to work on the next step.

I echoed her and did the same. "Remember I told you about the Mini Donation Libraries and V.L. Breedlove's newsletter?"

Mom let out a little moan and clutched a carrot to her chest, looking to the sky. "You promised to talk non-stop with me about Breedlove's books today!"

I giggled. Across the room, Darcy seemed tuckered out, leaving his catnip guitar in the middle of the floor and leaping up his cat tree to the very top level in order to take a nap.

"I would *love* to," I said. "But that leads me to tell you... I'm more sure than ever that I've met her."

"Who?" Mom adjusted her glasses up her nose.

"V.L. Breedlove!" I squealed, and just one of Darcy's ears went back. Before Mom could even reply, I launched into the story—meeting Allen and Val at Bodhi and Rory's, the job Allen had hired me for, spending yesterday hanging out with him.

Skipping the *spending-the-night* bit just yet.

And of course, my theory about Val being V.L.,

especially since Allen had confirmed he was the author's PA.

"So I have this man to thank for getting my whole Book Club wet," Mom said as she picked up a knife to start chopping.

"*Mom*," I said, settling a potato on my cutting board and about to do the same. Still, I snickered at the thought of half a dozen New Mexican retirees getting into a tizzy together over Breedlove's books.

"I mean, I guess you could thank him for, uh, *livening up* your book club. Allen *had* put the books in the condo's Ooh-La-La Box. Which led me to recommend them to you. And just about anyone else I could." I still had to gush about Breedlove to Milly. I didn't think she'd had time to read more than a book or two. "We're launching a V.L. Breedlove Book Club here, Evangeline and me." Evangeline was swinging by my place after dinner for a bit so we could hash out some of the details.

Mom pursed her lips. "A whole club devoted to one author?"

"Well, just to start. I'm sure we'll turn to other romance books soon enough. Hey, I bet Allen would love it if you and your Book Club took pictures with a copy of one of the books, too. For the newsletter."

"I bet I could arrange that," Mom said. "We already selected *Riding My Baby* as our book for next Saturday." Which meant every single member of her book club had to have at least read all of the other books in Breedlove's MC series. Then again, it did stand alone.

It was just so much more compelling when you had the full picture of Aaron's development over the previous books in the series.

"About that... I got to read it yesterday." I squealed again and almost forgot for a second that I had a sharp knife in my hand as I lifted it up to do a little dance.

"Whoa, careful, daughter of mine. You'll poke an eye out." Mom laughed, and I dropped the knife guiltily to the cutting board. She stared into the camera, her own chopping coming to a halt. Then her eyes widened. "Wait, did you just say—"

"I read it! I got an ARC direct from Allen and he let me spend the afternoon reading it at his place. I was there for the, um, job." I winced. "I mean, I don't *have* a copy, so I can't share it with you—"

"Oh, I've already pre-ordered." She shook her head. "Still, I have to admit I'm a bit jealous."

I thought of the paperback issue Allen and Val had been dealing with when I'd left them and my smile fell a bit. "Well, you won't be able to take pictures with the paperbacks this weekend. I think there's been a delay in printing them."

"Oh, most of us use Kindles anyway. We can hold up the Kindles with the cover." That would still work. "But who do we talk to to get signed copies of some of the other books?"

"Me," I said. Then I blushed at my gumption. "I mean, Allen—he's the PA in charge of that. But I can ask him for you."

That wouldn't be weird, right? We were definitely

friendly. It seemed as if he might even give me future Breedlove ARCs if I played my cards right.

And if that meant another night or two of being pampered and treated like a romance novel heroine, I certainly wasn't complaining.

"Hmm?" Mom nodded thoughtfully as she stared me down. "Anything *else* you might want to tell me? Anything *new* going on in your life?"

"What's that about something going on in your life?" Dad appeared just slightly out of frame. He was bald on top, with short-clipped, white hair wrapped around the back and sides of his head. He wore a cardigan even in the hundred-degree weather he often experienced down there.

"Our daughter is positively *glowing*." Mom gestured at the screen.

I fought the flush of heat spreading across my body and scraped the first wave of chopped potatoes into the slow cooker. "I'm just excited about the book we were talking about. But I don't want to spoil you—"

Dad put both hands over his ears and said loudly, "Spoilers! La la la la," before dropping one hand from his head to reach over and grab a piece of carrot.

"Hey. That's for dinner," Mom said as Dad popped it into his mouth.

They stared each other down, but they both smiled.

He gestured at the screen. "She was about to spoil this book you were talking about. I had to distract her."

"Oh, like *you* care." Mom smacked her hip against

his side playfully and Dad made a big to-do of "tumbling" off-screen.

"It's probably better than the second book in the series, though," I said, referring to my favorite in the MC series so far.

"*Nothing* can top that." Mom dumped her cutting board's contents into her slow cooker.

"Oh, you'll see. But maybe I still like Gideon and Bianca best?"

"That's a whole different series."

"I know. I just can't get them out of my head. That bonus short story didn't help."

"So sweet," Mom said, nodding and agreeing. Of *course* she'd gotten the bonus newsletter story, too. "Who'd have guessed Gideon would have made a great dad?"

"I did," I said, though I thought about it more, my knife hovering over a carrot. "I mean, I know he's pretty introverted—"

"Though also a playboy."

I tittered. He was that, too. But when not cruising for women, he liked staying home. Working. Indulging in hobbies. But mostly working, always focused on the next thing, the next crisis to come across his plate.

Kind of like Allen himself.

"What's occupying those thoughts of yours?" Mom asked. "You keep getting distracted."

I quickly got to chopping the carrot, focusing myself on the moment. "Just books."

It wasn't a total fabrication.

Books and my new favorite author and... one hunk of an author PA.

I hacked the top of the carrot and the frond went flying across the kitchen.

My stomach fluttered. Despite warning myself not to take it all so seriously, I was pretty sure I had it bad.

Chapter Twenty-Two

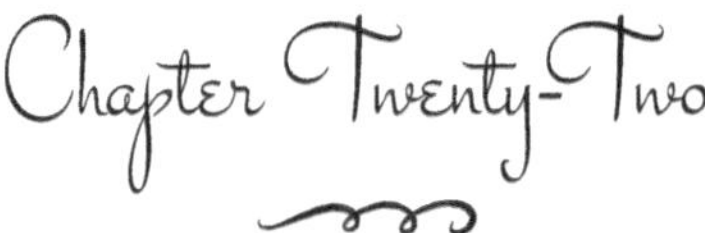

"Hey! Oh, hello, Darcy."

Evangeline beamed from my open front door in jeggings and a baggy, fluffy pink white sweater, Darcy apparently having skittered down the stairs without me noticing as he was currently weaving around my ankles and then Evangeline's in turn.

She bent down to offer him scritches, adjusting a cream-colored tote bag with a picture of an open book on it up her shoulder as she did. "He probably thinks I'm here to give him dinner again."

"Which I already gave him, so don't fall for his tricks." I stepped aside and gestured for her to come in. Darcy followed her, not looking where he was going as he stared up at her, his tail straight and tall in the air. He could barely wait for her to slip her shoes off before "guiding" her up the stairs and to his bowl.

"Oh, you have to let me at least give him a treat,"

she said, crouching down and cooing at him as he slammed his forehead into her body over and over.

I rolled my eyes at Darcy's machinations. "All right." As Evangeline moved to shake his can of treats, I wagged a finger at him. "You know, your namesake would never be such a welcoming host."

"He would be if he particularly liked his guest." Evangeline let a couple of treats clink into Darcy's bowl. "And you particularly like me, don't you, Darcy?" She rubbed his back, but he was too focused on eating to care whether or not his particularly-liked guest vanished into the ether at that very moment.

"Welcome to the inaugural meeting of the Ooh-La-La Book Club." I gestured at the coffee table in front of my couch, on which I'd set out some popcorn and hummus and carrot sticks, as well as Evangeline's preferred non-alcoholic choice, a ginger ale with a shot of cranberry juice. I'd been grocery shopping between making and eating dinner, letting the meal cook in my Crockpot while I'd been out.

"Oo, like the club name," she said, sitting down beside me but leaving enough space between us for another guest. Though she was it for tonight.

"Sorry it still smells like curry a bit," I said. I'd had the window cracked open, but it had gotten chilly after dark, and it was shut now.

"Is that what that is? I should have invited myself over sooner." She winked at me as she started taking things out of her tote bag. "The kids and Lucas wanted pizza, and I'm trying to cut back on dairy, so I was stuck with a salad."

"Oh, yikes. I don't know if I could stick to a salad when pizza was in the same room."

"You and me both." She laughed and arranged her tablet and phone on some space on the coffee table in front of us, grabbing for a carrot stick. "They promised to finish it off before I got back. Benjamin still has some homework to do, too, and Lucas claims he'll be able to handle supervising. We'll see. Benjamin tends to get frustrated."

"Are Sundays a good day for this club, you think?" The residents with kids would be busy getting them settled down for school the next day—and getting ready for work themselves, at least the ones with typical 8-5 jobs.

"I'll send out a survey." Evangeline took another carrot stick and dipped that one into the hummus before picking up her tablet and a stylus tucked into the case. "I'm leaning toward Saturdays myself, but maybe not every week." She glanced at me as she brought up a notetaking program and started writing on the screen. "Unless you want to have weekly meetings for those who can make it and sort of make it casual? We'll email out the book of the week, then people can drop by if they have time and are able to read it?"

"Sounds good to me." I looked around my condo, counting the spots for seating. If I got some fold-out chairs, I could maybe squeeze six or so. Then again, Bodhi and Rory had managed to do the most with an almost-equal space.

"I can host the first meeting," I said. "But how many people are we expecting?"

"Well, I haven't sent out the news in the community newsletter yet." Evangeline seemed to think of something and jotted it down. "But I did run into Bodhi and he's all on board—he offered to have the first meeting at his place."

"That would probably work better," I said, thinking of the dinner party last week. Had that really been less than a week ago? My cheeks grew flush. It felt like I had known Allen for much longer than that.

My phone buzzed from the counter where I'd left it, but I ignored it. Milly and I had arranged a lunch date on Tuesday already, Mom and I had chatted earlier in the day. Anything else could wait.

Or so I thought.

My phone buzzed one more time, but I didn't get up.

"Do you need to get that?" Evangeline asked as Darcy sauntered by, headed for the window, even though it was closed.

I shook my head. "I told my friend to text me." Milly was supposed to let me know when she got to her parents' house safely. Sure, it was sort of worried-Mom of me, but I knew she wasn't overly fond of driving alone.

Evangeline nodded and smiled—a little too wickedly if you asked me.

"What?" I asked.

She rested her tablet in her lap and grabbed a handful of popcorn, popping it one kernel at a time from her palm into her mouth. "Does this have anything to do with last night?"

"What? Oh, no." I laughed nervously and snatched my own carrot stick. "Just a friend from out of town. A girlfriend. I mean, a girl *friend*. Who has a boyfriend."

"You promised to spill about what you were up to last night. You don't often request me to be on cat-sitting duties." She downed a sip of ginger ale. "Don't get me wrong. I more than owe you, considering how often you let my dog out. But count me intrigued. I believe you told me you texted me from Mr. Hottie's bathroom...?"

My mouth opened, then shut again. I grabbed for my own ginger ale and swallowed half of it down in one gulp.

"Hmm?" Evangeline said. "Well, I *may* have let the cat-sitting thing slip to Bodhi, and hinted you were very coy about the reason why, so if he's asking you a bunch of questions next time he sees you, that'll be why—"

"I did spend the night. At Allen's."

Evangeline let out a little gasp. "I *thought* so! I mean, I saw you flirting with Mr. Hottie in the afternoon, and when I talked to Bodhi about it, he told me *all about* the sparks flying between you two at his party—"

"Flirting? *Sparks*?" I squeezed my chilled glass and stared down into it. "It's nothing so serious as that."

"Oh?"

"I went over to help with his Mini Donation Library planning."

Evangeline leaned one elbow back on the top of the couch. "And that took all night, did it?"

"Well, no." I swished my drink and took another sip. "He let me read *Riding My Baby*."

I didn't even have to explain who by.

All playfulness fell off of Evangeline's face. She leaned over and slapped my shoulder playfully. "He did *not*!"

"He did." I put my glass down. "And you are going to *love* it!"

"Well, spill the details!" Evangeline brought one leg up onto the couch and leaned forward, clutching her tablet. "You can't just tease me and leave me hanging."

At least that had gotten all thought of Allen out of her mind. For the moment.

"I wish I could, but I'm sworn to secrecy." I held one hand up as if in a scout's pledge as Darcy made his way out of the windowsill and crossed my lap to sit between us on the couch.

"You *tease*!" Evangeline stuck her tongue out at me after giving Darcy another pet.

"I know you'll love it, though."

"I don't doubt that. What do you think about making it the first book for a sort of trial run of the club this weekend? I don't expect a lot of people to show on short notice, but—"

"Not the first book in the series?" Mom had said her club would skip to the new release, too.

"Well, we can talk about the whole series when we get together. But anyone in the neighborhood who has even *a little* interest in romance has read everything Breedlove has put out so far. I know that much."

We spent a little while longer hashing out the details of the email Evangeline was going to send out the next day, and she texted Bodhi to confirm he was fine with hosting this Saturday. When Bodhi found out I'd already read *Riding My Baby*, he sent an angry face and a pouting face emoji and said it wasn't fair for Allen to hold out on him like that.

That was true. He'd introduced *me* to Allen and he hadn't gotten a sneak peek at Breedlove's next book like I had?

Unfortunately, that brought all the focus back to me and Allen. And Bodhi the gossip king wasn't even in the room with us.

"There's not much to say," I said truthfully. Not yet, anyway. Or ever? I really wasn't sure.

"All right. Keep your secrets. For now." Evangeline slipped her tablet and phone back into her tote, Darcy's little snores rhythmically filling in any awkward silence between us. "But you're going to let him know about club this weekend, right? Didn't he want some pictures for V.L. Breedlove's newsletter?"

"Yeah..." I cleared my throat as I stood along with Evangeline to escort her to the door. "I told my mom to send pictures of her club reading some of Breedlove's books, too."

Evangeline slipped her tote over her shoulder and spread her arms wide in the air above her, as if reading off a marquee. "Breedlove Fans Across the Nation."

"And Across Generations." I laughed.

"Hey, my mom's a snowbird retiree, too." She poked at my shoulder playfully. "And I made a Breedlove fan out of her this week."

"It's spreading," I teased.

"Like a wildfire."

"Or a cult." I stuck my tongue out. "Bad analogy."

"Honey, if *this* is a cult, then call my therapist because I'm in deep."

We both devolved into a fit of giggles, which was interrupted by my front doorbell. I glanced at my microwave clock. It was past seven.

"Expecting someone else?" Evangeline asked. Her eyes gleamed and I knew where her mind was going.

"No." I glanced at my phone but didn't grab it yet. "Maybe Milly swung by tonight after getting to her parents'..."

The doorbell rang again.

"Coming!" I called down the stairway, though I didn't know if they could hear me.

"I'll get out of your way," Evangeline said, heading

down first. She stepped aside and slipped on her shoes as I peeped through the peephole to make sure it wasn't a delivery person with the wrong condo number or something.

It was Allen. Allen Cox was on the other side of my door.

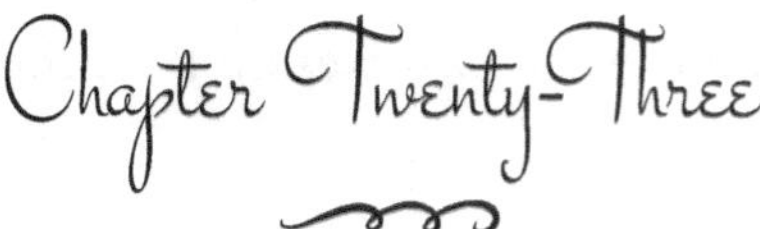

Chapter Twenty-Three

Allen's warm eyes widened just slightly as Evangeline nodded at him, clutching her tote bag handle over her shoulder with two hands.

"Oh, sorry. I didn't know you had company—" he started.

"I was just leaving," Evangeline insisted. She winked at me over her shoulder as Allen stepped aside to let her through.

"Oh, Evangeline, you don't have to rush," I insisted, although she'd been on her way out anyway.

It was just that the prospect of being left standing here alone with Allen all of a sudden low-key terrified me. In a "this will be terribly awkward" way.

"I have to get home. Don't forget to update him on the club!" She waved over her shoulder and Allen watched her head down the sidewalk for a second. I might have imagined it, but the moment he turned around, Evangeline turned around, too—and the look on her face was far too appraising. She smiled.

"Sorry. I texted. But you didn't answer, so that means I shouldn't have come, of course. But I was in the neighborhood..." He slipped his hands into his jeans pockets and left the rest unsaid.

"Um, sure." I stepped back to make room for him. So that had been the text I'd ignored? I didn't know if it would have been better if I'd read it or not. Would I have told him to stay away? Certainly, since I'd been with Evangeline at the time. "That is... It's all right. You can come in."

"I won't take up much of your time," he promised as he closed the door behind him.

Why did that make my stomach sink?

It wasn't like we'd sleep together again so soon, was it? Was I even ready for that here? In my slightly messy condo?

His gaze flicked to my shoes on the welcome mat to the side of the entrance, then back to me, as if wondering if he should take them off.

Or wondering if he should stay long enough to do so?

My throat constricted. Why were things so *awkward* between us? Had I rushed into things too soon with him?

That was it. I'd gone and done something casual when I was too inexperienced to separate my feelings from my sex drive. He'd definitely wined and dined me, but my pattern so far had been more of a talk-and-flirt-and-talk-and-talk-and-go-on-multiple-dates variety.

What was it about Allen that had made me want to jump his bones so quickly?

I checked him out—he'd put on a plain gray T-shirt that clung perfectly to his chest.

Besides the obvious, of course.

"Didn't you want to see Darcy?" I asked, when no explanation on his part was forthcoming. I started walking backward up the stairs.

"May I?" His face seemed to shine in the dim stairwell light.

I took a deep breath. My core was vibrating just at the sight of him. "Just for a minute," I said quickly.

I *so* wasn't ready to hop into bed again. Not until I figured out how to say more than two words to him without fighting a compulsion to run and hide.

"It's... uh... I didn't clean or anything." I gestured around as we reached the top of the stairs. He'd left his shoes downstairs. Then I thought better of what I'd just said. "Actually, I did, since Evangeline was coming over. This is, uh... My place at its finest." I looked over the mismatched pieces of furniture, the somewhat threadbare towering cat tree by the desk. "Other than it still smells a bit like curry."

"Nice." Allen took his hand from the bannister and tucked it once more in his pockets as he took it all in.

My face flushed, as if he were examining my naked body. Something this gorgeous man had *already* done, I might remind myself.

"I haven't eaten yet," Allen said. "Been too busy. Smells good."

"You can have some," I said before thinking. I winced. *Sure, invite him to stay longer, you idiot.* "If you... don't mind... le-leftovers." I could barely speak.

My heart was just about jumping out of my throat.

Allen's face lit up. "Could I? I'd love that."

Now I had a dinner guest. After dinner was cleaned up and put away.

Well, I was the one who'd stumbled into that offer, so I figured I may as well go into hostess mode.

I brushed past Allen to head into the kitchen, pointing behind me at the couch. "There're snacks over there. Oh, and Darcy!" Wasn't that why I'd brought him up here in the first place?

I brushed past Allen again, my nose catching that hearty musk of books that I so loved, and guided him to the couch, gesturing at my lump of gray-striped cat.

Allen's shoulders seemed to relax as he neared. "Hello, Mr. Darcy," he said softly, reaching a hand out to pet him.

Darcy opened one bleary eye and then sat up quickly, as if he'd expected to see Evangeline and was shocked to find an intruder instead.

"Oh, sorry, fella." Allen stood straighter and pulled his hand back. He looked crestfallen.

Darcy sat up on the couch and I pet him. "You just spooked him is all, I guess. Since he was sleeping. He usually likes company." I spoke soothing nonsense words to Darcy, who stood up more on the cushion, pushing his butt into my pets. "This is our new friend Allen, Darcy. He likes kitties, too."

My eyes caught Allen's and his face lit up. I looked back down at Darcy again to focus on anything other than Allen's sexy smile.

"Hello again, Mr. Darcy. I'm sorry I didn't wait for a proper introduction." Allen held an index finger out for my cat to sniff. "I should have known you wouldn't deign to associate with someone so rude."

I laughed despite myself, thinking of Mr. Darcy at any given social event in *Pride and Prejudice.*

Darcy cautiously took a sniff that lasted quite a bit. I wondered if he smelled the other cats on Allen. Then my cat started licking Allen's finger, as if grooming him.

And then Darcy bit him.

"Darcy! No!" I said. "I'm so sorry—"

"It's all right." Allen chuckled as Darcy jumped down off the couch, bouncing quickly past Allen's feet to head under the kitchen table across the room. "It was just a grooming nibble." Allen held up his finger as if to prove Darcy's innocence. There was no blood or anything.

"Still..." I chewed my lip. "He shouldn't bite at all, even if he didn't mean anything by it." I glanced at Darcy, whose shining eyes flicked up from the shadows at me. It was me raising my voice that had gotten him so upset. Maybe I'd messed up the tentative relationship he'd been forming with Allen. *Crap.*

"I'll just give him some space," Allen said. "Why don't I help you warm the dinner up?"

"Don't be silly. After all the pampering you did of me?" My breath caught at the word "pampering," as if he might think I'd meant something other than the meals he'd bought and made for me. Looking down quickly, I indicated the snacks I'd left out for Evangeline, grabbing the empty glass she'd left on a coaster. "Help yourself to some snacks—though if you want to wash your hands first since Darcy decided to share his little mouth germs with you, it's down the hallway." There was no missing the only short hallway in this place.

Allen chuckled but took me up on the offer, and after washing my own hands in the kitchen, I went to work heating up a plate of curry on rice.

A few minutes later, Allen exited the bathroom and helped himself to a carrot stick as I brought the steaming hot plate of leftovers to my small kitchen table.

"What do you want to drink?" I asked. "I don't usually keep alcohol on hand, but I have soda and water and tea—"

"Tea's good," Allen said. "I don't usually have time to drink much, either."

I poured him and myself each a glass as Allen sat down in front of the place I'd set for him. "Sugar?" I asked.

"Yes, darling?" he teased. I could feel my face

flushing and he laughed. "Unsweetened tea is fine, thank you."

A man after my own heart.

"Hope you don't mind green," I said, putting the glass by him and taking the other seat beside his at the tiny table. We were kitty-corner to each other at the only two chairs. I'd never had a need for more than that after my parents had moved. In fact, I'd found the second chair rather superfluous, other than for the fact that sometimes Darcy liked to join me for a meal by sitting on it.

Which was what the cat did as soon as I sat down, using my lap as his cushion.

"Any tea's fine," Allen said. He took a deep breath of the steaming curry. "This smells wonderful. Thank you." He picked up his spoon and I lazily pet my cat. "I'm so sorry for dropping in like this. And here I am, taking advantage of your kindness, eating in front of you—"

"It's fine. I probably made too much to begin with. I was bound to get sick of the leftovers." I clutched my tea and stared at it, focusing on the vibrant, green color through the clear glass. "Evangeline and I were planning the Ooh-La-La Book Club when you texted, apparently. I didn't notice." *Didn't notice it was you who texted, anyway.*

"Oh? Is that what it's going to be called?" He started eating. His face lit up as he chewed, and I found myself blushing again.

"Well, for the newsletter's sake, you can call us

something like the V.L. Breedlove Fan Club. Then mention we might spread out into other books in the future. I mean, even a prolific author publishes a finite amount of books."

Allen scoffed. "Tell me about it. This is so good, by the way. You made this?"

I laughed. "Mostly. I used curry roux. Didn't put together the spices from scratch or anything."

"Hey, it's not like most cooks have time to make things from scratch. This is plenty homemade to me." He started eating again and I took a sip of my tea for lack of something better to do.

"But I like the 'Ooh-La-La Book Club' name," he said. "To go with the box. Yes, that's a nice way to tie it all together."

"For the newsletter?" I observed Allen as he stared ahead of him at the wall. The gears seemed to be turning behind those eyes.

"Yeah. If I can get a shot of you all with one of Breedlove's books—"

"My mom's book club in New Mexico offered to do the same thing," I told him.

Allen's smile grew wider as he caught my eye. "Really?"

I nodded and told him about my chat with Mom. "Once I got her started talking about V.L. Breedlove, we couldn't stop."

Allen's gaze traveled back to his curry real quick, and it looked like, in the warm yellow light of the lamp above the table, that his cheeks might have darkened just a bit.

"We're meeting this Saturday," I said. "And my mom's meeting with her group then, too. So the pictures would have to wait a week."

"That's all right. Plenty to write about this week with the book release."

"Of course." I rested my hand on Darcy's back in my lap. "I didn't forget. Now that I've read it, it's almost like it already happened—for me."

Allen chuckled and managed to finish off the rest of his curry. "I get it. My mind is so full of future releases at any given time, that the most current release seems like old hat whenever it's finally available to the readers."

He had to plan for future book releases even as Val was still writing them? "It must be hard to juggle all that," I said. "Did you get the cover issue sorted?"

"Oh, yes. Sorry about that." He leaned back in his chair and shook his head, though his hand still clutched his fork. "I panicked a bit this morning. Val got a hold of the designer, who sent over the fixes. Now we're just waiting to see if Amazon will accept it." Sighing, he put his fork down on the plate. "That's why I thought I'd swing by. To apologize."

"Apologize?" I cocked my head. "For what?" He'd said *sorry* by text, too.

"I got so wrapped up in that problem, I feel like you felt rushed to leave." He turned in his chair, facing me full-on. "And that was the *last* thing I wanted. Especially after last night."

My breath hitched and I had to stare at his knee instead. His knee... connected to thick, muscly thighs. Thighs that had rammed up against my own just the night before. Okay, I'd stare at his feet in black socks instead.

"Don't worry about it. I was intruding—"

"You weren't." Allen reached over and took my hand in his. "I wanted you there."

I finally looked him in the eye for more than half a second, my heart thundering in my ears. "I had a nice time. A wonderful time."

Darcy looked up from where he was seated on my lap to my hand connected to Allen's. He sniffed up at us and then jumped down off my lap, only to jump up onto Allen's.

Our hands broke apart as Allen grinned and pet Darcy's cheek. "Hello, Mr. Darcy."

I knew where *I* stood in this dynamic. But a warmth filled me. I was glad Darcy felt comfortable around him now. "Can I get you some more curry?" I asked.

"No, I'm good—but thank you, I appreciate it. When I get caught up with work, entire meals can get overlooked."

"I know what you mean. That's why I try to make a point of cooking myself something nice in my slow cooker on Sundays."

"That sounds like a wonderful tradition." Allen

beamed as Darcy settled in on his lap, curling up on his jeans. "Maybe I should join you in that." His jaw dropped a little, as if just realizing what he'd said. "That is, I should do the same thing. At home."

"Right. Yeah... Yeah, you'll like it, I think." I stood up and cleared his plate away, bringing it to the kitchen as Allen took a sip of tea.

"You were in the neighborhood?" I said after a beat, rinsing his plate and tucking it into the dishwasher. "Visiting Bodhi?" Evangeline and I had just texted him, though, and there was *no way* Bodhi wouldn't have mentioned Allen being there.

"Uh, no, not tonight. I had some extra copies of Book 1 in Breedlove's MC series, so I thought I'd put them in the Ooh-La-La Box. Maybe you can use them for the photo op. I know a lot of readers prefer e-books."

My hand froze over the dishwasher after I'd just slammed it closed. "There are copies of *Kidnapped Desire* in the Ooh-La-La Box? Right now? Signed?"

"Yeah. My dad said I could build the box for my condo at his place, but it'll be a few days at least before it's constructed and ready to go, so I thought I'd get rid of the extras here—"

But I was already headed toward the stairs, grabbing my keys for the little flashlight I kept on the keyring.

I needed to snag a copy for myself before the other neighborhood bookworms descended on the box and took them all.

Chapter Twenty-Four

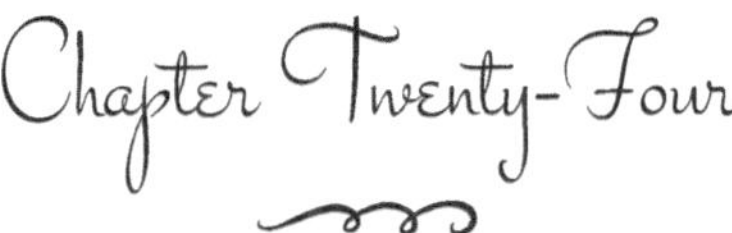

Cradling my signed copy of *Kidnapped Desire* to my chest, I entered the condo again, humming a tune to a song whose title I only vaguely remembered. When I reached the top of the stairs, a lightness in my step, I almost ground to a halt at the sight of Allen leaned over my kitchen counter.

How badly had I been lost in a bookworm fugue state that I could forget about the hot-as-hell house-guest I'd left behind for even one second?

"I take it you scored a copy?" he asked.

"There were tons left." Chuckling nervously, I put the book down on the table. It was cleared of his glass of tea—and probably wiped down to boot. It practically sparkled. "I guess I should have expected as much since it's dark out. I doubt the mini libraries get a lot of traffic this time of night."

"Another lesson for the student?" he asked, but he smirked. He was teasing me.

My fingers trailed over the cover of the book. "I thought you were done getting advice from me. You paid that invoice awfully quickly."

"It *wasn't* in hopes of getting rid of you," he said, coming around the counter. "On the contrary."

He stepped closer, the perpetually-smaller space between us almost crackling. I shifted my head up just slightly, my face warming as I caught sight of the way his eyes bore into mine.

Taking my face in both hands, he pressed his lips to mine, soft at first, then, after coming up for air, he pressed harder. The tip of his tongue danced at the seam between my lips, and my jaw grew slack, inviting, a tingling sensation shooting down through my core and to my toes.

But then, my fingers scraping against the paperback cover still under my hand, I took a step back, gasping for air.

Allen's hands fell from my face, and he gripped his shirt over his chest in one fist. His body grew unnaturally stiff, his Adam's apple bobbing at his throat.

"I'm sorry," he said. "I should have asked first."

"No, it's not—I liked it." I couldn't look at him, instead staring at the bare-chested biker on the cover of V.L. Breedlove's book.

"Then why...?"

"I just thought... We might be moving too fast. *If* you're interested in anything more."

"If?" He stepped closer again, the air beside me filling up with the *sense* of him. His alluring musk, his defined body hovering in my space. "I would have thought I'd made my thoughts clear last night."

"You showed me a closet full of toys," I pointed out. "And hinted that you may not socialize much, but you have a lot of women over—"

"That bothers you?" Allen took an uneven step back, and I finally turned to look at him. His chest hitched. "I may have given off the wrong impression when it comes to the *number* of women."

"No, it's not that." Why couldn't I articulate what I meant? Why didn't I *know* exactly what I meant? "I'm not slut-shaming you."

"Slut?" Allen cocked a brow, but there was a sparkle to his eye that had been missing the past minute.

"I mean, well, last night was *amazing*—"

"Agreed."

"And you do that kind of thing a lot. That's fine."

"I don't reenact book scenes with anyone else. At least not before they *become* book scenes." He dragged a hand down the back of his head, his eyes darting to my table and the book on it.

Wasn't that what I'd suspected? Maybe he gave Val ideas when it came to her sex scenes. Ideas he'd *experienced* himself.

But... there were *a lot* of sex scenes in V.L. Breedlove's books. If he coached Val on even a *fraction* of them from his own experience, that was a *lot* of experience.

"I'm a reader," I blurted out. As if he didn't know.

"And I'm not *used* to that much... See, I haven't dated anyone in a long time. Years, really."

Allen's jaw dropped. "*Years?*"

My stomach hardened. So now he realized how pathetic I was. How out of place I'd been in his bedroom.

That was it, really. That was what was bothering me. I could take last night as a wild ride, an incredible memory. But with Allen as gorgeous as he was, I wasn't expecting more... I was just a blip in the course of his empirical research. And I hadn't even done *that* right because we'd just roleplayed a scene Val had already incorporated into her books instead of inspiring anything new.

What did he see in someone as awkward and unsexy as I was?

Allen seemed to read something on my face because he quickly stepped toward me again, placing a hand lightly on my upper arm. "You're so beautiful, Quinn. I'm just surprised no one asked you out sooner than that."

My head grew a bit woozy. His voice was husky, and those words had melted most of the panicked thoughts circulating around my brain.

"Th-Thank you," I said. Of course he found me attractive. He could have *anyone*. Why would he bother with me if I weren't worth at least a fraction of his attention?

"But I can totally see how maybe we moved too fast." He reached over and tucked a strand of my hair behind my ear. "I mean—*I* was plenty happy not waiting. But I shouldn't have assumed you felt the same."

"I was happy not waiting, too," I mumbled. I patted *Kidnapped Desire*. "Blame Val. She put me in the mood."

Allen's breath hitched.

I searched his face for signs he was about to admit the jig was up. But his brow furrowed, his lips pinched together.

Stubborn until the end.

"When I thought we were just *having some fun...*" I paused and took a deep breath. "I was all in. Throwing caution into the wind. And I *did* have fun." I was rambling now, and Allen was staring at me, his lips pinched. The sparkle was gone from his eye, and I wasn't sure how I could fix that. "I just didn't think you were serious enough to want anything more. The toys, your mom acting like we were dating and you telling me you didn't *do* the kind of dating she wanted you to, that you were all about the flings..."

Every word of my mouth made his frown deeper. It was like I was chipping away at that light amusement that had colored his soul from the moment I'd met him. And I still couldn't stop. I plowed forward, as if somehow, I could explain my thoughts coherently.

I was a writer. Not a speaker.

"It just never occurred to me that you'd want much more." I took a deep breath. "I tried to school myself, to tamper my expectations. I mean, you were kind and gorgeous and charming—and you did me a *huge* favor, letting me read that ARC. I knew I owed you."

He looked as if I'd slapped him. "Did you think you had to sleep with me in exchange for that?"

"No!" Why was my brain so inept at explaining these feelings? My shouted word had woken Darcy, who stood up on the kitchen chair he'd apparently been lying on this whole time and stared at the two of us, as if wondering if we were about to hiss and launch into a cat fight. "I'm just saying. You were the perfect host. All that food—and then to give me something I wanted more than anything. The chance to read that book."

"And you thought it was all so I could get you into bed?" He sighed. "I mean, I *did* want you in my bed, but I still would have done those things even if you'd wanted to take it slow. Even if you hadn't been interested at all."

"I know that!" And somehow, I did. "I... I appreciate that."

"But you're not into sluts," he mumbled, an iciness to his tone. "Usually."

"I don't think you're a—look, I don't know what I'm saying. I like you, Allen. I'm... a bit in awe of you. And it's taking me a while to process that you were interested in having me in your bed *once*, let alone that you're coming around the next day, wanting to talk... Or..." *Had* he come over to try things on in my bed?

Did I want that?

Yes... And no. I needed time to process. Why was I so frustrating, even to myself?

"I shouldn't have come to your door when you didn't answer your text." He stuck his hands in his jeans pockets and stared at Darcy still on alert, as if confessing to my cat. "And bringing the books over—well, I thought I'd do that sometime, but yes, it was an excuse to see if you'd let me in. Because I came crashing down from my work crisis this morning and realized how I'd left things with you." He turned up to meet my gaze. "And I didn't want you to think last night was anything but extraordinary." He sighed and stared at my book. "But I can see I failed."

"No, you... That is, I..." I stared at the book. Things were hardly this awkward in romance novels. Sure, there were misunderstandings, but the heroines generally *liked* when alpha males took charge. They went with the flow, even if their brains screamed stubborn resistance at them.

But romantic heroines were guaranteed their HEAs. Life was so much more nerve-wracking. What if I sunk my heart into him and he didn't feel the same way? Great sex was one thing, but if I lost my heart to him...

And there was no guarantee of an HEA.

Silence hung heavily in the air between us. Darcy seemed relieved and jumped down from the chair, heading down the short hallway and to my room.

I scrambled to think of something—*anything*—to say. Anything *safe*, that is. That wouldn't put me in danger of risking my heart for just a small chance of a happily ever after.

My hand, shaking just slightly, rested on top of Breedlove's book. "I-I have to thank you. Thank Val. Her words have burrowed deeply into my heart, taking up space in my mind, haunting me—in a good way—in the moments before I fall asleep. They—" I stopped when my eyes met his.

This wasn't a safe topic at all, it seemed.

I'd just wanted to convey to him how much him coming into my life meant to me. How much *these books* meant to me. Books I'd always been happy to welcome into my heart. They were safe. Happy.

A real relationship... A scorching-hot, romantic relationship. That didn't happen to me. I was just a reader, not a heroine.

Allen drew in a slow, steady breath, after which he seemed to be grinding his teeth. He focused on the book on the table. "The books. That's all that's important to you."

"No. I mean, yes, but—"

"The books you insist wormed their way into your heart. The words you attribute to *my sister*."

I gasped. I could see how that would be awkward. I was supposed to be talking about *him and me*, not him, me, and his sister.

Oh, if only I hadn't met Breedlove in real life. This wouldn't have been an issue. Her books would have remained in the realm of safe escapism from real life.

My love for them wouldn't be like me praising Allen's sister more than him to his face.

"I'm glad." Allen's furrowed brow belied that he was anything but. "And I won't take any more of your time tonight. Thank you for the meal. It was delicious." His words were clipped, his gratitude more an add-on than a genuine sentiment.

He headed down the stairs before my brain could even process what was going on.

"Allen!" I called, flipping on the light switch for the stairwell and heading down after him. He already had his second shoe on.

He turned around, his hand on the doorknob. I hovered above him on the stairs, so he had to look up.

"I'll still send you ARCs," he muttered. "The author has too much of an ego not to hear praises from a fan like you."

"Oh... Thanks." Truth be told, I hadn't even thought about that. Despite the bookworm that I was, I hadn't been concerned about the potential loss of access to early copies of Breedlove's books.

"You can criticize them, too," he scrambled to say, his eyes dropping. "I'm not saying you have to be complimentary. And we have the book club thing to plan—I'll be in touch." He opened the door and stepped out.

I headed down the last few steps and grabbed the doorjamb, watching as he reached the end of the sidewalk.

I stared down at my shoes, then back up at him. He was moving so fast. Too fast.

And based on how I'd stuck my foot in my mouth, what else was there to say?

He'd be in touch. We would still be cordial. This was what I'd hardened my heart to expect after one amazing night that had seemed ripped out of a romance book.

I slowly shut the door and locked it, heading back upstairs and to nothing but my empty condo, my adorable cat, and my shelves and Kindle full of books.

Everything I could ever want in life.

Everything... Until I'd met Allen Cox.

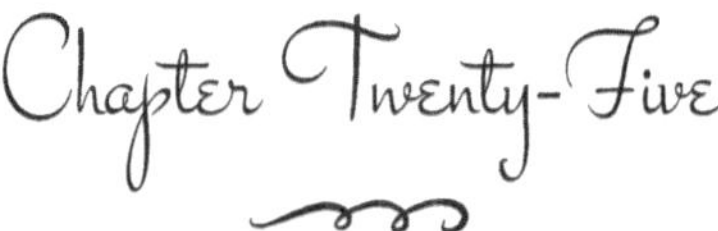

Chapter Twenty-Five

Monday had been a slog. Not because I'd been bogged down by too much client work—though it hadn't exactly been lightweight—but because it'd been hard for me to focus on writing a brochure, then plotting out SEO in a how-to article when my mind kept wandering to how terribly my interaction with Allen had gone.

It had started with kissing and ended with... whatever that had been.

I was doing no better on Tuesday, even though I'd taken half the day off.

I checked my phone for any sign of a text from Allen, but there'd been nothing in the past two days.

"Quinn? Did you hear me?" Milly dabbed at her mouth with a napkin. We'd met for a late lunch at her favorite mom-and-pop bistro near the interstate after she'd hung out with her parents all day yesterday.

I blinked and stared around. The bistro was only

about a third full. We'd met up a little later than the typical lunch hour, since my schedule was flexible and Milly had all day.

"Sorry...?" I said slowly.

Milly arched a dark brow. "You've been out of it this whole lunch." She stabbed at her salad, her brown eyes turned downward. She didn't seem hurt, though, by my lack of attention. Sunlight bounced off the dentist's office sign across the street and streamed into the bistro through the wide windows, sparkling off a golden barrette in her curly, brown hair. "Another book coma?" she offered.

"No. I've been busy with work." I cleared my throat and took a sip of my drink. I hadn't texted Milly a lot over the weekend, other than to confirm her plans to come here for a few days. We'd chatted about Breedlove last week.

"Ah. But work hard and you can reward yourself with a good book tonight, right?" Milly smirked as she waved a forkful of lettuce and cucumber into the air. "Isn't today Breedlove's new release? I haven't caught up with that series yet—"

That brought me back to the moment. "How? How could you not have caught up yet?"

Milly laughed and popped the fork into her mouth. "I had work last week. And Steve and I put together a new computer desk before I drove to my folks'. It's a miracle I read the first one. Though I do like the *Thrill Me* series more. Still haven't read the last two of those, either."

"But-But it's *Breedlove*!" I said. Louder than I'd meant to. Even though we were seated quite a ways from the nearest table of patrons, the people I presumed to be a mom and her two adult daughters all turned their heads to stare my way.

I leaned forward, practically hissing. "Breedlove is worth it. I promise you. Book binges are the best." A dreamy sigh escaped my lips.

Milly laughed and cradled her glass of sparkling water with her dark-brown hand. "You're preaching to the choir. To the *librarian*. But sometimes, life just gets in the way. And there's the crash afterward." She tipped her glass toward me. "Which I have to wonder if you're currently suffering from yourself. Your mind is wandering."

"I'm sorry." I took a bite of my sandwich. I'd only taken a couple of bites so far and we'd been here—I checked my phone screen again—forty minutes already. It didn't feel that long.

I got an alert that there was a new email in my inbox. I clicked on it.

V.L. Breedlove's newsletter. I was surprised she hadn't sent it out—or Allen hadn't sent it out, more accurately—right away this morning for all the morning birds.

Was Allen finding it hard to focus on his work, too?

"So you're excited about the new book, I take it?" Milly asked.

"I actually read it." I clicked on the alert,

responding to Milly, albeit matter-of-factly, but my eyes glazing over the email and the first image that popped up. It was of *Riding My Baby*'s cover, of course, a bit about Aaron's story finally "being out in the wild" the first part of text below it.

"That was fast." Milly laughed.

I turned my attention away from the phone and to my best friend. My poor, ignored best friend. "Oh, I don't mean this morning—I wasn't lying when I said I had work to do so I could take off this afternoon. I read an advanced copy a couple of days ago."

"I see." Milly's smile widened. "You got on the Street Team."

I opened my mouth, about to fess up. But to what? My one-night stand? The one that may have led to more, but I'd utterly blown?

Not that I was *convinced* it would have led to more.

"Ye-Yeah," I said softly.

Even though Milly and I had the kind of relationship that could generally be reignited as if we hadn't just gone weeks without talking much, I still felt like a failure not being fully in the present with her in this moment.

"Was it good?" she asked.

"Yes." I smiled as I dug into my sandwich, launching into everything I'd liked about the book—while avoiding spoilers. Which was no easy task.

Milly seemed genuinely interested, asking questions that I sometimes refused to answer so she could find out for herself. "But was the sex good?" she asked.

Then she giggled when my jaw dropped. "I mean, the sex scenes? In the book?"

My cheeks flushed, my mind going to some very *real* places at first. "Um-hmm," I said quickly, finishing off my sandwich for an excuse not to say more.

"Do you want dessert?" she asked. "I want dessert."

I nodded, trying *very* hard not to picture Allen just then. His strong hand on my hips. His mouth on my cheek, my chin. My chest.

Milly's phone buzzed. "Oh, but I have to get this first. Dad said he'd ask a friend if he could look at my car while I'm here. I need new tires. Do you mind?"

I shook my head as Milly took her call at the table, picking my own phone back up to fill the few minutes she'd need before we could order our dessert. I scrolled through Breedlove's newsletter, glad to see the paperback edition was available to order right away. So they'd fixed that issue, as Allen had told me.

And then I scrolled down to see Poe and Raven staring back at me, their fuzzy, black cheeks flush up against one another.

These are my cats, Breedlove had written. *The cutest possible writing accountability buddies.*

Her cats.

Allen's cats.

Allen had taken my idea to start sharing photos of his cats in Breedlove's newsletter. But Val had a dog. Cats may have had the slightest edge when it came to being an author's "writing companion," in my opinion, but dogs were popular among plenty of readers, too. And Val had one of those frou-frou ones. Readers would have a blast with her.

I scrolled to Breedlove's Instagram, and sure enough, there were a few photos of Poe and Raven thrown up on the account now—even a video of Poe, I guessed, chasing an automatic mouse toy around Allen's kitchen. Raven watched warily from the corner of the shot, her tail twitching, but she never moved from that spot.

They'd just been posted since yesterday, and already, the comments were reaching the hundreds. People asked if they'd been recently adopted and how old they were. A lot of people commented on them looking like shadows and voids, and a few people appreciated their bookish names.

At one point, Allen—as "Breedlove's PA"—commented that Breedlove had had these brother and sister cats practically their whole lives: five years. That just led to more comments about why none of the readers had seen them before, but neither Val nor Allen had responded yet.

"Quinn?" Milly's voice snapped me back to attention.

She placed her phone on the table and tilted her head toward our server, who stared at me expectantly, a customer-service smile pasted on her bright-red lips.

"Did you want dessert, too?" she asked.

I hadn't noticed her standing there. Or Milly ordering.

"Oh, yes. Uh..." I put my phone down and snatched the dessert menu from the stand on our table.

The server clasped her hands together tightly in front of her. "We have apple pie, key lime pie, chocolate cream pie, ice cream, sherbet—"

"The apple pie," I said, putting the menu back in the holder without even looking at it. "Thank—"

But my words caught in my throat. My hand still clutched the menu as I stared through the wide window at the front of the restaurant. At what I saw across the street.

Fortunately, the server didn't seem to notice the fact that I had gone silent. "A slice of apple and a slice of key lime. I'll get that prepped for you." She turned over her shoulder and walked away. "Hi! Thank you for joining us today. Table for three?"

I didn't dare look. Didn't dare see if the group I'd spotted walking across the street toward us had headed inside this very restaurant.

"Quinn?" Milly asked again.

She looked over her shoulder so she could see what I was looking at.

Gaping at.

Our server was greeting Allen, Val, and even their mom, Vera, by the front door.

Snatching the dessert menu back into my hands, I hunched down, covering the side of my head with it.

Milly arched a brow. "Do you know them?"

Wincing, I put the dessert menu back down. Why was I hiding?

"That's the guy I was telling you about," I whispered, folding my hands over the menu and straightening my back. "Breedlove's PA. And Breedlove herself, I'm pretty sure. His sister." I stared straight ahead at Milly's cup of coffee in front of her, wondering if it was better to pretend I hadn't seen them.

I'd say *hello* on my way out, but surely, it'd be too awkward for anything more than that. I didn't want to disturb them. Maybe they were taking Val out to celebrate her latest book release.

"Hmm." Milly's eyes sparkled as she had no qualms about staring at the door. "You said he was *fine*, but you didn't properly explain he was fine as all *that*."

My heart rate soared, but at least she'd spoken softly.

I wasn't going to have the excuse to pretend I hadn't seen them walk in, though, because Vera's loud, sonorous voice was impossible to miss.

"Oh, stop being such a baby, Valerie. It was *one little cavity*."

"*Mother*." Even Valerie's hushed rebuke was fairly loud.

The few other people in the restaurant turned to look as the trio followed our server to a table by the window.

Vera shielded her eyes and squinted. "It's a bit bright out to be so close to the window. Can we have something farther back?"

"Of course." The server gestured to the side. Toward Milly and me.

Valerie cradled her cheek, which did appear a bit swollen, and shook her head. "I told you, I can't even *eat* for half an hour—"

"It'll take that long before we get our food," Vera said. "Now hush. Today's supposed to be a celebration."

"If I'd known you could have gotten off today, Mother, you could have taken Val yourself—" Allen turned to follow the server, then cut himself short.

Because he was staring at me.

The server gestured to a table just a few feet away from our own.

"Quinn!" Vera noticed me for the first time. "What a surprise! I didn't know Allen invited you!"

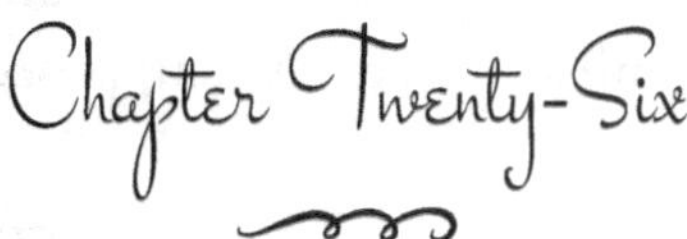

Chapter Twenty-Six

Milly gazed between Vera and me. "Invited you?" she echoed.

I shook my head. I didn't know what the woman was talking about.

Vera barreled straight ahead, practically knocking Val over to get to me. I noticed the twins giving each other an arched brow, a sigh escaping Allen's lips as Val sat down at the offered table and our server went back to put in our dessert orders.

Dessert. There was no chance we could up and leave this awkwardness now, was there?

"How have you been, darling?" Vera asked, as if we'd known each other for years instead of all of a few minutes. She stood beside our table like the manager of the place come to check to make sure we were enjoying ourselves, looking from Milly to me and back. "And who's this?"

"Milly," I said, too stunned at the situation to do more than numbly play along. "My best friend."

"Well, come join us! The both of you!" Vera beamed. She was dressed all business today, too, a bright red blazer and pencil skirt combo, her hair pinned back into a sleek updo.

"Mother, please, let them be." Allen slid in beside her, putting a hand on her forearm and sort of forcibly turning her back toward Val. He looked stunning—as usual. But he'd gone to a bit of effort, despite his protestations that he preferred the comfortable loungewear he wore at home. Pressed navy slacks that clung stiffly to his thighs. A pale blue button-up that was only missing a jacket and tie to put him somewhere in a board room. Business casual, then.

"Just being friendly," she said. "You know how rarely you introduce me to any friends. Excuse me, *clients*. Clients with whom you have tangible chemistry."

"Thanks for that, Mother," Allen said, forcing the widest smile on his face—probably wider than the server's had been.

"All right, I'll give you a minute." Vera fluffed her hand in the air. "Valerie Louise, stop cradling your cheek like that." She stomped over to the table and sat down beside her adult daughter, who was dressed in a floral blouse and sleek, navy pants that made her seem like the picture of a vintage pin-up model. Yet Vera was shaking her head at her as if she were a misbehaving toddler.

Allen let out a sigh as he watched her, then turned back to Milly and me. He focused on my friend, and I caught sight of the slight twitch of his jaw. "Hi," he said, his eyes flittering back and forth between us. "Nice to meet you. Sorry to disturb your lunch." He took a step back as if to go.

"Hi." Milly wriggled her fingers up at Allen. "Quinn's told me *all about* you."

My breath hitched as Allen froze, his gaze meeting mine. "Has she?"

I had, uh, not given her *all* the details. Yet. I'd still been processing everything that had gone on between us.

But she'd gotten the picture.

"Hi," I said softly, all other words having left my brain at the sight of his big, brown eyes. "I, um, saw the cats."

Milly's head cocked, but Allen was on my wavelength and picked up what I meant right away.

"On Instagram," he said.

"And in the newsletter." I nervously took a sip of my tea, cradling the glass in both hands in front of me. "Looks like readers loved my suggestion to include them."

Allen chuckled. "I won't let the cats know. They have big enough egos."

"What about Pearl?" I asked, feeling the tension I'd expected slipping from my shoulders. Talking to him was so natural for me. Which was strange because talking to people I didn't know never felt very natural.

Though I knew Allen intimately. I just didn't *know* him well. Yet.

"Oh, I thought about it for a second, but I didn't want to ask Val," he said. "Plus, then I'd be answering questions about dogs all the time and people would want to see how the pets all get along."

I giggled. I'd almost forgotten his aversion to canines. "But Val doesn't mind pretending the cats are hers?"

"Excuse me, hon." The server offered Allen a smile as she squeezed past, setting a slice of key lime pie in front of Milly and a slice of apple pie in front of me before heading over toward the table with Vera and Val.

Allen stepped back, his brow furrowed just a bit. "I'll leave you to it," he said, his voice short, clipped.

"What was that about?" Milly asked, a quiet hiss. "He seemed a bit insulted."

"I... don't know." She'd sensed something off about him, too. What had changed? We'd been talking like before, things had seemed so easy, and then... Just because our dessert had come?

Allen was seated between his mother and his sister now, picking up a menu and glancing it over, though his eyes seemed sort of glazed.

Vera spoke to the server, interrupting her daughter to ask about appetizers—the question rung out heavily throughout the restaurant and was hard to miss.

"So—are you and Allen, like, *seeing* each other?" Milly asked, digging into her pie.

I took a bite of my own, chewing slowly.

Before I could answer Milly's question, Vera leaned toward us, her voice growing even louder. "Quinn, dear, are you sure you won't join us? We're celebrating Vallen's new book release!"

Vallen's new…

Did she mean "Valerie"?

"*Mother*, would you *please* not make a spectacle—" Allen started.

"Oh, hush, Vallen Leon. I'm your mother. I'm allowed to embarrass you. I don't care how big you get." She reached over and pinched his cheek.

Vallen. Leon.

V.L.

Poe and Raven were V.L. Breedlove's cats.

Allen Cox was V.L. Breedlove.

Allen was my favorite author. Not Val.

I suddenly felt sick. Delicious, sweet apple pie was turning to stone in my stomach.

My fork clattered to the plate and I shot up. "Excuse me," I said to Milly, rushing to the back of the restaurant and to the bathroom.

I couldn't even look at Allen's table. My heart thudded wildly, dark stars at the edges of my vision. I practically shouldered open the bathroom door. It was a single-use, so I locked the door and leaned back against it, just catching my breath.

All this time. *All this time*, I'd been with my favorite new author. I'd been talking to him as if his sister were said author.

And he'd never corrected me.

I'd thought I was so clever, gathering all those "clues." Like the initials "V.L." even meant a thing. Anyone could write with any initials they wanted. Where had "Breedlove" come from?

I was so glad I'd stopped myself short of coming up with some asinine explanation, like Val's dog was a kind of "breeder" she "loved." *That* was how far ahead of myself I'd gotten in my foray into my amateur sleuthing this past week.

I'd *met* my favorite author. I'd *slept with* my favorite author.

I paced the bathroom, just flailing my hands wildly, taking deep breaths.

And he'd *known* I'd been off-base. And he'd said nothing!

Someone knocked on the door.

"Just a minute," I said, rushing to the sink and turning on the water. I sniffled and looked up in horror as I washed my hands—out of habit, if nothing else— to find two small tears streaking down my face.

I wasn't *sad*. I was embarrassed. Hurt.

I felt stupid.

"Quinn?" Allen's voice echoed out from the other side of the door softly.

Oh, god.

I shut off the water and took shallow breaths, as if he'd go away if I didn't make a sound.

Only this genius here had already called out and revealed she was inside, thinking it was someone else just waiting to use the toilet.

Shit, shit, shit. Think. Think, Quinn.

"I just wanted to make sure you're okay," he said through the door. "You got up from the table kind of fast."

"Yeah, um..." My voice squeaked, betraying the sense of calm I'd hoped to convey. "Sorry."

What was I apologizing for? I winced.

"Can we talk?"

Those were three words that almost never led to anything good.

I didn't *do* drama.

And not in some kind of judgmental sense. I was just... Quinn. Introverted, bookworm me.

Things happened to the people I read about.

Not to me.

"Outside?" he added.

Right. Nobody had a "Can we talk?" conversation through a bathroom door. Not comfortably, anyway.

Wiping my eyes and steeling myself, I reached for the handle and opened the door.

The corner of Allen's mouth quirked into an uneasy smile. "Hi again."

"Hi," I said softly. My heart melted.

There we were, falling back into a sense of easiness again.

But then the reality of everything that had sent me running into the bathroom crashed back into me.

"Milly," I said, looking at his feet. "I can't talk long. I should get back to her."

"And your slice of mostly uneaten pie," he added.

Oh. That, too.

"My mother will *most definitely* miss me if I'm gone too long." He let out a deep breath. "I won't take too much of your time. Promise." He gestured to the back door of the restaurant, which led out to a patio that no one was currently using. It was only just warm enough to stand an outdoor conversation, let alone dining out there.

"Okay," I said quietly, and I followed him outside.

Allen pulled out a chair at one of the restaurant's patio tables and hovered behind it, as if waiting for me to sit in it. I did, unable to make eye contact with him, my hands clenching the rough khaki material of my Capri pants.

He took the seat across from me and folded his hands over the table.

"You feeling all right?" he asked.

I nodded, biting my lip.

"I thought maybe, given how quickly you got out of there, it was because my mother revealed something you didn't know."

"You're V.L. Breedlove," I said, finally meeting his eyes. They narrowed slightly, his Adam's apple bobbing at his throat. "Not your sister."

"I wanted to tell you earlier."

"But you didn't."

"Because you seemed *so convinced* you'd figured it

out." He sighed and ran a hand through his dark hair. "It got more and more awkward. The more sure you were it was Val, the stranger it felt to admit the truth."

"But you didn't correct me," I said softly.

He furrowed his brow. "I'm not in the habit of revealing my author identity to every person I meet. That's why I use a pen name."

"With your initials. Your birth ones."

"It's a nod to both my grandfathers," he said. "And my sister—my family. And my past. And I thought it had a better ring to it than 'A.L.' anyway."

"And 'Breedlove'?"

The corner of his mouth twitched up a bit. "No particular significance. It's a real surname I found when trying to come up with one. I just thought it sounded racy. Though, if you Google it, you'll find it means something more like 'catches wolves,' rather than having anything to do with romance."

"Oh, I can think of a few *wolves* that have something to do with romance," I said. "Wolves of the alpha variety."

"I really need to write a shifter romance, don't I?"

I opened my mouth to retort, but then I realized I really wanted to see his take on the genre.

His take. Because *he* was my new favorite author.

"But why hide even your gender?" I asked.

Allen's mouth pursed. "The majority of romance authors are women—"

"But you don't think they'd read books put out by

a man? Especially one as smoking hot as you are?" I gestured across the table at him. He smirked.

Oh, no. This wasn't the time for me to be stroking his ego.

His ego. He'd kept hinting that V.L. Breedlove had a bit of an ego.

"Well, I wouldn't put a picture of myself up anywhere either way," he said. "And I'm careful to only refer to the author as 'they'—"

"You mean, instead of 'I'? Why do you pose as your own PA anyway? Do you even have any other clients beside *yourself*?"

Allen tugged at his collar. "Well, just my sister and her business. The writing and marketing takes enough of my time. And so far, it's been plenty for me to count it as my full-time income. I've been fortunate that way."

I thought back to him telling me he'd had an agent once—had written a book that would never see the light of day. Yeah, *one* book that would never see the light of day.

"What about your agent? The book you tried to publish traditionally? Did you jump on the romance genre because you thought you could milk it or something?"

Allen let out a slow, steady breath. "My agent and I parted ways a while ago. And I *did* try to write more marketable books once I thought about self-publishing. But that didn't mean I was trying to 'milk' it. I did my research and really dove into the genre—and I loved it. Writing it is so much fun. My mother was always a casual romance reader, and I was aware of the big-time authors growing up—but the indie landscape changed things up a bit. The more I read, the more I couldn't wait to try my hand at it."

"Your mother knows," I said. "That you write these sexy books."

"She does." Allen winced. "Val knew and there was no keeping it from my parents. Not after the books took off and they kept asking what, exactly, I was doing working from home that was keeping me from helping out with either of their businesses. Val, too."

Val's fiancée, Maya, had even mentioned Val and Allen worked together.

"So what *does* Val do?" I asked. "If you're your own PA..."

"She has an editing and proofreading business—which I help her market. She mostly edits for me. She's always been good at that, even if she's never been that interested in reading fiction."

My jaw dropped. "You said she wasn't much of a reader."

"She's not." He shrugged. "Just because you're good at something doesn't mean it's what you choose to do in your free time. She mostly edits for businesses outside of my work. But she does enjoy my books. Or at least she claims to."

"Val doesn't strike me as the type to lie to boost someone's ego," I pointed out. "Not even for her brother. Maybe *especially* not for her brother."

Allen chuckled, his eye twinkling. "You know my family so well already."

Heat shot from my cheeks down to my toes. He was only teasing me, of course. I hadn't even *met* all of his family, and the ones I *had* met...

My eyes darted back to the restaurant. Milly seemed engrossed in her phone, but she kept looking my way. Allen's mother and sister were positively *staring* out at us.

I shivered. It was just *slightly* too cool to be outside for too long in the shade.

"I shouldn't keep Milly much longer," I said, getting to my feet. "She has to meet up with her dad to get her car fixed later today."

Allen cleared his throat and stood, too. "Right. And my mother will be descending on us like a vulture with carrion if I don't show my face again soon."

He walked with me to the door but caught my elbow as I went to reach for the handle. "I don't feel like we're done here—are you free tomorrow evening? I thought I might invite you..."

What more was there to say? He'd been under no obligation to reveal the truth to me, not after just a week. But I felt like an idiot for guessing so wrong—and he'd only made it worse by not correcting me.

I tried to keep my reply cool, collected. "What's going on tomorrow?"

"The fruit of our efforts."

Allen had insisted I invite whomever I liked to his condo today—and had warned me to expect not just his family, but Bodhi and Rory and C.J. and Jake, too.

I didn't have many people to invite beyond that, so I'd extended an invitation to both Evangeline and Milly, as long as Milly was still in town for the week. Evangeline had had to pass since her son had a soccer game, but Milly had agreed to come with me.

She was especially eager after the strange scene at the restaurant yesterday.

A strange scene I'd finally spilled my guts out to her about last night, after we'd put the restaurant far behind us and she'd finished with the stuff she'd had to do with her parents the rest of the day.

"So, you ready to christen some new mini libraries?" Milly asked from my passenger seat. She nudged me. "And are you sure I won't be a third wheel?"

"From the sounds of it, there's bound to be about a dozen wheels." I gripped the steering wheel tighter, even though I'd already shut off the engine. We were in the parking lot of Allen and Val's condo complex. I could only see the very edge of the courtyard from where we were, but it was clear there was a small crowd gathered around something.

"You didn't get to talk much with him at the restaurant," Milly said.

"There's nothing to talk *about*." Even as the words left my lips, I knew they were a lie.

I didn't know what I wanted from Allen—I didn't

feel right expecting an apology. But if he'd invited me over to talk—just the two of us—maybe I'd have the right to hope for... something.

Then again, he had invited me here. Even if it was for a group activity. That meant he wanted us on good terms. I was his fan, after all.

His fan. I still couldn't get over that.

I'd re-read *Corrupt Me* last night and had continued thinking about it in a haze all day today while trying to get some work done. It was probably my favorite of Breedlove's works. Now I couldn't stop seeing Allen as the hero. I knew not every protagonist of his was identical, that he wasn't just writing himself into every story, but there was something about Gideon in that book. Now that I'd met Allen's mother, I couldn't even separate her from Gideon's mother in that book.

And he'd said she *knew* about his books? Hopefully, she didn't see herself in those pages, because that fictional woman had been overbearing to the max.

Perhaps Allen only took some inspiration from real life and exaggerated it.

Perhaps that closet full of sex toys... Perhaps he hadn't reenacted *every* steamy sex scene down to the very detail with a bevy of gorgeous women he'd picked up at clubs.

Allen had told me himself he didn't even *like* going to clubs.

"Come on." Milly opened the car door. "I know

things are going to be awkward between you for a while, but better to rip off the Band-Aid."

She had a point. I hadn't yet spread the news about Allen's identity far and wide—that was his secret to tell, not mine, but given the things Milly had overheard and seen at the restaurant, I figured she'd deserved to know the details.

Evangeline and my mom... Well, they didn't *need* to know just yet. Even if they were Breedlove superfans, too.

I caught up with Milly at the end of the parking lot and we slipped in behind Bodhi at the edge of the crowd.

Everyone was talking amongst themselves, or helping with the installation. Allen and a man who could have been his twin brother, but for the overly tanned complexion, the wrinkles working into deep lines across his face, and the all-white hair, were hammering a very well-built mini library structure into the ground. Other people I didn't recognize were working on patching the grass, several bushes that had once been in the dirt stacked in one parking spot next to a landscaper's truck. Beside Allen and the man I presumed to be his father, Jake was painting a second mini library already installed. One side depicted a pirate ship on a stormy sea, and the other blank side he was working on was shaping up to be a collection of fairies flying through a forest. My dad would have been impressed. They sort of made our boxes look simplistic in comparison.

"There you are." Bodhi did a double-take as he looked over his shoulder and then turned fully toward me. "Allen promised me he'd invited you, but I was starting to worry."

"My fault we're a bit late," said Milly with a tight smile. "We had dinner with my parents before coming over."

"Hello," said Bodhi, his gaze flicking back and forth between us.

"Milly," I said, by way of introduction. "My best friend. She's visiting her parents this week. Milly, this is Bodhi, one of my neighbors."

"Enchanted," Bodhi said, offering his hand for a shake. "But why is this the first time I'm hearing about her?" He eyed me suspiciously.

"What? You wouldn't believe I had friends outside of my head," I said, only partially teasing him. "Weren't you the one who constantly harps on me getting too lost in books?"

Bodhi fought back a smile. "I believe my exact words were you had to get laid."

"Oh, she did." Milly elbowed me.

"*Milly!*" My eyes widened. Was this the thanks I got for going into too many details?

Bodhi gasped. Then he looked over at Allen, whose back was to us as he and his father shifted the mini library's base a bit in the dirt. Bodhi looked back to me, his brows arched. "I had my suspicions, based on the gossip Evangeline and Val shared with me."

"Where is Val?" I asked, making a great show of

looking around the small crowd gathered. "And Rory, for that matter?"

"It's a casual wine-and-dine sort of event." Bodhi waved a hand at the condo I knew to be Val's, which had its door propped open. Almost as if on cue, Rory stepped out, two glasses of white champagne in his hands.

Bodhi threaded his arms through mine and Milly's, guiding us toward his husband. "So. Are you going to spill the details or make me wring them out of you?"

My face heated. "I can't... He's right—" I looked over my shoulder as Vera's familiar voice let out a great cry of delight.

"Oh, it looks marvelous!" Vera stepped out from where she'd been talking to the landscapers and clapped her hands as Allen and his dad stepped back to look at the second mini library. "I almost didn't let you convince me to pull up the landscaping, but they look marvelous. That art! I can't wait to see the second one fully painted."

Rory met up with us and Bodhi dropped his grip on Milly and me to grab his glass of champagne. We exchanged *hello*s and I made another introduction.

"Do you want anything to drink?" Rory offered.

Milly shook her head, and I answered *no*. I couldn't stop looking back at Allen with his parents. He hadn't seemed to notice I'd shown up yet. Not that I could blame him.

I hadn't gone up and said *hello* or anything.

"Pearl!"

Far off down the courtyard, Val's shout echoed out toward us. She and Maya were small figures in the distance, both setting toward us at a jog, but they were no match for the creamy ball of fur barreling down the grass, a long, black leash dragging behind her.

"Uh-oh," said Bodhi, taking a step back and lifting his champagne glass into the air. "That little fuzzball is stronger than she looks."

And she was headed right for us.

"Quinn?" Allen's voice grabbed my attention.

His jaw was slackened, his eyebrows drawn together. His gaze darted to the super-sonic sphere of fur plummeting toward me—and he leaped out between us and the little terror.

Chapter Twenty-Eight

"Pearl!" Allen blocked the little dog from reaching Bodhi, Rory, Milly, and me, taking the brunt of the dog's intense affection as she jumped up and slammed her front paws against his shins over and over.

His arms were out wide, as if the little creature could jump five feet and launch herself at us on either side of him.

I laughed. Allen's gorgeously-sharp jawline all tense, his eyes squinting as if he couldn't bear to look. All over the little dog who, admittedly, was yipping loud enough to burst some eardrums.

"All right, girl." Rory handed Bodhi his glass and bent down to take up Pearl's leash. "Let's go back to your mommies."

Bodhi took the last sip of his champagne and then finished off his husband's in his other hand for good measure. "Thought for sure she was going to get dirt on our pants. Close one. I offer my thanks to our dashing savior."

Milly laughed.

Allen turned around sheepishly as Rory managed to direct the trotting dog back toward Val and Maya halfway down the courtyard.

"Hi," he said to me, his eyes locking with mine.

"Hi," I said back. "Thank you for… the rescue. I know dogs make you nervous. Even Pearl."

"Especially Pearl," he said.

"Um, Milly, dear? Do you want to come with me inside?" Bodhi tilted his head toward Val's open doorway. "I could use a refill." He held up both empty glasses.

"Sure." Milly sent me an amused smirk.

She always had liked a man who could make her laugh.

I did, too. But I didn't know if I should keep laughing at Allen's obvious fear of canines.

After Bodhi and Milly had walked away, Allen and I stood there a moment. People moved and conversed around the courtyard, reminding me that we weren't alone—but for now, with Allen looking longingly down at me like that, it felt as if the world around us had slipped away.

I had to force myself to look behind him, or I might have melted right there on the spot.

"You got those installed really quickly," I said.

"I talked my mom into rearranging the landscaping just yesterday morning," he said. "And then my dad and I built them last night. Jake's supposed to finish the paintings by the weekend, but I thought you might want to swing by and give it your stamp of approval. It's Val's turn to host dinner for her friends, so we sort of made a thing out of it." He gestured around.

"They look great," I said. "I can't wait to see the finished paintings. I'm worried whatever Jake comes up with for the romance box will put the Ooh-La-La Box to shame."

"Never." Allen took my hand in his and squeezed it. "That mini library is the one that started it all for me. In fact, I was wondering if we could name this one the same thing. The 'Ooh-La-La Box Junior.'"

"I think the 'Junior' part might cause a few mix-ups if you don't want kids rummaging around the steamy reads." Though my stomach practically leaped into my throat at his touch, my hand felt warm and secure in his. "What about..." I tapped my lips with the fingers on my free hand. "The 'Va-Va-Voom Box'?"

Allen clamped his lips together. "I like the sound of that."

"The Va-Va-Voom Box it is. Too racy a name for my neighborhood, but since *yours* is home to a real-life steamy book author..." My voice lowered. "Tell me I'm not the only one who didn't know."

"You're not." He pointed toward Rory, who was still speaking to Val and Maya. Pearl, securely attached to Val's hand on her leash, was running circles around them, practically tying their ankles together.

"I haven't told Rory, Bodhi, Jake, or C.J. They're

Val's friends more than mine, and I don't need that kind of pressure. Though I think Bodhi has it pinned down to being Val or me."

"That's one step further than I got, considering I was so stuck on it being Val."

"Because you assumed it had to be a woman," he said. "And that is precisely why I try to keep it vague. Women authors have fought hard to earn their spots on top of the genre. I respect that."

"And take advantage of it to hide your identity," I said.

"That, too."

"You know, the majority of romance readers are women, too. And plenty of them would *gobble up* any information about a sexy male author who writes sexy books. You already have a newsletter. Some of the other male authors I follow sort of, like, share all sorts of details about their lives. And they get fan mail about it, too, judging by their replies in the next newsletter."

"That's one thing I *want to* avoid, though," he said. "I'm not big on sharing those kinds of details with just anyone." He grimaced. "Other than maybe the themes from my life that work their way into my books."

"Aren't you writing about a green-skinned alien hero soon?" I teased.

He smirked. "I did say *themes*. Not details."

"Unless you're hiding something else from me."

"I'm not from Mars," he said. "I promise you that."

I laughed despite myself. If I'd found out there *were*

an alien among my social circle, I'd have probably guessed it was the wrong person, judging by my track record thus far.

Good thing the stakes had been a lot lower than alien invasion.

Though knowing V.L. Breedlove, the next book was going to be about one *sexy* alien invasion.

My hand was growing a bit clammy in his grip. But the last thing I wanted was to let go. "Did you ever think, 'God, what an idiot. She keeps thinking Val's the author?' at any point over the past few days?"

"No." All amusement vanished from Allen's face. "If anything, I patted myself on the back for keeping it from being too obvious."

"Of course you did." I smirked.

He smiled back, but then grew serious. "After the other night, I thought it might be time to confess."

"But you didn't."

"I got distracted by that paperback crisis. And then when I went to speak to you again later that night—"

"I kept putting my foot in my mouth," I offered. A sigh escaped my lips. "I'm sorry."

"You have nothing to apologize for."

"I sort of do. I wasn't sure what kinds of expectations you had. Don't get me wrong—the other night was *amazing* for me—but I thought maybe, well, maybe you didn't want a repeat of it. Maybe I was just too vanilla. Or out of practice. Or too nerdy."

"Are you kidding me?" Allen dropped my hand, his

jaw growing a bit slack. "I haven't been able to *stop* thinking about that night ever since. And I knew I fucked something up between us—I knew it was getting to be a bit too late to tell you the truth, too. I didn't know what to do." He took a step forward, his face lingering over mine. "But I can't focus. I've tried to keep busy, but I can't write—all I want to do is jump to the sex scenes and write down every little thing I wish I could do to you."

I hiccupped, my voice coming out like a squeak. "*To* me?"

He chuckled, his voice a deep rumble. "With you. With your permission."

"Does this mean you haven't finished writing the next book?"

Allen winced, his eyes fluttering rapidly. "You sound like my sister. She keeps riding my ass to put more space between release dates."

"She's probably right about that," I said, taking a hold of his thick bicep and drawing my lips closer to his. "I can feel the tension in your muscles. You'll burn out if you push yourself too hard."

"You could help me relax," he said, each word a promise of more.

"I'd like that," I whispered, his breath warm against my face.

He pressed his lips to mine, a sweet, short kiss. Then he seized another hungrier one, his palm sliding through the hair at the back of my head in order to press my mouth harder against his own.

"Allen! Oh, Quinn! You came! I *knew* you were dating, you naughty things. You must meet my husband." Vera's voice broke through my focus, bringing me crashing through to the moment—and the fact that we were hardly alone.

Allen and I broke apart, but he stayed slightly bent over, his forehead pressing atop mine. His dad seemed to be keeping Allen's mom from stepping closer just yet, their conversation a murmur in the background.

"Help me work all those sexual fantasies I've been writing into the draft of my alien romance out of my system?" he asked, his voice hardly more than a whisper.

"Only if they don't involve alien tentacles."

He snorted. "And if they do?"

"Well, I can't promise I'll react like your heroine actually would in that situation. I'd probably be laughing too hard to play it serious. But even so, you have to swear not to cut a single one of those scenes from the draft."

He leaned back and arched a brow at me, his lips curling into a smile.

"Hey, I'm V.L. Breedlove's fan," I said. "And I've got to make sure I campaign on behalf of her readers. His readers. *Your* readers."

He kissed me again. "The trouble with dating a bookworm is—I'm not sure I can match the fantasies she's had while reading."

"You put a whole lot of them there," I pointed out.

"Oh, I've only just started."

If his parents hadn't chosen that moment to slide into our conversation—his dad throwing me an apologetic look as Vera prattled on and introduced him—I might have dragged him back to his condo right then and there.

Epilogue

"I really didn't think I'd be up for an alien hero romance, but Breedlove has scratched an itch I didn't even realize I *had*." Evangeline stopped stacking the plates of mostly eaten snacks left over from the Ooh-La-La Book Club meeting just long enough to put a hand on her waist and wink at me, her hip jutting out toward the cover of V.L. Breedlove's *Alien Lover Daddy*.

No, Allen and I hadn't roleplayed with Allen as an alien. Yet. We'd been too busy trying out other fantasies.

Evangeline wasn't too far off. After reading this book, I was starting to come around to the idea of the alien roleplay.

"I'll be sure to tell Lucas that," Bodhi teased as he walked by with a garbage bag and started gathering anything else the other members of Club had left behind.

Evangeline's cheeks pinked, most likely at the thought of her husband knowing about her newfound penchant for green-skinned alien men.

I knew the feeling. When everyone had talked about their favorite scenes in the book, Joanna had brought up the one sex scene Allen had still been *working the kinks out of*, so to speak, over the past month and a half. I *may* have had a bit of empirical input into that scene, even if we hadn't gone so far as to pretend to be an alien and his human captive.

No wonder Allen didn't want people to know he was V.L. Breedlove. For one thing, he'd already let people know about his "empirical experience" in the author bio alone. All because he'd been trying to spice it up. And now he was stuck with having told the world something secret and sexy.

Well, that and he'd written so many books that had turned so many people on, it'd be arguably a little weird to put a face to the one responsible if that face didn't want that kind of attention.

Though I still believed *his face* could sell even more romance books.

"What's that on your Kindle?" Evangeline asked as she brought the plates over to Bodhi's sink. I was gathering the wineglasses, slipping the stems between my fingers, and forgot I'd woken up my Kindle Fire in order to get a picture of everyone with their *Alien Lover Daddy* signed paperbacks for Breedlove's newsletter before they'd left.

As everyone had started exchanging their goodbyes

for the week, I'd snuck in another chapter of a certain unpublished manuscript. The screensaver on the Kindle hadn't gone off yet.

"Oh, Allen's first—" I cut myself short. "Allen wrote a book a few years ago. I finally convinced him to let me read it."

"Ah." Bodhi smacked his lips as he reached the trash can in the kitchen and started emptying it. "The infamous story about his family that he's never let a soul read. Outside of his former agent and a dozen publishing house editors who rejected him."

"Your author PA boyfriend's a writer, too?" Evangeline asked. She lowered her voice. "I don't suppose you ever got him or his sister to admit that she's really—"

"My lips are sealed." I set down the last of the wineglasses and made a zipper motion over my mouth.

"I see, I see." Evangeline's eyes sparkled. "Maybe *whoever* V.L. Breedlove is will stop by for an Ooh-La-La Book Club meeting one of these days." Evangeline looked to Bodhi as he tied the garbage bag up. "I see Allen's sister in our neighborhood fairly often."

"Oh, they won't spill the beans," Bodhi said. He locked eyes with me—and I had a feeling he actually knew the truth. "And I'm not going to pry. I wait for *others* to slip up. More fun that way."

I yelped at his hard stare. I wasn't sure when he'd figured it out. *If* he really knew it was Allen and not Val. I had to look away and cleared my throat, closing out Allen's unpublished manuscript.

It really *was* good, even if not quite the typical book I'd read. I could see why he'd garnered some professional interest with it.

But the more I got to know his family, the more blatantly obvious their respective counterparts became in this manuscript.

If *that* book had seen the light of day—and he'd put his face to it—he would have been a thousand times more embarrassed than he would have been to be known for publishing dirty romance books.

Not to mention, there was a sex scene in what I'd read so far, too. A little rougher than the ones he'd perfected over time, but it was there. The spark of something to come.

I chuckled to myself. I felt like some kind of book critic now.

I *was* a trusted beta reader for every one of Breedlove's books going forward.

And I'd taken my "super fan" cap off enough to make a few valid criticisms. On occasion. If the manuscript warranted it. So I thought.

"Oh! It's late." Evangeline rushed over to the couch where she and I had been sitting and grabbed her paperback and purse. "Thank you for hosting, Bodhi. Let me know if you can come next week."

"You mean, when we're not reading a Breedlove book for once?" Bodhi chuckled darkly. "Who'd have thought we'd get through their bibliography so quickly?"

Their. He was playing footsy with the gender of the author.

He couldn't hide his smirk as our gazes met.

"Well, that and Breedlove finally slowed down her release schedule." Evangeline headed for the top of Bodhi's staircase. "Gives us time to catch up."

She said her goodbyes and Bodhi followed after her, bringing his garbage down to his attached garage.

Yes. The release schedule.

As a fan, I kind of hated myself for that—even if I had early access to anything Breedlove put out. But as Allen's girlfriend, I'd agreed with his sister. He'd been pushing himself too hard.

His income from backlog sales was fairly consistent from month to month. Even if switching to an every-other-month release schedule meant every other month was a dip in income without that new release bonus, he was doing just fine.

What had really convinced him was that the relaxing in schedule allowed him to not scramble to get the paperback versions and audiobooks ready before the release of the e-books.

That, and he *may* have wanted to come up from his computer a little more often to do things with me. We'd only known each other a few months, but they'd been jam-packed. I'd even had to take a *little* cut in the number of freelance jobs I'd accepted. We didn't go far —even just going for a walk together downtown was fun, or curling up together with a cat or two to watch a movie at home—but I'd enjoyed so many good meals, cooked by someone who had too many damn talents for one man.

If he'd gotten out from behind his computer more than for an occasional hookup, he'd have been snatched up long ago by now.

Then again, it would take a special kind of woman to embrace our "alone together" time, too. In the quiet or with some soft music playing, he'd be writing, I'd be reading...

A paradise to a bookworm like me, especially knowing he was writing more things for me to read. And when we were done having alone time for the evening, well, there were plenty of other things for us to do. He *did* have a closet full of sex toys, after all.

My phone buzzed from my purse on the couch, and I dug it out. I pushed aside a couple of alien-hero-related messages from both my mom and Milly that I saw on the screen—it was release week, and I could finally talk spoilers about the book with other readers—to see a text from Allen.

Book Club over? Should I walk you home?

I laughed. *I live a building over from Bodhi's,* I wrote back.

Can never be too cautious, he replied almost immediately. *Besides, I got the pic from you and figured your meeting was about over. I'm waiting out front.*

Bodhi appeared at the top of the stairs, humming a rather loud tune. He clapped his hands together. "Quinn, I love you, and thank you for helping me clean up—but Rory's due home any minute and that book has got me *hot and bothered*, little green men or not, so…"

"I think you mean 'big green men,'" I pointed out.

He arched an eyebrow. "*Very* big green men."

We both laughed and I gathered up my paperback and phone, which I tucked into my purse, then snatched my Kindle from where I'd left it on the counter. "Thanks for hosting," I said as I passed him at the top of the stairs. "Enjoy your evening."

"You, too." Bodhi stuck his tongue out. "I *might* have seen a familiar vehicle out front when I closed the door after Evangeline."

"That's my escort."

"Look at *you*," Bodhi shouted down the stairs, chuckling. "Positively beaming. I knew you needed some action. You kids have fun!"

"Yes, Mr. Nosy," I shot back up to him, slipping on my shoes in front of the door.

"You tell your *author boyfriend* I want to read his unpublished manuscript someday," Bodhi called as I grabbed the door handle. "Since I've read all the other books he's written."

I turned and looked back up the stairs.

Bodhi smirked.

I made another zipper motion over my lips and headed out into the night.

It was fairly warm, despite the sun having set, on this summer evening. The crickets chirped as I headed down the walk from Bodhi and Rory's condo leading to the sidewalk out front. Allen exited from his jeep, then grabbed me by the waist as I approached, planting a quick kiss on my lips.

"Good evening," he said as he leaned back and smiled.

"Hello, you." I poked at his chest with the Kindle Fire he'd crushed between us. "I just saw you this morning."

"And it's been a long few hours without you."

He kissed me again.

We parted, and I took a deep breath, my eyes closed, his forehead pressing against the top of my head.

"I *did* miss you," I admitted. "But I've been reading."

He chuckled and pulled back. "I'd take that as an insult, but I know you better than that."

My cheeks darkened. "I just mean—"

"The time flew by," he said, shifting to my side and wrapping one arm around me. "I get it. Just please tell me you weren't reading—"

"Your trunked manuscript."

He winced.

"Come on," I said as we started walking toward my condo. "It's not *that* bad."

"Just a little bad," he muttered.

"No!" I hadn't meant that. My tongue stuck out. I would never get better at speaking around him, even if I felt more and more comfortable with him every day. Of course, he still made my heart race—and *other parts* of me tingle—every day. So that didn't help matters.

"It's just that I see so much of your family in it," I said.

He snorted. "Yeah. I was working through some things when I wrote it. Still am, maybe."

"The protagonist's mother winds up losing her business because she's so rude to an important client, though," I pointed out. I didn't know how any of the plot would be resolved yet. Between Ooh-La-La Book Club and my gorgeous boyfriend showing up, I hadn't quite had the time to finish it.

"I know. She'd kill me if she read that."

"What about Val?" I said. "The protagonist isn't a twin, but his sister is awfully *annoying* and—"

"Yeah, she's never reading it, either." He grimaced. "Maya might kill me *for* Val."

"Maya? She seems too sweet."

Allen squeezed my arm as we reached the area with the mailboxes. "She's ferocious when it comes to defending her lady love. I made the mistake of being crabby at Val over some editorial suggestions once." He shuddered. "I was lucky Maya didn't sic Pearl on me."

"Pearl doesn't need an excuse to latch on to your legs."

"True." He rolled his eyes.

"So Maya and your family know about Breedlove. But no one's read your first manuscript?"

"Well, outside of some agents and a few editors... No."

"But you trusted me to?" I stopped, clutching the tablet to my chest as if to cradle it. As if to cradle the very feeling of trust and love that him offering me the chance to read this manuscript provided.

Allen kissed my forehead. "I couldn't say *no* to you."

"You did the first few times I asked to read it."

"Well, I'll never say *no* again." He winked.

I poked him in the bicep. "I'll try to keep my requests reasonable, then."

"Hmm... An obsessed fan who's reasonable."

"I am *not* obsessed." My jaw dropped in pretend shock. Then I laughed. "Okay, maybe a little. You're just too damn good an author, Allen Leon Cox."

"Don't you mean V.L. Breedlove?"

"I said what I said. But Breedlove, too."

"You know exactly how to feed my ego." Allen gave me another kiss on the forehead and we started shuffling back toward my building.

"Whatever it takes for you to feed me more books. And delicious food." I stood on my toes and pecked his lips.

We froze for a while, enjoying a longer kiss, my heart thudding and a jolt of electricity shooting up and down from my core to my head and the tips of my toes.

"I love you, Quinn Simmons," he whispered.

"I love you, too, Allen Cox."

The creaking sound of a hinge in need of oiling drew our attention. No one was getting their mail this late at night, though.

"I forgot to tell you," said Allen. "I checked on the stock of Breedlove books in the Ooh-La-La Box while I was waiting for your meeting to disperse, and the hinges need some WD-40. I can grab some next time I come by."

"Checking on your autographed book stock." I nudged my hip against his, still clutching my Kindle to my chest. "Any copies of *Alien Lover Daddy* left, Mr. Author PA?"

"Just one," Allen said. "Though I suppose everyone in the neighborhood who's interested got their copy and joined the Book Club."

A dog barked and Allen stiffened. It was the higher-pitched toy dog variety, like Pearl. Allen's tension was immediate.

"It's all right," I whispered. Ahead of us, where the mini donation libraries were, a figure stepped out from the warm, orange light illuminating the boxes.

"Cupcake! Be quiet!" Someone hushed.

Mrs. Whithouse. Taking her little obnoxious beast for a walk in the dark.

"Good evening, Mrs. Whithouse!" I shouted.

Some of the tension in Allen's arm loosened as the woman turned around, tugging on her little dog's leash.

Cupcake barked and barked at the sight of Allen and me several feet behind them.

"Don't scare us like that!" shouted Mrs. Whithouse.

As if we'd done anything but walk down the public sidewalk.

Mrs. Whithouse struggled to keep Cupcake's

energy contained, and a book fell from under her arm to the concrete. She let out a little cry and snatched it up, almost losing control of her dog while she was at it but just managing to yank her back in time.

"We have a noise ordinance after nine P.M.," I reminded her. Not above being a bit petty, considering she'd sent Evangeline a long email about how it *dragged* the neighborhood's reputation to be holding Ooh-La-La Book Club meetings celebrating such *filth*.

Mrs. Whithouse paled, her eyes flicking from Allen to me, and she turned on her heel, without another word to us.

"Come, Cupcake," she said quickly, her back stiff as she practically dragged the dog away and into the night.

Allen let out a deep breath, and I gave him a side hug. The only time he'd ever written a man's fear of dogs into one of his books had been in this unpublished one, the one that was closer to real life for Allen than his stalwart, unbreakable romantic heroes.

But I found it a little cute. Though I felt bad dogs made him so nervous, of course.

We walked past the mini donation libraries and Allen stopped.

"She didn't shut it all the way," he said, pointing to the Ooh-La-La Box.

The Ooh-La-La Box.

The book she'd dropped. Mrs. Whithouse was *so* against my mini donation libraries, I hadn't even *considered* she'd be taking or adding a book to either of the libraries, but push come to shove, I would have guessed perhaps the All-Ages Box.

But she hadn't latched the *filthy* romance box.

I swung open the Ooh-La-La Box's door to check on the squeaky hinge. Sure enough, it let out a grating sound. "We'll fix it tomorrow," I said. "I think I have some WD-40 myself. I *am* in charge of the boxes' maintenance, after all. I should have taught you that when instructing you on how to create your own."

"I should have known you'd have it in hand." Allen smirked, but then his eyes traveled over the box's contents. It was about half full—and I'd just filled it from another thrift store run this morning. Leaving plenty of room for Allen's latest autographed copies, of course.

"The last copy of *Alien Lover Daddy* is gone," Allen said.

Frowning, I ran my hands over the remaining books' spines as if to verify his statement. "You don't think...?"

"I *just* saw it. Not ten minutes ago." He looked around. "Not a lot of people out here taking books, other than that woman."

"But Mrs. Whitmore *hates* the Ooh-La-La Box. She —" I cut myself short. "She doth protest *too* much."

I snickered.

Mrs. Whitmore was a V.L. Breedlove fan. Or at least she'd seen the hot, green-skinned alien man on Breedlove's latest book cover and had said, *"Yeah, I have to have me some of that."*

"What's so funny?" Allen asked. He playfully pinched my shoulder.

"You have more fans than I thought. Including some of the *very* uptight variety."

"Huh." He grinned. "Good thing you're not uptight. Not unless you're roleplaying one of my more buttoned-up heroines."

"Is that a request for tonight?"

"I'll let you decide." He leaned over and whispered softly. "Whatever you choose, I won't say *no*."

I fingered his shirt collar and drew closer. "Good. Because I *might* want an alien lover daddy to capture me, after all."

The Succubus Sirens Series

Read sexy reverse harem stories set in the Succubus Sirens world of superpowered heroes, villains, and elves:

These standalone, interconnected books can be picked up in any order, but if you want to avoid spoilers, it's best to read *Lips*, *Heart*, *Rebellion*, then *Soul*.

Praise for *Succubus Lips*:

"This is probably one of the most bizarre yet satisfyingly creative books I've ever read... If you're into kickass heroines and book boyfriends that make you swoon, this one is for you!" -The Lovely Books

"*Succubus Lips* is well-written and subversively funny, willing to toy with the reader's expectations and do the opposite... sexy without being tedious." -The Romance Reviews

Praise for *Succubus Heart*:

"This book kept my interest from the very beginning, and I enjoyed every scene. Absolutely recommended." ~The Romance Reviews

Praise for *Succubus Soul: Veras Academy*:

"With a great storyline, a bunch of brilliant characters (both main and supporting), plus some very steamy bits, this was a great book to read to while away the hours." ~The Romance Reviews

Four superpowered women. Fifteen gorgeous, roguish men, each a distinct hero—or villain— eager to make these women theirs.

Succubus Lips: Her lips have the power to boost. Her love can grant power unparalleled. In an ongoing conflict against ravishingly beautiful beings from another dimension, Aurora's abilities allow her to turn the tide of the battle.

Succubus Heart: Her aura takes powers away. Ally or foe, no Natch or Nelian can rely on their supernatural strengths in the proximity of the Nelian princess. Superpowered battles devolve into pandemonium when Alanna enters the fray.

Mutiny's Rebellion (novella): Superpowered Natch law school student Joey O'Shea, a.k.a. Mutiny, has a secret past and a promising future... If only she could focus and get her mind off the three hunks who represent the three sides of her: the good, the bad, and the shades of gray.

Succubus Soul: Veras Academy: Blessed with the power to protect. A princess born to two worlds. But despite being the star pupil at Veras Academy for superpowered young adults, all Bryony wants is to be "normal."

My Racy Reverse Harem Book Club

STANDALONE CONTEMPORARY REVERSE HAREM

Nothing can keep Rose away from Romance Book Club at the library—not even the snowstorm of the century. Catching a ride home through the storm with Lance, the stunningly attractive librarian who happens to be her neighbor, and Vaughn, his chiseled, alluring housemate, Rose takes them up on their invitation to drop by sometime and join them for their own book club. Rose gets more than she bargained for when she's introduced to Rafael, their magnetically charming third roommate, and the surprising genre of books they love to read and discuss. As the blizzard rages, Rose joins the Racy Reverse Harem Book Club, whose members are open to trying just about everything together to get warm.

A standalone novelette by Lina Jubilee, author of the reverse harem urban fantasy series Succubus Sirens.

<h1 style="text-align:center">Revere Me</h1>

FANTASY ROMANCE ADVENTURE

Brecc

I've waited an eon to find you. You, my bride, the other half to my soul. But I noticed you too late, the annual fete that was supposed to bring us together not your time to shine. My need for you threatens us all... Nonetheless, I will have you. The world is meaningless without you. Love me. Bow to me. Revere me.

Edony

I was supposed to be safe. My years as an eligible maiden were behind me, so no fae should have sought my hand at the Fae King's Fete. Yet you caught me breaking the rules, and my fate rested in your hands. Instead of banishing me to the labyrinth of madness surrounding your castle, you vowed to let the world crumble to have me at your side. But I won't let you sacrifice everyone I care for—everyone in your kingdom—for me. To escape you, I'll go willingly into the maze. I'll keep running so you never find me. You will never break me. I will never yield to your desires.

Even though I crave you. Even though when I close my eyes, all I see is your face.

Revere Me is a steamy fantasy romance recommended for ages 17+ for mature themes and scorching romantic tension. First serialized on Kindle Vella, this episodic novel reads as a dark fairy tale in the vein of Beauty and the Beast.

About the Author

Lina Jubilee loves reading, writing, drinking tea, and rooting for her favorite fictional romances. When not lost in a book, she cooks dinner at lunchtime, plans errands in fewer trips, and does everything she can to get back to romping through fictional worlds ASAP.

Ravenous readers, if you liked this book, please consider joining my Facebook street team! Connect with me:

Join My Mailing List (Get a Free Novelette!)

Visit My Website

amazon.com/author/linajubilee

bookbub.com/profile/lina-jubilee

instagram.com/linajubilee

x.com/LinaJubilee

facebook.com/authorlinajubilee

The Madrid Mistake: Wander & Lust Book 1

When Layla arrives in Madrid for her sister's wedding, she's brokenhearted and ready for a rebound. What she finds is more than a rebound: She finds Mateo, the first man to truly see her for who she is and make her feel worthy of love. And he just happens to be an international superstar.

As the wedding approaches and family drama escalates, it becomes clear that secrets will come out. Secrets that just might ruin the wedding—and cost Layla the love of her life.

A Beautiful Risk: Love at Lincolnfield Book 1

One stolen kiss. One wild fantasy. One big risk.

When a gorgeous Viking-like stranger plants a smoldering kiss on Passi in the thermal baths, she goes home with more than relaxation on her mind. The stranger sparks a fantasy hot enough to overcome the climax-killing side effects of her very necessary anti-depressants. When she walks into work to find the same devastatingly handsome man as the hospital's new risk manager, she frantically emails her best friend, detailing the fantasy starring her hot, new coworker. Only, instead of emailing her friend, she accidentally sends the X-rated message directly to *him*.

Insert leg in mouth. Quit job immediately. Or not...

Single dad Magnus is intrigued by the lovely woman he kissed at the baths who got away before he could learn her name. Even more so when he opens his email and discovers he was responsible for her breakthrough orgasm. But she's now his new HR director, and the reason she needs the medication means she won't date guys like him.

Exchanging risqué letters at work may be good, nail-biting fun, but the only way he can have her outside the realm of fantasy is to convince her to bend her rules and risk her heart on all that he has to offer.

A single dad, second chance, office romance, *A Beautiful Risk* is the first book in the Love at Lincoln-field series, heart-warming, hot page turners about the love lives of men and women who work at a Chicago hospital.

www.ingramcontent.com/pod-product-compliance
Lightning Source LLC
Chambersburg PA
CBHW030711190726
48286CB00001B/275